A Lunar Eclipse

A LUNAR ECLIPSE

Robert Edric

Heinemann : London

William Heinemann Ltd
Michelin House, 81 Fulham Road, London SW3 6RB
LONDON   MELBOURNE   AUCKLAND

First published 1989
Copyright © Robert Edric 1989

British Library Cataloguing in Publication Data

Edric, Robert, *1956–*
  A lunar eclipse.
  I. Title
  823'.914[F]

  ISBN 0 434 23910 0

Typeset by Deltatype Ltd, Ellesmere Port, Wirral
Printed in Great Britain by
St Edmundsbury Press, Bury St Edmunds
and bound by Hunter & Foulis Ltd, Edinburgh

For Rebecca and Holly

An odd comfort
that the way we are always
most in agreement
is in playing the same game
where everyone always gets lost

Thom Gunn *Elegy*

PROLOGUE

Memories of a three-year-old wedding: Colin with his arm around Rachel's shoulders, a drink in his hand; another in hers, already uncomfortable in the dress she has chosen and in which she looks like someone completely different, her hair styled differently, her lips and eyes made up differently, having already kissed another hundred guests, most of whom she would not have invited by choice, television people, few of whom she will ever see again.

I kissed her and became as much a part of the deception as the dress, the other kisses and touched glasses.

'We're glad you could come, we really are.' She looked beyond and around me as she spoke.

'It makes all the difference.' Colin was already half drunk, and every time he looked at her he smiled.

Later, there were telegrams from the other side of the world and the exclusivity of the group was infinitely extended.

Rachel removed the headband of her veil; without it her hair fell forward and she continually brushed it back, the same practised motion every time, until she became aware of it and stopped herself.

'We'll see more of you.' She was still looking over my shoulder, this time at new arrivals. Someone beside us had his hand on Colin's shoulder and Colin had half turned to speak to him.

The room was filled with guests, few of whom I knew. Waitresses in black with white aprons served us drinks. People remembered the occasions of their own weddings.

Later still, the routine became more familiar – meal, speeches, more toasts – and afterwards the tone of the proceedings changed with a slipped tie, a spilled drink and a laugh too loud for the room to hold.

Colin returned to me. 'We've done it, but what next?' he said.

Beside us was a mound of presents, but having already lived together for four years there was nothing in the pile they needed, only what they were thought to need by others. He was distracted by Rachel's laughter; she was surrounded by a circle of her own friends. The woman holding her arm was laughing and crying at the same time. Colin picked up an electric toothbrush and pretended not to know what it was. He slotted in one of its attachments and pretended to clean his teeth, laughing for my benefit at its uselessness.

'Rachel's list.'

'Whoever bought it . . .' I suggested, indicating the people around us, any one of whom might have been waiting to overhear his comment.

He looked back to Rachel. 'The dress is wrong. She said as we arrived that the dress was wrong. She bought it four months ago and now she's saying that it's all wrong.'

'Does it matter?'

'Of course it doesn't matter. What matters is that now, here, she bothers to tell me. Look at it: does it look wrong to you?' He caught the table and several packages fell to the floor.

'They all look the same. White.'

'Four months and she waits until now.'

The six young bridesmaids sat together near us: young cousins and the two daughters of a close friend. They wore peach dresses with white sashes and socks which made them look younger than they probably were. Colin pulled a face at them and they laughed.

'She's supposed to know about these things. It's her job.'

The music resumed and couples returned to the small dance floor.

'There's nothing wrong with the dress.'

'Will you come and see us – afterwards, I mean?'

I said I would.

'I mean it. Everything's going to have to change.'

'You'll be able to clean your teeth more quickly.'

There was something in his face as distant and as far removed from what was happening as the telegrams of congratulations. He told me where they were now living. Then he told me where they were going for their honeymoon.

'Change: it's what all this is about.' He indicated the people around us, and then the presents, most of which remained unopened. 'They might as well *all* be electric toothbrushes.'

'Perhaps they are.'

He smiled. 'It might make more sense.'

'Your secret's safe with me.'

He looked at me as though I'd told him more directly that his voice was raised, and that people were watching him and deciding for themselves what was happening.

An older couple shook his hand and gave their apologies for

4

leaving early. Colin asked them if they'd enjoyed themselves and thanked them for coming. It was clear he had no idea who they were. The woman wished him . . . she hoped . . . she knew he and Rachel were going to be happy together. We waved them out.

Then he led me from the presents and introduced me to the group of people standing around Rachel.

'Susan agrees with me,' Rachel said.

'I didn't agree, I said I could see what you meant. When you said the drop from the waist – ' Susan had tried to be kind and was now being humiliated.

'Oh, I know, I know,' Rachel said. 'And you're right.' She poured drink from one of the two glasses she held into Susan's and they were friends again, like the schoolgirls they might once have been together.

'What I meant was . . . ' Susan began telling me.

Colin kissed Rachel and then Susan.

The curtains were half drawn and there were moments of stillness in the room as people posed to have their photographs taken: Colin and Rachel's wedding; us enjoying ourselves; a hot, perfect day. The bride wore . . . The service was . . . The reception . . . The meal . . . The evening.

Susan tried again to explain what she meant about the dress and Rachel lifted her arms to indicate where she thought it was too tight or badly fitting. Susan was drunk. When she couldn't explain herself she looked about to cry. She knelt down and pulled a pleat into the material.

'Pissed,' Rachel mouthed over her shoulder. She tried to stop her, but Susan persisted.

Colin made a joke about the electric toothbrush and it became our duty to laugh. I saw the faces of another couple, the couple who might have brought the toothbrush, and who might now hate everyone in the room who'd bought something else.

Having demonstrated what she meant about the dress, Susan stood up and then almost fell.

Rachel took a flower from someone and clumsily worked it into my buttonhole. Someone else had given her a ribbon to hold back her hair in place of the veil. Like the bridesmaids in their white socks, it made her look younger.

'You were drunk the first time I saw you,' I said.

'You're guessing.'

'No, seriously.'

'Perhaps I'm drunk with happiness, perhaps that's it.'

5

'Susan's right: your dress is wrong.'

'I know. I knew four months ago. It stinks. It absolutely stinks.' She began to laugh.

'Why not change into something else? Isn't that what people generally do?'

'"People" might. Everyone else is telling me how marvellous I look. Marvellous, beautiful, adorable . . . A genuine blushing bride.'

'And are you?'

'Of course.' She lifted her glass from the table and drained it. She put a hand on each of my shoulders as though we were about to dance. 'For your information,' she said, half closing her eyes, 'I've been to bed – well, not actually bed, perhaps – with five of the men in this room. All of them a long time before Colin. There's no point looking because it's the last thing you'll see. Do you think I'll make a good wife?'

'I don't know. What am I supposed to be looking for?'

Here are fifty women, twenty-five of whom are married. Of that fifty, thirty are good cooks, but only ten are 'good' in bed. Of the thirty who are good cooks, fifteen are not married. Of the ten who are 'good' in bed, five are married and none are good cooks. What makes a good wife?

Beside us, two women admired everything the other was wearing.

Colin returned with a tray of drinks. Either the curtains had been fully drawn or it had grown dark. When Rachel let her arms fall from my shoulders the room was already half empty.

What do people talk about after weddings? How nice the dress was, how beautiful the bride looked, how perfectly everything went? Would the slightest imperfection become a disaster, something worth remembering simply because it had happened and shouldn't have?

'It was Colin's choice.'

I didn't believe her. 'It hardly matters now.'

'No, I don't suppose it does.'

Someone took a photograph of the younger bridesmaids, who had fallen asleep in a row where they sat, their heads on each other's shoulders.

'I can barely stand,' Rachel said, and we returned with her to the company of the other women.

'The trouble with the dress,' she said to Susan, 'is that you haven't got the first idea about these things. Look at that skirt, look at that blouse, look at those earrings, for Christ's sake. Look at – I'm sorry, I'm sorry, I'm sorry, I'm sorry.'

6

Susan stood up and left us. A man followed her.

'I'm sorry, I'm sorry, I'm sorry. Will she come back? Make her come back.'

Colin held her face into his chest. The man who'd followed Susan returned and told us she was outside, crying. He was as embarrassed as Colin by what had happened.

'Ask her to come back in, make her come back in.'

'She's upset.'

The other women were patting Rachel's arm in light, reassuring touches. Someone told a story of something similar happening at his own wedding.

Susan reappeared and Colin manoeuvred her into Rachel's arms. They said, 'I'm sorry, I'm sorry, I'm sorry,' together, and the few people still watching them stood as though they were about to applaud. The dress was perfect; it had become a detail.

I went back with Colin to the table of men with whom he'd been sitting. One of them said he remembered me and I pretended to remember him. We talked about women, wives, wives-to-be. There were men who regretted having made bad decisions and it showed in everything they said and did. Occasionally they left the table to dance with each other's wives.

Fifty men at a wedding. Thirty are married. Twenty are not. Ten of those who are not are with women whom they might marry. All ten watch the proceedings very carefully. The thirty who are already married tell the twenty who aren't either to do it or not to do it. Of the ten who might soon marry, four are with women who are 'good' in bed. Of the four, none is a good cook.

Rachel and Susan are friends again. They are dancing, holding each other as tightly as the men are holding each other's wives, most of whom have become good cooks, and several of whom –

PART ONE

1

Rachel sat where the silver pipes left the ward, entered the conservatory, turned at right-angles through the glass and continued outside. The glass roof and wall caught the sun, but where she sat there was a triangle of shade cast by the wall, and another beneath the extended branch of a tree which overhung the lawn. She sat facing away from the door and at a distance from the few other women already there, all of whom looked up from their empty laps or their books or magazines or the letters they were composing as I entered. It was warm beneath the glass and several wore sunglasses and sat in pink or mauve tracksuits with towels around their necks.

Rachel, too, wore dark glasses, and she neither turned nor looked up at me.

'Rachel?'

She pressed the lenses closer to her eyes.

I told her I thought she might have been asleep.

'I *was* asleep. Now I'm awake.'

Eight weeks after Colin's death she'd broken down, and four days later had come to the clinic. There had been many changes in those eight weeks, changes which gave an edge to everything she now did and said and planned.

She tapped the empty chair beside her. The floor beneath it was spread with magazines. I shifted the chair into the shade and sat down.

'Before you ask, let me tell you something,' she said. 'I came here because it was recommended. Everything had stopped, and for the first time in my life I had no idea about what happened next. I'm here on recommendation. Being here makes as much sense as being anywhere else right now. Being here is like being asleep as a child, when everything is going to be better, wiped clean and forgotten in the morning. Being here, I can pretend the implications don't matter. Out there is where everything that matters begins. Out there you're either running or you're stopped dead.' She indicated the wall separating the lawn from the rest of the hospital. 'The public domain,' she added. 'I imagine Hampstead to be somewhere along a straight line running at right-angles to that wall.' She held out her arm and looked along it.

An order had been lost where previously no order had been apparent. Now, only the details mattered.

I took off my jacket.

'You had no problem finding me?' She lifted her face and traced a line with her finger from her chin to the top of the robe she wore. 'What can I offer you? Shout. Someone will come running. It's that kind of place.'

'Water,' I said.

'Playing safe.' She shouted, 'Water, water, H_2O, H_2O.'

The other women looked up and watched us. An orderly shouted back from inside and came out a moment later with a jug and glasses. She collected up empty jugs, refilled them and brought them back out.

'Thank you, dear,' Rachel said in an affected voice. I nodded my own thanks, but the woman ignored me. No one else spoke to her.

I told Rachel that on the phone she'd sounded pleased with the way things were going at the clinic.

'I know. I sound pleased about a lot of things. It helps. It's all a question of what we seem to be, you see. We all have to be very careful.' She indicated the other women by tilting her face and looking over her glasses. She lifted the jug and poured two glassfuls of water until they overflowed. 'I could leave tomorrow. I won't, but I could.'

I asked her how long she thought she'd stay. It felt as though we were having two separate discussions, neither moving towards the same point.

'You knew about Colin before I did,' she said accusingly.

'Only at the beginning.' Only when it didn't matter.

I turned the conversation by asking how she spent her days.

'Like that.' She pointed to the other women, some of whom looked back at us before being distracted by a group of joggers running past the glass on their small circuit of lawn. The second time around only half of the runners passed us; the others sat where they had stopped, their legs splayed on the grass.

'Is it what you expected?' she asked. 'Seriously.'

I told her it was considerably better than I'd expected.

'Apart from the crappy architecture. Don't tell me that's better than you expected – being an architect, that is.'

'I try never to expect too much in that respect.'

12

I remarked that the conservatory looked to be in need of some repair.

She said I ought to mention it to the authorities.

I asked which 'authorities' and she said she didn't know, that it was one of those words.

When the water in the jug grew warm she shouted for more. The orderly came out again. She asked if we would prefer orange juice, or perhaps coffee, or perhaps tea.

'We asked for water. W-A-T–'

The woman was constrained to stand and listen. Several of the others in the conservatory were amused by the way Rachel was treating her, and when the orderly had gone I asked her if what she'd done had been entirely necessary.

'None of this is *entirely* necessary. What is?'

The roof directly above us was stained green with lichen, with clear lines through it where water had run down and drained away. There were handles along the cast-iron supports of the glass wall by which a line of high panes could be slanted open to allow a flow of air. Looking up and watching the play of sun on the glass gave me the impression of being under water.

Rachel unfastened her robe, revealing a one-piece swimsuit in black and yellow. 'The solarium is for the exclusive use of the exclusive members only.' She leaned back in her chair, her head and shoulders still carefully positioned in the shade. On the lawn a woman in a bikini walked to the edge of the shadow cast by the tree and then walked carefully around its perimeter, holding out her arms to balance herself. Having completed a full circuit she bowed to the women sitting on the grass.

'It won't change anything,' Rachel said. She lifted the jug and shook the melting ice cubes. 'When Colin died I watched plays and films and read books and magazine articles to find out how to respond. I still don't know. I tried out one or two of the better scenarios, and for all I know this might be just another.'

In the two months since his death she'd started drinking heavily, and now not drinking had become part of her recovery. She worked as a freelance writer for the better-quality women's magazines, and until Colin's death she'd been successful and in demand. It was a competitive field and I'd always accepted that it was one of the reasons she drank. Not being able to return to work was what she feared most, and it was something she already knew she was losing during those two months.

'One minute it all makes perfect sense and the next it leaves you where you are: nowhere, and waiting for the next best thing to come along and push you another inch in the right direction.' She stopped, surprised by her confession. 'W-a-t-e-r. Someone ought to make a list of all our jokes on the subject. No more cannibals or headhunters to track down, only us: self-indulgent and pathetic, a dying breed crawling through the sand and shouting for water.' She repeated the absent gesture with her finger, running it from her chin to her navel, as though unzipping herself.

The other women had stopped watching us and several were asleep.

'If you squint at the light,' she said, looking directly up at the roof, 'it breaks down into its composite colours.' She squinted and I copied her. She stopped and shook her glass; the ice cubes had melted. She sipped the water.

When you squinted at the conservatory roof the composition of the light became perfectly revealed; everything else became indistinct and unimpressive.

'The centre of the universe,' she said. There was a sun in each of her dark lenses. 'I'll apologise to her when she next comes out to ask if we want any more water.'

I asked her if she was still receiving any medication. I used the phrase 'under the doctor'.

She clapped her hands together. '"Now Starring.' West End Comedy Sensation. *Under the Doctor*. Destined to Run and Run and Run." Doctor chasing blonde buxom nurse. Doctor with silver disc on his forehead, stethoscope flapping, maniacal leer. Nurse's uniform unbuttoned, excited panic. "Oh, Doctor, Doctor, Doctor." "Just a Little Injection, Nurse. One Little Prick." Run and Run – '
The other women looked at us again. 'Call all this a passing phase. Tell anyone who asks.' She stopped looking at the roof and removed her glasses.

Outside, the women on the lawn gathered in a group and started running again.

'Clip clop clip clop.' Rachel wiped a hand across her face and then looked at its wetness. The sun had moved and her head was now in the sharpest angle of the shade. The robe had Colin's initials on the pocket and was too large for her. Her finger- and toenails were painted the colour of acorns.

'Do you think she'll come out again for me to apologise to her? It can't be much of a job.'

I said that one day the woman would come out and pour the water over their pampered heads.

14

I saw beneath her gown and her swimsuit, imagined her sitting beside a pool, her feet kicking in the water, tossing back the rope of her hair extended in a spray, the whole of her body still wet, the broken outline of someone beneath the surface ready to grab her feet and pull her back in.

2

Colin and Rachel met inside a whale.

'Did I ever tell you how Rachel and I met? You won't believe it.'

All couples meet in precisely the same way; only the irrelevant physical details differ, and these matter only to them, not to anyone else. Couples – still then strangers to each other, or perhaps not – might miss each other by a glance, a second, a crowded lift, a full bus; they might meet as the result of a spilled drink, an insult, someone else's unwelcome intervention. These are the things that matter.

What won't I believe?

Apparently –

It makes him happier for me to become incredulous when I'm told. (A whale! How? You're joking! Ridiculous.) A whale.

(What possible bearing can any of it have had on what happened to them afterwards? Perhaps none. Perhaps such incidents – the distinction of before and after – matter far less than the incidental details in any life.)

Colin's unbelievable story of how he met Rachel inside a whale:

'I was behind her in the queue of visitors to a recently opened exhibition of whales and whaling, the centre-piece of which was the reconstructed skeleton of a humpback whale, through which people were directed in single file by arrows on the floor. Rachel was in front of me – not that she was Rachel then, of course – with a pencil and a pad, taking shorthand notes, not so much of the details of the exhibition as her impressions of it.'

These details become inconsequential for him in his urge to get to the point at which they met, but despite this they have remained part of the story and cannot now be abandoned. They must persist, because to discard them would be to strip a layer of truth and understanding from the event. Everything, even the pencil and notepad, have a place in the natural flow of minutiae; even the way he remembered watching what she was doing and interpreted it for himself there and then, before they met.

'She had a way of closing her eyes as she began to write, then opening them and speeding up. She'd paused too long, I suppose, and the people in the queue continued coming into the skeleton of the whale behind me.'

You were pushed forward into her. Forced. You met and the details of 'before' became indistinguishable from the details of 'after'.

'There was a small child somewhere inside the open jaws, being posed by his father for a photograph. But the child was frightened and became frantic to get out. Unfortunately, everyone else had seen what a marvellous subject for a photograph the situation provided and they were all trying to persuade him to stay where he was. His father's camera was an expensive one and the man took his time in focusing and setting up the shot. When he was ready he shouted almost angrily for everyone who'd been trying to keep his son in position to get out of the way. I remember that as well as anything.'

The type of photograph which wins five pounds or a book token in the Sunday papers.

'And Rachel?'

'I was pushed into her from behind and knocked the pencil out of her hand. I tried to retrieve it for her and she said it didn't matter, that it was too short anyway. She sharpened her pencils away to nothing when she was working. She had a callus on her right hand on the piece of loose skin between her thumb and forefinger.'

He held out his hand and plucked at his own web of skin.

'When she stopped working for any length of time it vanished. There was no time to look for the pencil and we went out of the whale to relieve the bottleneck we'd caused.'

'It sounds like the name of a type of whale: a bottleneck whale.'

'Yes, I suppose so.' He stopped to recount for himself the precise sequence in which the events had taken place before going on. The joke had been an intrusion. 'We were both interested in whales, wildlife, conservation in general. I suppose everyone was; most of our friends were, certainly. I remember that parts of some of the forward ribs had been sawn away to create a doorway out of the skeleton. Plastic model kits of it were on sale and I offered to buy her one for having caused her to lose her pencil. One of those things. Then we went and had coffee together on the mezzanine over-looking the main exhibition.'

At this point – and I heard him tell the tale again – he held his hands together and opened them, emphasising the gesture with a sigh. 'And that was that,' he might say, or, 'Believe it or not, that was how it all started.' Afterwards, he waited for people to respond.

'And all around the mezzanine there were maps and charts showing the breeding grounds and migratory paths of the various types of whales. Where they fed and how they followed the same annual routes. Most of it we knew already. There was a chart showing where they were hunted, with variously sized red circles indicating how many were killed and who took them. We drank four cups of coffee. It was how we knew, I suppose. Ask her – she'll tell you the same.' It was clear by the way he said it that the thought had only just occurred to him. But only the details would be the same: the skeleton, the pencil, the four cups of coffee, the charts.

'Above the counter they'd mounted a blown-up black-and-white photograph – it must have been six feet by six – of a dead polar bear hanging from the rigging of one of the whaling ships. It had been gutted and looked flattened, like a heavy waterlogged rug hanging out to dry. There was a small cub beneath it, jumping up and trying to reach the body until it had become an elongated blur. The men around it had stared into the primitive camera and their faces were fixed.'

'Valuable fur, I suppose.'

'I don't know. I doubt it.'

'Anyway, it was how you met.'

'Did you know that Rachel's great-grandfather owned a substantial shareholding in a whaling fleet working out of Whitby, Hull and the North East? He's supposed to have made and then lost a fortune.'

'But none of it trickled down to Rachel.'

'She inherited from her father a collection of pieces of scrimshaw. Pieces of carved whalebone and ivory made up into trinkets by the whalers in their spare time: jewellery, boxes, knife-handles, combs, small ornaments. It was always a big embarrassment to her – feeling as she did, feeling as we both did, then – and, in addition to what her great-grandfather managed to collect, it appears that her grandfather and even her father continued to add to the collection. We still insure it.'

'And so the meeting in the whale was somehow appropriate?'

He responded to this as though it were a criticism. 'Not really. One thing would have led to another, given time.'

'Demonstrators at a recent international meeting calling for a moratorium on whaling threw plastic bags full of blood at the delegates beneath them. They were protesting at the way in which quotas were being ignored.'

'Red dye. They threw it at the Japanese.'

18

'Was it dye? The papers said blood.'

'Some papers said blood.'

He offered me a drink, standing the bottle on the low table between us. Rachel had been in the house earlier, but had left us to interview someone living near by. They hadn't been married long, and were no longer living in the house they'd shared beforehand.

'And was she writing about the exhibition?'

'I think so. She used to give some pieces of that kind of thing to a magazine stapled together in Camden. "This magazine is printed on recycled paper using only —" That kind of magazine. Not exactly Rachel's kind of magazine. Ideals, I suppose.' The word embarrassed him. 'We went again at least three times to the exhibition. When the crowds had eased off we used to go in the evenings.'

We were interrupted by Rachel's unexpectedly early return. Colin looked at his watch. He shouted to ask her what was wrong.

Rachel came into the room. 'Some people are so fucking unreliable. She *knew* I was going round to see her. She fucking well *knew*.' She sat beside us, looked at the bottle and glasses. 'Enjoying yourselves?'

'I was hearing the story of how you met.'

'Of how we met?'

Colin put the cap on the bottle.

'And how exactly did we meet? At a party, over lunch, over drinks, over drinks, over drinks?'

'You met inside the skeleton of a whale.'

'She's joking. She knows precisely how we met.'

'Inside a whale, I know. "Oh, how unusual, how exciting, how novel. How different: a whale!" We met inside a whale like a pair of Jonahs. She *knew* I was going round to talk to her. She fucking well *knew*.' She dropped a tape recorder from her bag on to the sofa.

'Perhaps something important came up,' Colin suggested.

Only my presence stopped her from responding as she might have done had they been alone.

'A whale of a time,' she said. She made a telephone call and waited impatiently as no one answered.

'I was saying how interested we were in that kind of thing.'

'That's right – you name it and we'll show some concern. Come on, answer. You hold out a tin and we'll drop something in. It might not be much, but it'll make a noise and rattle around.'

'She's having some problems workwise,' Colin said to me.

'*She's* still here,' Rachel shouted. 'She may not be her usual rational happy-go-lucky self today, but she's still *here*.' She phoned again but there was still no answer. She held the receiver a foot above its cradle and let it drop. 'Fuck you, then. Stay to dinner,' she said. I had no other plans. 'Colin will no doubt find something which urgently requires his attention, or someone will call and he'll have to go out. Colin, you see, is still very much in demand.' She turned to him. 'What is it this month? Death, mayhem, looting, burning, raping . . .?'

Colin made documentaries and was a television news reporter. He'd already told me about the work he was doing on the reporting of natural disasters and the way in which –

'Followed by an hour-long discussion in which Colin will answer questions and everything will become perfectly clear and respectable. They'll push up the viewing figures by having an announcement beforehand warning people with weak hearts, impressionable children and relatives who died in natural disasters reported on the news.'

Three months earlier Colin had won an award for a documentary filmed in the Andes about a group of climbers who used scarcely any equipment. In the pieces of film he'd shown me in the house, the men were wearing shorts, vests and training shoes, and appeared to be actually running up the mountains as though they were no more than the gentle hills of the streets outside. He pretended otherwise, but he was proud of the award. He'd been elsewhere with the climbers since.

'Make another film about the whales,' Rachel suggested, still angry that her own plans for the day had been disrupted. 'He has a piece of film showing a killer whale leaping out of a pool somewhere in America and biting off the arm of the man stretched out on a diving board offering it a fish.' She made the motion of the surfacing whale with her hand, opening her fingers to suggest its mouth. 'Clean off at the elbow. Marvellous. In front of hundreds – millions, I suppose. Irresistible news. "What you are about to see may prove disturbing." Imagine it, year after year, going round and round and round, and then one sunny morning deciding to come up and do that. Splash, crunch, splash.' She made the same motion, moving her hand in a curve. 'They had to kill it, of course, after that. A marksman.'

She asked me again if I'd stay to dinner and I accepted.

'We're working things out,' Colin said to me when we were alone. 'I think she was expecting to get something exclusive from the woman she was supposed to be seeing. It would have led to something else. It shouldn't matter to her all that much when these things don't come off, but it still does.'

20

Later in the evening Colin brought down a book on whales. He asked Rachel if she remembered it and blew away the non-existent dust before opening it, another fondness, heightening the moment. In the book were Blue Whales, Rorquals, Sei Whales, Humpbacks and Finbacks, Killers and Pilot Whales and Dolphins. There were pictures of each, and charts which measured them against a man and an elephant and which made their lives simple and understandable. He rested the heavy book in my lap. There was an inscription. Case proven. This was how it had once been. See for yourself. See it: a childlike drawing of two whales spouting the single word 'Love'.

Seeing it, Rachel kissed him and apologised for her behaviour.

3

'I had an abortion. We never told you that, but others knew.'

'Am I supposed to be shocked?'

She went on as though I hadn't spoken. 'Children were never a part of the master plan. They would have made an absolute balls-up of all our plans, of everything we were going to do.' Her voice tailed off.

'Before or after you were married?'

'Before. Years before. Years before anything. Thinking about it now I don't suppose it can have been part of any plan. Not then, so long before.'

The woman sitting nearest to us had her hair in a turban and a crescent of silver foil beneath each eye. A thin line of shadow crossed her face diagonally from her forehead to her chin and occasionally she touched it as though it were an insect. She rubbed cream into her hands until they were dry and then blew on them.

'I don't know why, but I'd always assumed Colin would have wanted children – daughters,' I said.

'It's hard to tell. Do you think so?'

I'd sometimes seen it in him.

The sunbathing woman was joined by two others. She peeled the foil from beneath her eyes and gently stroked the skin with her forefingers. She asked if they could see any improvement and they told her they could. One of hem raised the question of the possibility of tanning under glass.

'Colin had a friend who was a doctor. Did I tell you? It's beginning to look as though I'd tell anybody with time to listen everything there is to know about us. How's the house?'

'The house is fine.'

By then I'd been living with them for almost a year. I'd moved in originally as a temporary measure between leaving one flat and finding another. Since Colin's death I'd been waiting to leave. Rachel asking me now about the house was another pressure to stay.

My room was on the second floor, overlooking the road and the

22

traffic. Little of the noise of the street penetrated the foliage of the plane trees, and only the faintest of yellow streetlight shone up through their translucent leaves. I had access to all the other rooms, of which, including the basement, there were twelve. There was a handwritten notice on the basement door, saying *Utility Room Ha Ha*'.

'Colin had a friend who was a doctor,' I reminded her.

'Nothing to it, really. In, out, problem solved. It was all above board and perfectly legal, but it's one of those things that never feels it. Can you understand what I mean?' She held her flat stomach. 'We had a long and careful discussion about it. One of those long and careful discussions where you both decide on a conclusion before-hand and then work towards it separately.'

Had they never considered trying again?

She shook her head. By then the master plan really was in existence. 'By then I was thirty-one.'

The women beside us were no longer making any effort to hide their interest.

'Of course, the real problem with this place' – Rachel said loudly, and they turned away – 'are the awful opening hours.'

The women left us.

'You could have afforded to have had children properly looked after and gone on working.'

'You're actually suggesting that to a woman who can barely look after herself?'

'I'm not talking about now; I was talking about then.'

'There would still have been too much involved. I was infected afterwards. Antibiotically saved. I didn't mind; I'd expected it. It made the whole thing feel somehow – '

At the far end of the corridor a bell rang but no one paid it any attention.

'The big tablet giveth and the little tablet taketh away.'

She took off her glasses and pinched the top of her nose.

'Other people said that of the two of us, Colin would be the one to want children most. Can you really see that kind of thing in people?'

I said I supposed you could see it in them when they were around other people's children.

'Other people's children are a different species entirely.'

I said I thought the same was true with pets.

'He had a dog when we met. He has films of it with him on the Heath. It used to jump into the ponds and swim, scare the ducks. He must have a thousand photographs of it. When it died we had

23

another of our long and careful discussions about whether to get another one. But he was out of the country so often, and usually at such short notice, that it had been a mistake in the first place. Can we change the subject?'

I tried to remember having seen any of the photographs in the house.

'Yesterday the doctor actually suggested – as casually and indirectly as he knew how – that I might be a suitable case for regression under hypnosis. I told him we'd never get back through the wall of empty bottles. It isn't the kind of thing they like to force. For most of them' – she indicated the other women – 'being here is just another way of passing the time, something they think might help them and something they can afford. They get told something better than they remembered. They lap it up. I've seen some of their husbands. I won't stay much longer.'

I asked her if she intended coming directly back to the house and she said she did.

'Bird!' she said suddenly, as I was preparing to leave.

Bird?

'Bird was the name of the dog. I think it was named after a musician, or perhaps someone he knew. Bird. Definitely Bird.'

'Charlie Parker.'

'I don't know. Perhaps. Bird. That was it, Bird.' She closed her eyes. 'Definitely Bird.'

I knew from her voice that it was something she had never forgotten. She was only one step ahead of everything behind her, but she had stopped moving and the past hadn't.

Two days later she discharged herself from the clinic, four days ahead of the intended date; it was her way of keeping ahead.

4

She was in the house when I returned in the early evening, sitting at one of the first-floor windows, looking down. As I approached the door she tapped on the glass and waved. I let myself in and went upstairs.

'Nothing's changed,' she said, before I could remark on her unexpected presence. Beside her were her two cases. They were new and she asked me if I liked them in a voice which said she didn't. In one of the third-floor rooms was a pile of cases and bags stamped with the mosaic of Colin's journeys.

'The trains are disgusting,' she said. Beside her on the window seat was a neatly arranged line of cigarettes and their empty packet. 'I spilled them. I used to travel everywhere on the train before Colin. I had an entire carriage to myself.' She started coughing and stubbed out her half-smoked cigarette.

I turned on the fire and she left the window to sit beside it. It was not particularly cold, but in her absence the room hadn't been used. She moved around, fingering surfaces and straightening already perfectly straight pictures.

'I've been back an hour,' she said. 'I came straight up here. I'm thinking seriously about a holiday. Seriously thinking. Somewhere warm, somewhere tropical perhaps.'

Why not?

'Do you think I should? Wouldn't it be too much like recuperating all over again?' She lit another cigarette and sat without smoking it, letting it burn to ash and fall. I gave her a small copper pot and she tried to pick up the ash already on the carpet. 'Colin was very particular around the house. We both were. Once a month he used to go round with a dozen small pots of paint, touching up where the woodwork had been chipped. It mattered to him.'

We went downstairs to the kitchen. She sat at the table and talked about preparing a meal.

'When will you go?' I asked, referring to her holiday.

'When I decide where. China, have you ever been to China?'

I told her I hadn't.

25

'I could go and look at the Great Wall. Colin's been. I think he might have walked the length of it on his hands. I think deep down he always wanted to be one of those men who sat up in the trees talking to gorillas.'

She prepared a meal, but ate little, smoked instead. She asked if it bothered me, her smoking while I ate. When I said it didn't she called me a liar and dropped the cigarette into a glass of water. She shook it, watching it disintegrate. Beside the fridge was a full wine rack and she told me to take a bottle.

'It worries you,' she said. 'Me sitting here and watching you. It's an imposition – it imposes a strain. It's good wine.' She tipped her own head back as I took my first drink. 'The top six bottles are just for show. I think they were a present from a fawning writer. He wanted Colin to do something with him in the New Forest. Can you believe it? Perhaps they might have found a gorilla together.' She stopped. 'I'm being ridiculous.' She was speaking to fill every silence.

She went to the door leading down into the long rear garden. It was dominated by the trees which rose on each side and interlocked over half of it. The ground beneath them had been laid with a herringbone of red brick.

'We had all this laid out to exact specifications,' she said, indicating the interwoven initials 'R' and 'C' at the centre of the brickwork.

I asked her when she intended resuming work.

'I can get back into it any time I like. I know all that kind of people . . . Is that good English?'

It made sense.

'Did you know that practically everything in this house and garden, from the television aerial down to the sewers, is insured for twice what it's worth?' She stood with her back to me before returning to the house.

She sat at the table and pushed her uneaten food into small mounds. 'I was reading on the train about solar heating. Do we get enough sun here?' She looked up at the ceiling. I answered her as though she were a client asking me the same question.

'I'll sell the house,' she said when I'd finished. 'Not just yet, perhaps, but eventually. What do you think?' She asked me to go back out with her into the garden. We walked through the shade of the trees to the open space at the end, where she turned and looked at the house. She held a cardigan over her shoulders.

'I don't know what's going to happen,' she said. 'Or does my knowing matter?'

26

The holiday?

'The holiday was only an idea, but not a particularly good one. Listen –' She stopped talking to listen to the drone of a remote-controlled model aeroplane. She told me where it came from. 'It interferes with the televisions and radio. Colin used to phone up and complain. It sometimes used to interfere with the equipment he had in his study. He'd stand out here shouting up at it. Then he threatened to buy a gun and shoot it down.'

I searched the sky between the houses and the trees.

'You won't see it,' she said. 'You never see it. That was the whole point.'

Back in the house she ate a forkful of the cold food.

We went into the living-room. She switched on six lamps, counting them when she'd finished. There were oil paintings above the marble fireplace, each lit by a spotlight. She switched these on and then off again. She asked me what I thought of the paintings.

'The paintings are nothing remarkable,' I said. 'Let me guess: they were Colin's choice and you never liked them and now you're going to get rid of them.'

When I finished she applauded. And then she laughed: the kind of laughter that turns into a woman crying and holding her face in her hands because everything she'd wanted to be right was wrong and because everything with which she'd once been intimately familiar was now unknown to her.

When she stopped it was with a long breath of realization. 'Shitty pictures,' she said.

'They're not that bad.'

I switched the spotlights back on.

In one picture there were two nuns, one of whom was digging a grave. It was dusk. There were evergreen bushes around them and the sky above them was cream and grey.

'It's an "original",' she said, pronouncing the word slowly.

Nuns Digging a Grave?

'I could tell you who painted it but I've forgotten. It's unsigned.'

The second nun was sitting with her clean hands clasped around her knee; there was a fresh wreath beside her and her rosary was laid flat across the creases of her habit. She was looking directly at the artist. The digging nun stood in the partially excavated grave with her sleeves rolled to her elbows and with a spade full of soil in her hands. Whoever had painted the picture knew how a spade should be held, and how the body of the digger compensated for the weight of the soil. The excavated soil looked clayey, heavy and wet.

At the top of the grave the exposed soil was either yellow or had caught the last of the sun. There were mounds on either side of the hole. The sides of the grave were clean and sheer, which might also suggest clay. The digging nun's headdress was tied behind her ears and her robe had been folded up to reveal a white underskirt. She was looking away from the artist, concentrating on her task.

'Nuns digging a grave looking down at you every night.'

The look on the face of the sitting nun was an apology for the work of the digger. The sky was streaked, and the horizon of the graveyard was broken only by trees and the focal point of a cupola mounted by a cross and holding a bell. The sky directly behind the small dome was cream-coloured.

'Do you have any idea who might have painted it?'

I said I didn't, but that it looked French.

'"It looks French." Is that it? "It looks French."'

Or perhaps Belgian.

'Or perhaps – '

Or perhaps Dutch, German, Danish, Swedish . . . Two nuns – white – dressed like all nuns – digging a grave – probably for another nun.

People would refer to the painting as being strange, if not particularly inspiring. That kind of painting.

'It might even have been another gift. The house is full of un-wanted gifts. Colin kept a list of who'd given us what. He honestly did. Some of them were absolutely fucking hideous. Somebody once gave us a stuffed mongoose fighting a stuffed snake on a stand coiled round a piece of bleached wood. Or at least the mongoose was stuffed; I think the snake had probably just been skinned, stitched up and filled with air. A cobra.'

I'd seen them upstairs in Colin's study when I'd been in to watch his films.

'God knows where it is now.' She knew precisely where everything was in the house. 'When we knew people were coming to dinner or to stay we'd get whatever it was they'd given us out and make sure it was prominently displayed. That's the type of people they were. That's the type of people *we* were.'

'Everybody does it,' I said.

'Everybody does it with the odd vase now and again; they don't do it with probably one quarter of all they possess, and they don't do it with a fucking mongoose fighting a fucking snake.'

What about the second painting? What did she think of it? What did I think of it?

28

The second painting was an imitation of Grant Wood's *American Gothic*, a display of exhaustion and hopeless pride. The original had long been a favourite of mine and I told her what I thought of it. 'She's his ageing spinster daughter,' I said. 'People assume she's his wife, but she's not.' There's an arched window in the frame-built house behind them, hung with a patterned lace curtain; terracotta pots on the porch over her shoulder; a pitchfork in his hand and a brooch at her clean starched collar. 'It's an awful copy,' I said. Only the seemingly insignificant details mattered: the curtain, the brooch, the pots, the tiny needle spire of a hidden church.

'It came from America. It might be an original.'

'It's still a copy.'

'Take it down and put your fist through it. It's insured.' She watched me, daring me like a child to do it. When I didn't, she said, 'Music, we need music.'

There were four hundred records in Colin's collection, each filed according to type and artist, each catalogued in a small index.

She asked me what I wanted and I told her to choose.

'I never choose,' she said. 'What do you want?'

The music began and she listened to it for a few seconds. Then she ignored it. When the first side had finished she turned the record over. When the second had finished she changed it for another.

The lamps around us were positioned to cast few shadows.

She told me to help myself to a drink.

'What should I do with all the letters?' she said, referring to the mail which had accumulated during her absence.

I suggested reading them, which she disregarded. Even then there were small parts of the past, unwanted connections, which she was able to cut loose and let drift without a second thought.

'I'm running out of cigarettes.' She found a full packet in her handbag.

'I went round this room with the paint pots the day before the funeral,' she said. She pointed to the invisible spots on the door frame and skirting board. 'It was considered a good idea not to come back here afterwards. They were all there.'

'He was a popular man.'

'So they said. Much liked and respected. Much missed.'

When the second record finished she said she had a headache.

I heard her moving around the house during the night. I heard her in the room beneath me and in the kitchen. She opened the door leading to the garden and might have gone outside.

In the morning I left before she was awake.

She rang me mid-afternoon to find out what time I would return. I asked her how she'd found out where I was. 'What time?' she said. I guessed at the time. She said she was cooking a meal and needed to know. The lie was too obvious to challenge.

When I returned she'd taken the fighting mongoose and cobra from the study and had positioned them at the centre of the kitchen table. She'd stuck a cigarette in the mongoose's mouth. The head of the cobra was drawn back, ready.

'We ought to have a curry,' she said. 'We'll open one of the more expensive bottles and what you don't drink we can pour away.' She told me to go through to the sitting-room until the meal was ready. I heard her singing. She sang 'Take Me To The River' and 'Tea For Two' – a few lines of each.

5

I'd started watching Colin's collection of films during Rachel's absence; it was how I spent most of my evenings alone in the house. They were films he'd made himself: records, often without sound, of complete and seemingly insignificant events of their past together. Rachel was the star of them all, and there were times when he'd filmed and photographed her at every opportunity. Although absent from many of the films, Colin became a part of them through his technique, through the angles and movements he repeated, and through Rachel's eyes watching him and the expression on her face as she listened to and then followed his instructions.

The film I watched on the evening before her return began as most of them did with empty frames and a few seconds of flickering light – something which, given Colin's expertise, it would have been simple enough to have avoided.

And then Rachel standing in a jacket and skirt and high-heeled shoes, smartly dressed as though for a wedding or a christening with a simple, black, glossy handbag and a matching band around her hat. She held the bag under one arm and pulled on a pair of white gloves to her elbows. She appeared unusually self-conscious, as though she knew or had guessed she was being watched by someone else, frequently smiling or making small dismissive gestures. I expected Colin to mount the camera on a tripod and take his place beside her, equally smartly dressed, perhaps with a flower in his lapel, a clue to what was happening. There was a wall behind her and I saw that she was standing in one of the third-floor bedrooms. The indoor lighting had been expertly done and there were no shadows behind her.

She made a small turn, pulled a face at the camera, pouted, laughed, covered her eyes, and then signalled for the film to stop. When it didn't, she crouched down and moved quickly to one side. The camera followed her until it caught her with her hands on her hips staring directly into it. Then she laughed again and went back to modelling, balancing her hat on one finger.

A hand appeared in front of her and inched her into a more central position. The film ended and she vanished.

And then Rachel in a completely different outfit, and with different accessories. She moved less and looked less often directly into the camera. Still smiling, still striking poses as directed. She was standing in the same room.

A few seconds later she was dressed differently again.

The breaks continued, and after each she appeared wearing new outfits.

In some her eyes were heavily made up, and in others her lips were made fuller with lipstick.

The changes continued until eventually the clothes mattered less than her repeated signals to the camera.

She turned as she was directed, into profile and then away, facing the wall and then with her back to it.

She lifted her leg to reveal the split of a skirt and the stockings beneath. She leaned forward slightly – the way people lean forward to hear something more clearly – and lifted her leg again, this time higher, bending it until her heel touched her thigh and she almost overbalanced and fell. There was no sound to the film, only the intuitive compensatory gestures of word-forming and smiling and looks to one side. After almost falling, she swore and formed her hand into a fist.

Her irritation was most evident when she appeared wearing a short skirt and a T-shirt too small to tuck into her waistband, which rose to reveal her stomach. She pulled at the openings of her sleeveless arms and looked embarrassed by what she was doing. She held up her arms to the camera. She lifted the front of the T-shirt as far as she dared. She looked ridiculous in clothes she would never wear.

After posing a little longer she held out both hands and came forward until she covered the lens. When her hands withdrew, her cheek and eye filled the screen. She was laughing again.

There was a longer break between outfits, and again the contrived amateurishness of a blank screen.

She was back against the wall wearing something as elegant as the first outfit. Elegant clothes suited her. Her hair was styled differently and when she faced the camera she was slightly above and to one side of it.

Three more outfits followed.

In another film from the same box she wore a headscarf and posed with a telescopic umbrella. She was complaining about something and trying to slip her fingers into a small waist-pocket never intended to be penetrated.

Next she wore a pair of faded jeans, moccasin-style shoes and a baggy white sweater. The outfit was intended to suggest casualness, but instead looked as carefully planned as all the others. She blew upwards at her fringe until it rose horizontally from her forehead. The camera swung to one side and revealed a full-length mirror in which she was able to watch herself. It revealed what lay around her like a narrow doorway into another, brighter room. I saw the reflection of strong light in her eyes.

The films were filed in as precise an order as Colin's record collection. They imposed no real order on the past, their past; nor did they create any true idea of continuity or change. All they really did was keep that past accessible, and allow comparisons with what had happened since and what was happening now.

6

A week after her return, Rachel announced that she'd been invited to a dinner party and that she wanted me to accompany her. She held the invitation between her thumb and forefinger.

'We are warmly invited. We are cordially invited.' She flicked it to the table. It was a simple printed card with handwritten details.

'Not "we" – you.'

'Us. The obligation-stroke-embarrassment factor. You are a convenience. Or should that be "oblique"?'

What sort of party?

'Oh, the absolute best: polite people, polite conversation, polite remarks behind other people's backs as they make polite remarks behind yours. That kind of party.' She sounded like a bad actress rehearsing the lines of a play she scarcely knew.

And were we really going?

She pretended to think, picking up the invitation and fanning herself. 'I should think so; don't you?'

I said I wouldn't know anyone there.

'That's preferable to what I'll know. Let's look upon it as my coming-out, my return to society.'

'Which it won't be.'

'Possibily not, but at least I'll have been seen to have made the effort. It shouldn't matter, but it probably does.'

I said I'd go with her, as though my compliance were still in doubt.

'You're reliable,' she said, almost contemptuously.

She had once again tipped her cigarettes from their packet and spread them across the table. 'I ration myself. A hundred a day.'

Seriously?

'No, not seriously. Forty, perhaps fifty. I'm making up for lost time. I'm going shopping again later. It's quite a little social event; I quite enjoy it.'

Quite.

'I sound like Mrs fucking Miniver. The butcher, the baker – '

I asked her when the party was.

'Friday night.' She asked me how accomplished I was at polite

34

conversation. 'I'll feed you some good lines. You can wait until the first awkward silence – the word "clinic" may occur, for instance – and then remark as loudly as possible that I'm looking well. Or that I'm looking much better. I'll be drinking as much water as a horse so everyone else will have a good excuse to chip in about how many improvements they've spotted.' She started tearing small rips into the card and then folded it into four. When she realised it betrayed her nervousness she threw it down.

It was eight in the morning. She told me how Colin had had the door leading to the garden enlarged to let in more of the morning sun. Then she explained how he'd also had two lime trees chopped down to increase further the amount of sunlight.

'You think I might embarrass you,' she said. 'You'll probably never see any of them again.'

'Which would make it easy for you.'

'How much do you think they care?' She studied the room around her.

I left her.

When I returned in the evening, the kitchen was exactly as I'd left it, the breakfast dishes still on the table.

She appeared a little later and said simply that she'd been asleep. She came into the kitchen and dropped heavily into a chair.

'I've lost the whole fucking day.' She held her face in her hands and pushed her hair back. She looked at me through her fingers. 'You had a good day, I suppose.'

Not particularly.

'I intended making a start on the house, finding something to do. And then this.' Her face was still creased with sleep.

I sat beside her. I told her I could go out and come back in an hour.

'How about getting out and coming back in five years? Is that funny?'

We went to the dinner party the following Friday. Everyone made a great deal of her arrival.

Rachel announced herself: 'Back from the dead,' went to each of the six men and kissed them. Two wore dinner jackets. She flirted with them and, having raised the subject of the clinic herself, spoke disparagingly about it. They agreed with everything she said, but with the tacit reservations of shared glances.

In her absence, people remarked to me how well she looked: it was something they hadn't expected. Everything they said made me careful about my answers.

I met Rachel alone outside the bathroom.

35

'Jesus Christ,' she said. She closed her eyes and blew out her cheeks. 'I've known some of these people almost twenty years. Did they send you up to see where I was?'

One way or another. I asked her if she wanted to go.

'I think leaving early would undo all our good work. I've even been on holiday with some of these people.'

She went back downstairs. I waited a few minutes and followed her. People were passing round photographs and remembering. I saw how much of it was being done for her sake alone. Looking at all the unknown faces I was excluded even further. The woman who took the photographs from the wallet was careful about what she chose to let people see.

In the hearth of the unlit fire lay a sleeping black Labrador. Someone pointed out that it was twitching, having a nightmare. We watched and several of the men laughed at it. Then someone stroked it and it stopped.

The conversation turned to dogs. Four of the six men were drunk. The remaining two made a point of saying how sober they felt. Rachel had drunk nothing but fruit juice and tonic all evening.

We waited until others began suggesting it was time to leave before leaving ourselves.

On the short journey home, Rachel said little.

The following day she slept until mid-afternoon.

'"She awoke as if from a deep, drugged sleep and walked as though still in a dream."'

'It could be worse.'

'"And this is us in Cyprus. And this is us in the Seychelles. And this is us – "' At least in the clinic they either said next to nothing or kept their mouths shut about what mattered. What date is it? I feel worse than I used to feel on the mornings-after before. That dog – it stank. I suppose they'd seen one in front of a hearth in *House & Garden*. Central heating and logs in winter and a vase full of dried flowers and a dog in summer. It stank, absolutely stank. It's usually kids. They wheel them down and you pat them on their heads and they perform. At least they're clean.' She sniffed her fingers.

'There was nothing wrong with the dog. All old dogs smell.'

'"Stank"', I said. I'll ring them up and thank them, send some dried flowers or something.'

She made coffee and filled the house with the aroma. 'Coffee, toast and bacon,' she said. 'They all smell better than they taste.'

I asked her if she was hungry.

'Are you listening?' She'd eaten almost nothing for the past three

36

days. She complained that the food in the clinic had caused her to put on weight. She was wrong: she'd lost weight. 'We had a better coffee jug, but I can't find it. If I knew where it was . . . Blue. It used to be kept – ' She carefully put down the kettle. 'I haven't seen it.'

Broken, perhaps.

The house had undergone an upheaval and nothing had changed. She was simply a woman who had misplaced a coffee jug, but neither of us could keep it at that. She created the kind of silences which could only be broken by something being smashed or slammed.

She took out an inferior white coffee jug.

'Delicious,' she said. '"And this is us in London – not London, Hampstead. Healthy, healthy place."' She sat at the table and read the headline news. There had been an earthquake in Bolivia. 'Another small one. Colin went to Mexico. For his film. Then he went to California. People know what's coming but they never believe it until it arrives. Even then – That was what interested him, not the disasters themselves. Their homes crack up around them and every year the sea comes in halfway up their walls. Freak waves, twenty to thirty dead, a dozen missing, a few hundred homeless, people out in the streets praying for salvation between the cracks. Salvation with a capital "S". It would have been a good film. Might still be.'

I asked her if someone else had taken it on.

'How should I know? Television people: you only matter to them if there's a red light on somewhere. Before disasters he was interested in the reporting of strikes. He was at Grunwick. Was it Grunwick? He might even have won an award for that, too. They're very good about giving each other awards. Do you know how dull earthquakes in Bolivia or Turkey are? Where is it, for Christ's sake? Does it matter to you? Should it? Mexico mattered. Football, the World Cup. California will matter. California would have been a nice one for him to cover.'

'Did you travel with him much?'

'Sometimes. If there was time to arrange it. There seldom was. It gets through to you in the end, all that disaster stuff – not how it should get to you, perhaps, but after a while you begin to see it for what it is. It begins to matter and then you stop going. Most of the modern, four-star hotels he stayed in had earthquake-proof foundations, whatever that means. That kind of thing mattered. The only things which shook in them were the glasses in the bar.'

She shook her empty cup.

37

'I'm not supposed to know this, but there's even the chance of a short film being made about Colin. A profile. There's a lot of nice footage. Too good to waste. A car crash in Africa is to being killed in Beirut what Bolivia would have been to California. It's a crying waste, but there you are. In the minds of the men who make the decisions these things should not be lost.'

In Africa, in a car crash, was where and how Colin had died.

'I'd intended getting up early today and doing everything I hadn't done during the week.'

Such as?

'Such as – ' She was ready with a list. Everything she'd done as a wife for Colin. She made a remark about his clothes. They were too good to give away and she'd decided to keep them. She'd washed and ironed them all after his death, and many of his suits and jackets hung in the wardrobe in their dry-cleaning bags. There was a pile of untouched washing in the corner of the kitchen beside the door leading to the basement and the washing machine. She opened the door and kicked the clothes down the stairs. She went out and returned with the dress she'd worn the previous evening. 'The dog.' She threw it down the stairs, making sure it landed clear of the others.

'The ground should have opened up and swallowed him. Somewhere newsworthy – that much at least.'

7

Surrounded by trees at the centre of the park was a small hothouse, and inside was a narrow gravel path around a green pool stocked with overgrown and sluggish goldfish. The glass roof rose in a dome, touched at its centre by the fronds of a palm. A sign nailed to the trunk indicated that the tree was over a hundred and thirty years old and had been the reason for the construction of the hothouse in the first place. The fish came to the surface of the water and made sucking noises as they fed. Rachel walked around the path ahead of me.

'Colin and I used to come here on Sundays. Collect the papers, come in here and then sit on one of the benches outside. In winter the vagrants get in.'

Outside, the grass was covered with families, fathers playing with their sons. There were decorative flower beds and a larger pond with ducks.

'You'll have noticed that that was another of my "Colin and I used to – " memories. There are nine hundred and ninety-nine more. They went for a while but they're starting to come back.'

She stopped by a table of cacti and held her hands an inch from the spikes of the largest. She lit a cigarette and almost immediately a capped and uniformed attendant appeared and asked her to put it out. He watched her to ensure she didn't drop it into the pond. She pinched it out between her fingers without taking her eyes from him. He screwed up his face at the imagined pain.

There was a film of Rachel and Colin in the hothouse, and on the grass outside, chasing each other, behaving like teenagers, one being careful with the hand-held camera, the other being careful to remain in frame. Another shot of Rachel stealing cuttings by pinching off the tips of the plants with her fingernails and palming them into her pocket, in which there was a plastic bag, proof of predetermination.

She lifted the heads of some of the plants beside the cacti and studied them. She disarmed the attendant by apologising to him and then asking him about the plant he held. An antler fern. She touched it. The man took off his cap and began to tell her about it. She asked him if he didn't suffer from being beneath the glass all day. He told her he'd grown accustomed to it. Everything he told her she repeated to me, thus allowing him to feel twice as knowledgeable and important. He apologised to her for the rule banning smoking, explaining unnecessarily how the decision had come to be made.

'I've been coming here for ten years,' she said.

There were times when everything seemed to be about to be revealed.

He surpassed her achievement: eighteen years, himself.

The running costs of the hothouse were subsidised. The boiler, pump and pipes by which it was heated were all the originals, almost as old as the palm. When they eventually broke down or became too expensive to maintain –

'People don't appreciate,' she said.

In return, he said he thought he recognised her and invited her to sit with him on the two seats in his own working space. He told her he definitely remembered her and she encouraged him. She described Colin to him, and he said, 'That's right, that's right.' The description she gave him was of someone else.

'Blondish hair.'

'That's right. Fair.'

'Short.'

'Shortish.' He too was a short man and he indicated a point a few inches above his own head. He took off his cap and held it in his lap. Between them they had created something substantial out of nothing. When she offered him a cigarette he accepted, opening the window beside them. They blew smoke out together in a single plume. She had also created a small conspiracy of which we were all a part. She gestured with her finger and I moved further away from them. She told him that Colin had moved to another part of the country. She said he'd written in one of his letters that he missed visiting the hothouse. The man said it was kind of him and Rachel said she'd mention their conversation when she next wrote back. The man took her finished cigarette from her and flicked both through the open window. When she told him she had to leave he said it had been a pleasure talking to her.

We walked away from the hothouse towards the larger pond.

'There was no need for that,' I said.

'You needn't have stayed.'

I asked her what she'd hoped to achieve by it.

'Why should I have wanted to "achieve" anything? Perhaps it's just

40

a relief not to have to drag so much baggage around with me wherever I go. Perhaps it's not important to have to know even the slightest thing about anybody else. What do you suppose he made of you, the supplanter of an admirer of his hothouse? You see how easy it is.'

In the film of her stealing the plants, she and Colin left the hothouse and immediately started running, the camera making wild leaps into the sky and then down to the grass around their feet. I'd watched her tip out the contents of the plastic bag and stamp on them. The end of the film showed their crushed remains. Colin had superimposed 'Fin'. Shared jokes with no common currency.

She stopped suddenly and sat on the grass, pulling it in handfuls from beside her. She positioned herself to face the sun and closed her eyes.

'If I never came here again none of it would matter.'

She could have gone back to everywhere she'd ever been with him and said the same.

'It's called coming to terms,' she said sharply. 'There, now there's no need for *you* to have to say it.' She leaned back. 'I'm still considering that holiday before I think seriously about getting back to work. Do you suppose I might find a place where everyone would believe everything I told them about myself?'

'It shouldn't be too difficult.'

'Even it he found out, I doubt he'd be offended.' She looked back to the hothouse. 'I probably made his day. He'll tell all his other little workmates what happened. I can just imagine it.'

I told her I thought she was being ridiculous.

'So what? If you knew how perfectly behaved I've been over the past few years – '

I left her and walked alone towards the entrance of the park.

She returned to the house an hour later carrying the newspapers we'd forgotten to collect and with cans of beer in each deep pocket of her dress. She took them out and stood them on the table.

'Peace offerings.'

I took one and opened it.

She spoke again about the holiday she intended taking and tried to sound enthusiastic.

'Do I need a holiday?' she said firmly. 'Do I really need one? A change is as good as a rest. What do I do except rest? There has to be a point to these things.'

Did I agree?

We sat in the sun until the heat defeated us and we couldn't even make the decision to move.

8

I next saw Colin four months after the wedding. He'd recently been out of the country and was heavily tanned. He'd also had his hair cut close to his scalp so that even from a short distance I almost didn't recognise him. When he spoke loudly he had a penetrating voice and it was this which attracted my attention. He was with several others and when he saw me he shouted across a busy street and then ran through the traffic to reach me. The people he'd been with – two men and a woman – waited for him. I asked him where he'd been and he showed me the large pale patches on the backs of his hands where the burnt skin was already peeling. My impression of him at that time was that he'd always just returned from somewhere or was about to leave for somewhere else. All his travels were organised down to the smallest detail by someone whose job it was to do just that. He asked me to have lunch with him. I accepted and he shouted to the three others to go on without him. He was self-conscious of his shorn head and stroked it repeatedly; it made his face look rounder.

He led the way to a small restaurant, one where he was known. It looked full, but after a few minutes at the bar a table was found for us.

It was only as he picked up the menu that I saw that the index and forefinger of his left hand were strapped together in a sheath. I asked him what had happened.

'A car door. We were sitting waiting for someone to appear. I had my hand on the roof. Slam. Two good breaks.' He held out the fingers in a gun and fired.

The waiter recommended our meal and wine, and, while he was still with us, Colin said it was the only place in town where he allowed them to do it. The waiter thanked him and left us. Later, I heard him say the same elsewhere.

When the first bottle was empty the waiter brought a second.

'And what happened then?'

'Pain happened. My fingers came up like tennis balls. I had them cooled down and fastened up over there and I've had them X-rayed since I've been back. No real problems. The grip's still there.' He tried to bend his fingers and then winced at the pain, exaggerating to hide it.

He asked me about my work.

We were frequently interrupted by people arriving and leaving who knew him, people he pretended he wanted to avoid. Customers at surrounding tables watched him when he stood up to greet them. I recognised an actress and she asked to be introduced to me. He refused, telling her I was the last of his uncorrupted friends.

'You're not in television, then?' she said, making the tired joke more for his sake than for mine. She kissed him and then kissed his injured fingers. Someone shouted for her and she left us.

'You were telling me about your work,' he said, sitting back down.

'But you weren't really listening and I didn't want to tell you in the first place.'

'We could make an afternoon of it,' he suggested, indicating the second empty bottle. I accepted.

The conversation turned to Rachel and I asked him how she was.

He took a deep breath. 'Rachel's fine. Rachel's not working. Rachel hasn't done a page of real work for the past four months, since the wedding, since before. To quote Rachel herself, Rachel is resting, Rachel is sick of doing all the running around while others take the credit.'

'Is that bad?'

'It's a lot of empty space. I think she expected a lot more. Come and see us. The trouble is, when she puts her mind to it she's good. Too bloody good, in fact, for the toilet rolls she works for. The other trouble is that she's done too little for too long and has just about overdrawn on her reputation for reliability. She used to be reliable. She used to know how to work everything to her own advantage.'

Two separate waiters asked us if the meal had been okay. The 'okay' made everything casual, relaxed. Colin held his fingers to his lips and said the meal, as usual, had been perfect. The waiters behaved as though they had cooked rather than served it.

'She was offered a decent editorial job: more reliable, more money. She turned it down. She's been at it ten years but it still counts for nothing. Miss a deadline and there's always something else to slot into its place. There's no real security – not that kind of security.'

We sat in the restaurant a further hour. I promised to visit them. I still didn't know where he'd been to burn his hands and break his fingers.

I phoned him several evenings later and Rachel answered. For a few seconds she didn't recognise my voice. I'd expected Colin at least to have told her we'd met. She sounded impatient as I explained to her what had happened.

'He's gone to France,' she said.

I asked when he'd be back and she said she didn't know. I apologised for having interrupted her.

'No, wait. He's back on Wednesday. Come round then if you like.'

I told her we hadn't planned anything, that it had only been a casual invitation.

She paused before answering. 'Wednesday. Any time in the evening. He should be back.' She hung up. Even then, before I really got to know her, she had a way of suggesting that she knew everything that might have been said about her in her absence.

I went to see them, relieved when I saw Colin's bags in the hallway. Rachel showed me into the living room and then left me, returning a few minutes later with Colin, who had clearly been asleep. It was also clear that he too had not expected to see me so soon. He'd only had an hour's sleep but insisted he was pleased I'd arrived. Rachel said little to either of us, and when she was next out of the room Colin told me they'd had an argument: something to do with someone with whom he'd been working in France. When he called her back in to join us she said she was busy. 'See what I mean?' he said.

He told me what he'd been to film in France. His broken fingers were still in their sheath, but a different one, black instead of white, making his injury look somehow more sinister and permanent.

Rachel returned shortly before I left. Colin asked her if she'd finished her work. She poured herself a large drink and he watched her drain most of it in a single swallow. 'Work,' she said. 'Work work work work work.' She asked me if Colin had kept me amused with tales of his *expédition française* and refilled her glass.

9

Before I had a chance to speak, Rachel said, 'Her name's Valentine; she's American; she loves our wonderful wonderful country.'

Valentine introduced herself. She'd been waiting for the opportunity and quickly pulled her seat closer to the corner where I sat with Rachel. Once beside us she lay back and closed her eyes. I recognised her as the woman who'd had the foil beneath her eyes during Rachel's first stay at the clinic.

After which Rachel had dismissed herself, gone home, stayed a month, decided she'd returned too early and made arrangements to go back. She told me of her plans on the morning before she was due to depart.

She spoke of it as though it were a country hotel, or perhaps a spa. She said that as long as she paid the bills she could think of it as being whatever she wanted it to be. She said originally that she didn't want me to visit her and then helped me decide on the best time to go.

'Everything Valentine does is off-hand, casual and desultory,' Rachel said.

Valentine tried to suppress her laughter.

'Valentine's a big Anglophile who – '

'Valentine's a big everything.' Valentine shook in her chair.

I asked her where in America she was from.

'Television America,' Rachel said.

'American out of Italy. My grandfather, he was Italian. You're wondering how I came to be here.'

'Bo–ring,' Rachel yawned.

'Only to you,' Valentine said. She told me about her four husbands. 'Men put us all in here,' she concluded defiantly.

'That's right,' Rachel said.

'Men,' Valentine repeated. 'And it's always "Valentine", never "Val". You get a name like Valentine and it's something worth holding on to. Right?'

Right.

'I like you. I know straight away. Some people I like, some people

I don't. You I like. I knew right off with Rayche. This place is full of idiots – '

'Except we're desperate cases ourselves,' Rachel said. 'Why don't you go and tell *them* some of your stories?'

'That's all the thanks I get. You invite me over and then it's "Goodbye, Valentine." '

'Valentine loves everything about America. She hasn't lived there for seven years, and only her first and last husbands were American, but she's taken the entire continent to her heart.'

'Big heart, big heart.' Valentine pushed herself up and her body fell out of shape. 'And it's where I was born and raised. You listen to us,' she said to me. 'Me and her. Start listening to any of the others and you'll believe anything. I'm here on account of my weight. I got a projected weight loss this week of four pounds.' She took a card from the pouch fastened to her waist and checked it. 'Four pounds.'

'She's enrolled in Health and Beauty. It's a joke.'

Valentine agreed. 'Everywhere else I've been took it too seriously.' She left us and tried to walk like a model along the conservatory.

'Everything she does she's been to lessons for: walking, sitting, posture. She used to drink; we have an affinity. They project her weight loss and all she does is talk about it. She's been in so many clinics of one sort or another over the past ten years that she's stopped making any distinction.' She stopped the conversation by flicking over the page of a magazine.

It was easy, being enclosed and being beneath the glass, not to have to think about anything beyond what she could see outside. It was what the clinic allowed her to avoid, and why, ultimately, she had returned.

She watched as a gardener drove a mower in broad sweeps across the lawn and then as he tipped the cuttings into a gulley between the walled enclosure and the rest of the hospital.

'We've started doing voluntary work, me and Valentine. Except she calls it "missionary work".'

Where?

Talking about Valentine had become her diversion.

'The ward, parts of the rest of the hospital. They send us out to do good.' She was silent for a minute and then said, 'This isn't the problem you think it is.'

We heard Valentine's raised voice.

'Valentine's good on dead husbands. Ask her, she'll tell you all their names and exactly how much they were worth to her at the time of their "demise". She's a walking handbook of handy euphemisms.'

A group of women came into the conservatory from the corridor.

'They come in here to warm up. Valentine – she read it in a book – thinks we're like cold-blooded lizards that need to be out on a rock in the sun every morning before they can think about moving.'

The women unfolded chairs and sun-loungers and arranged themselves in a semi-circle.

Valentine reappeared and shouted to us. Rachel groaned.

'She's a pain. If anything gets me out of here sooner rather than later it'll be her.' Valentine was the only other woman in the clinic for whom she felt any affection. 'Do you want to know how I really found out about this place? One of Colin's friends did a programme on it. Shock horror revelation falls flat because nothing really happens. Rich women lying around. Shocking misuse of medical facilities. Except that they were all taken away and given to the NHS when the place was sold.'

We were finally interrupted by Valentine, who set down a jug and three glasses.

'Nothing ever goes any place in here,' she said. 'Things just keep moving round and round.'

'It's why we're here, Vee. It's what makes it so dependable.'

Valentine explained to me that her second husband had called her 'Vee'. 'Valentine' had embarrassed him. 'Valentine was probably some great goddess of love. I think perhaps he expected too much of me. His fault, not mine. "Vee" – that brings him back.' She slapped Rachel's leg. 'I let her call me that because we understand each other.'

'Saint Valentine was a man,' Rachel said.

'You can't know that. How can she know that for certain?'

I sided with Valentine.

'You're getting mixed up with Rudolph Valentino, that's what you're doing.' Valentine asked me if I believed her. 'Rayche walked into this big hole,' she said defensively. 'This Colin died and Rayche walked slap into a big hole.'

I watched Rachel tense and then relax. 'She read that in a book,' she said.

'I worked that out in my head, sister.' Valentine's voice had changed, her accent and tone. She looked from Rachel to me to the glass in her hand. 'I used to call everybody sister – sister, brother. That gives me away if nothing else does. Four pounds they expect me to lose. Do I look as though I need to lose that much? I only put

47

weight on because of all the water they make us drink. People don't believe me when I tell them that we're ninety-nine point nine per cent composed of water. It's true. It weighs a ton, that stuff.' She fingered the glass.

'Valentine is a great strength.' Rachel hooked her arm through Valentine's elbow.

'I ought to rent myself out,' Valentine said. 'Anybody's going to look one hundred per cent habeas corpus sitting beside me.' She remembered another husband. 'Laugh in adversity. The shit. He never drank water in his life. Ice was the nearest he ever got.'

'You make *me* laugh,' Rachel said.

'It's a gift. You two carry on. I'll just sit here.' She was silent for a few seconds. 'She tell you her theory about the lizards yet? Well it's mine. She stole it from me. But it can't be right: lizards are quick, come and gone before you see them. Now I'll shut my mouth.' She pulled her sunglasses down from her forehead and lay beside us. She tried to give the impression of being unconcerned by what we said. She sat up only as I prepared to leave. 'We'll meet again,' she said dramatically, holding out her hand. She said she intended returning to America at the end of the following week. She said she'd given Rachel her address. 'We walk in a twilight world, me and Rayche, remember that.'

'For Christ's sake, Vee.'

Valentine was hurt. 'Well, what am I expected to say? You don't like a bit of excitement, romance?'

'In here?'

'Sure in here. Why not? Where else do we find it? Doctors are very romantic people.'

'She watches too much afternoon television,' Rachel said.

I shook Valentine's hand.

'It's life,' she said to Rachel. 'They show life. You've got to believe it.'

'Okay, Vee, we all believe it.'

Rachel walked with me into the corridor. She stood at the glass door overlooking the car park.

As I left it began to rain. I didn't see her, but I imagined her running back along the corridor into the conservatory, where Valentine would be waiting to question her and tell her what mattered and what didn't matter, what was worth having and what was worth forgetting.

10

Children were playing in the adjoining gardens. Their parents, Rachel's neighbours, sat among them and held conversations through the shouts and screams. I was on speaking terms with several of them, but little more. Some sat in silence in the last of the day's sun.

With its cane blinds drawn, Colin's study was cool. I pulled out one of his neatly stacked cassettes and a dozen others fell to the floor. The growl in a man's throat slowly became a note released from his trumpet, and at the end of each sequence – already interrupted by the noises from outside – came a ripple of applause and the calls for more from a twenty-year-old audience. I could see out through the thin strips of the blind, but to anyone outside looking in I would have remained a shadow. The trumpeter introduced each quiet song, paying no attention to the audience around him.

The projector showed a film of Colin and Rachel sitting beside a river having a picnic. I'd watched the beginning of it on the day of her departure. There was still no soundtrack, only another tape.

"By the River", "A Picnic", "A Typical Summer's Day".

Words to the camera were clearly formed. Colin and Rachel standing together. Introduction. Colin's arm around Rachel's waist. Rachel's arm across Colin's shoulders, their similar heights making it difficult for him to appear comfortable, slipping from her at the first opportunity. The trumpeter's note falls back to his breath. It sounds as though he wants to laugh at his achievement, at the relief of having completed something he hadn't even been certain of how to begin.

When Colin and Rachel sat down and then leaned back into the long grass they were almost completely hidden by it. The middle distance was lost to the camouflage of patches of light and the shadows of trees.

Rachel knelt by the river and scooped out handfuls of water. Colin rolled up his trousers and waded in up to his shins. He looked for fish; he looked hard because he could not believe in the possibility of their existence. Rachel threw the water at him and he was unable to defend himself; he almost fell. She ran away from the bank and threw herself back down into the long grass. He waded from the water and kicked his legs dry.

He returned to where Rachel was hidden and lay down beside her, supporting himself on his elbow. He pulled up a stalk of grass, put it in his mouth and made a funny silent voice for the camera.

Rachel prepared a picnic and Colin retrieved dripping bottles of wine from the river. Neither of them looked any younger, but the way they ran and fell and chased each other made it easy to believe.

Occasionally, the camera was lifted from its tripod and taken to look up and down the river and then to follow the wooded horizon. Rachel pointed and it moved quickly upwards into the glare of the sky to focus on a hawk hovering above them. The camera waited, followed its dive, and then lost it. It held the spot where the bird had disappeared in the hope of seeing it rise with its prey.

Then Rachel held the camera and Colin stood in front of it with his hands on his hips and performed a clumsy dance.

They returned together to the long grass and were again lost to view. For almost five minutes nothing on the screen changed. Then Colin's hand rose and waved, followed by Rachel's, followed by his grinning face, followed by hers. She pushed herself up into a sitting position and brushed seeds from her face and shoulders. Colin stood and tried to pull her up, but she refused. She covered her face until he left her. She waved for the camera to be turned off, but instead he ran to it, lifted it from its stand and ran back to her. She turned away from him, holding the straps of her dress over her shoulders. Colin picked something small and white from her feet and held it up. She snatched it from him. He tried to lift her dress and she ran away, lifting her legs high to clear the tall stems. Colin chased her and then stopped. Rachel paused, saw that she was no longer being pursued, and went back to him. They pressed their faces together and smiled into the camera. Colin put a finger into his mouth and popped his cheek. Rachel hit him playfully. It was something I'd seen him do on other occasions – another of their intimacies. Rachel gave a thumbs-down sign into the camera and Colin pulled a face of dejection. Then she laughed, held her arms around his neck and kissed him. She drew the figure seven over the figure ten a few inches from the lens. Colin pretended to rub it out and drew an eight in its place. She pretended to think about it and then nodded in agreement.

There was further film of them lying in the grass facing upwards, and of them clearing away their plates and remains of the food. Rachel began carefully packing everything into a basket until Colin picked up the cloth by its four corners and held everything in a bundle at arm's length.

Then Rachel lay on her side at his feet and he rested his toes on her shoulder in the stance of a big game hunter with his kill. She growled and he made an invisible rifle and shot her. The film ended a second later.

When it returned they were together in the car with all its doors open and windows wound down. Rachel's hair was wet, as though she'd been swimming. She rubbed it with a towel and then shook it in the warm air. Colin walked in a circle through the grass where they'd eaten, looking down for something they'd perhaps lost or forgotten; whatever it might have been, he seemed unconcerned. Rachel sat sideways in the passenger seat. She fanned herself with the plastic lid of a container and drew her dress up almost to her waist. Colin returned and kissed her arms. It was later in the day and the shapes and outlines around them were sharper. Several hours had passed, been lost. Colin made a familiar gesture towards the camera, and I guessed later that he was asking Rachel to check how much film remained. The camera jarred and Rachel apologised to it. Colin performed another of his dances as he lifted the bundle of crockery and food into the boot of the car. He held out the two empty wine bottles and pretended to be drunk. Rachel left the car and danced around him. He took half a cucumber from the bundle and made an obscene gesture with it. Rachel tried to grab it from him, but he held it away from her and then threw it high into the air. The camera remained on them as they craned their necks to watch it rise and fall. Rachel covered her head and ran back to the car. Colin cupped his hands and tried to catch it, pulling them away at the last moment. He picked what remained of the cucumber from the grass and threw it towards the car, but the watery pulp fell apart a few feet from his hands. Rachel checked the camera again and waved to him frantically. He ran to join her and stood with her immediately in front of it. The lower edge of the sun had fallen into the sky behind them and the shadows of individual trees had coalesced into a dark band. As they composed themselves for their finale, the film ended.

The music continued; a penetrating insistence over the silent room. And when it stopped there was the pause of a disbelieving audience letting out its breath before beginning its applause.

11

'Tell me something: you worry about Rayche? Tell me to mind my own business.' Valentine leaned forward conspiratorially – 'Me and Rayche, we understand each other' – and rested her hand on my arm. She looked at it and said that contact was important to her; it was what one of the doctors had told her and what she believed. It was the kind of question Valentine enjoyed asking. I waited for Rachel to appear; she knew I was waiting.

Valentine sprang out of silences and plunged back into them.

'"Perhaps" is a good British answer,' she said. One of her dead husbands speaking. '"Perhaps", "I don't know", "What do *you* think?" They're all good answers. She doesn't need this place.' She leaned forward again and shielded one side of her face with her hand.

Meaning?

'Meaning she doesn't need to be here.' What else?

I'd offended her.

'Everything about this place is supposed to be voluntary, voluntary this, voluntary that, voluntary making your mind up. Don't you believe it. Take me, for instance: I should have gone a month ago.'

Why hadn't she?

She seemed uncertain. 'One thing and another.'

The temperature in the conservatory felt twice that of the grounds through which I'd walked from the car.

'My first husband – and whatever anyone tells you, they're always the best – used to say that you could know somebody better by asking two good questions of them than by living with them for a month. You believe that?'

For her sake, I was prepared to.

Rachel appeared in the doorway and watched us. I stood up. Valentine said, 'Gentleman,' reached up and held my arm. She shouted Rachel over to us and when she arrived told her I'd been keeping her company and she could take that any way she liked. Rachel sat beside us. Her eyes were dark and her hair fell down over one of her cheeks. Valentine signalled to her to push it back.

'I look a mess.'

'He didn't come expecting to see no beauty queen.'

I was surprised by Rachel's appearance but told her she looked fine.

'Of course I do.' She held her hands to the warm glass. 'Miss America, 1941,' she said, indicating Valentine.

'Pearl Harbor,' Valentine said.

'I've lost my appetite. Hospital food.'

'It's good food,' Valentine said. 'Our own kitchens, special diets, everything.'

Rachel looked away from us as she spoke.

'It was still good of him to come,' Valentine prompted.

Rachel agreed with her and then grew impatient with her presence and persistent interruptions. 'Go tell sombody else about Pearl Harbor,' she said eventually. The severity of her voice made me uncomfortable. Valentine stood up and searched her seat for the book or magazine she might have had with her.

'We're good friends,' Rachel said, watching her go. 'Good Buddies.'

'You were abrupt and rude.'

'She'll be back. You must understand that none of this, nothing of what we do or say to each other in here, none of this matters. It only matters out there. What's wrong with Valentine is that for too long people have been telling her she's funny, that she amuses them, and now she considers it her duty to live up to their expectations. Everything's a joke, or waiting to become one. Half of what she says she doesn't mean; she makes entrances, that's all. I sometimes wonder how much of the original there is left. It's something I'm beginning to wonder about myself.'

'You treat her no differently from any of the others.'

'It's what she expects: she'd be offended if I didn't.'

A vicious circle.

'If you like.' She pushed the loose hair behind her ear. 'Actually, and contrary to all appearances, I feel quite good.' She sat back to keep her face out of the strong sunlight. The small shadows beneath her eyes and in her cheeks disappeared.

I showed her the letter I'd received from an estate agent. It was addressed to me and in it he said he'd been directed by her to put the house up for sale. I'd called him and asked him to wait until I could confirm the decision.

'Is it why you came?' she said.

I asked her if it was what she really wanted. I said it seemed an unwise decision under the circumstances and waited for her to become angry at the implications.

'It felt like a good idea at the time,' she said. 'You're right – tell him to wait. I don't suppose he's planted any signs yet.'

I told her the agent had suggested a valuation.

She said that was a joke, that she could write 'For Sale' on the back of a postage stamp, stick it in the window, and that they'd be queueing within the hour to pay whatever she asked. 'The price isn't what matters in places like that. Where ought I to go? You build me somewhere.'

I told her she couldn't afford it and I couldn't afford to build it.

'Then tell Valentine that you'll follow her to America and build something for her. She's loaded, and sitting in here she just gets richer.' She searched the conservatory for Valentine.

There was a woman who resembled her on the lawn and I pointed her out.

'Valentine doesn't walk like that. Valentine strolls, Valentine ambles. It's important. When I said 1941 – ' She screwed up her eyes. 'No – tell him definitely not to sell it.'

It was important to her to believe she'd made the right decision, and that she'd made it independently. She rubbed her face. In the still air the smoke from her cigarette betrayed her hands. She noticed and watched it, forcing it to stop. She held up both hands.

Then she saw Valentine and shouted to her.

Valentine almost ran, slowing as she neared us. 'So I came back to be insulted again. What difference does it make? Listen, I made a joke: black Japanese kamikaze pilot – every December he gets bombed and attacks Pearl Bailey. Pearl Bailey the singer, actress maybe.' She told it as though she herself didn't fully understand it. No one told her it wasn't her joke.

Rachel almost choked laughing.

'She likes it,' Valentine said to me. 'Perhaps it's a better joke than I thought. When she said 1941, what she meant was I'm age forty-one.' She drew in her stomach. 'You believe that?'

'Then what year were you born?' Rachel asked her.

Valentine worked it out slowly on her fingers.

'Vee, you're an idiot.'

Valentine ignored her. '1946.'

'Give or take ten years. Do you think I should sell my house, Vee?'

'Property's property.'

'Valentine says: "Property is property." Valentine is some kind of oracle.'

Valentine told her she needed to get out in the sun more often. She held her tanned arm alongside Rachel's. 'See?'

'Valentine says I need to get out in the sun more often.'

Then she told Valentine that I was an architect, but Valentine was unimpressed. There was something she wanted to show Rachel in one of the magazines she'd brought with her. Writing for magazines impressed Valentine. She found the article.

'Food presentation, table-ware, that kind of thing. It's important.' What did we think?

'Some of these tables have five glasses per place-setting.'

'Would that be enough, do you think?' Rachel said.

'"California wines: A Coming of Age."'

'Vee thinks I should go back and live in America with her. Did you ever hear a worse idea?'

Valentine continued to read to us about the importance of the presentation of food. She showed us pictures and licked her lips. She turned the pictures for us to see, tried to read the text upside down and was quickly defeated.

'You get the feel of the dish,' she said.

'Except that when you've separated what might be edible from what isn't, there's nothing left,' Rachel said.

'She knows about these things. These are the kind of things she's worked on. Perhaps this is the kind of food I should be ordering. Perhaps then there would be less left of me.'

'We could walk outside,' Rachel suggested to me. We stood, but walked only a few paces along the conservatory.

'There's nothing here worth the breath it takes to say it,' she said.

I told her I'd contact the estate agent as soon as I got back.

'Do you think a valuation is a good idea?'

I told her that she'd at least have a realistic idea of how much the house would fetch if she changed her mind.

She said nothing for a minute, watching her reflection in the glass, seeing the figures of the women outside move across her face. 'I've been thinking about going back with Valentine just for that promised holiday, two or three weeks.'

'Valentine isn't going anywhere.'

She said she knew. 'She thinks she is.' She continued watching herself in the glass. 'I sometimes used to look like this when I'd been working away. I once went to the south of France and caught malaria. I lost nearly two stones. Jet-setting Rachel. I ought to recommend it to Vee.' She shouted to Valentine that she had the answer to all her problems.

'You and ten thousand others,' Valentine shouted back.

12

A week after her return, Rachel took out her collection of carved whalebone and ivory and spread it piece by piece over the table for me to inspect.

'*My* collection, note. In company it was always *my* collection.'

Each piece was wrapped in tissue and then newspaper. She handled them fondly.

He didn't know how to respond to them, I suggested.

'He still knew what they were worth. It would have been the easiest thing in the world to have taken them out and disposed of them, or sold them and donated the proceeds to one or other of our worthy concerns.'

I saw how successfully she had concealed from him her true feelings on the collection.

The smaller pieces of carved bone were little larger than thimbles; there were several hundred buttons and a cup of carved dice. There was a walrus, a small bear and several men with their arms linked like paper-chain men. Some of the pieces were yellow, others clean and white. She explained to me about the different types of bone and ivory from which the pieces had been carved. The yellowing was not due to age. She told me how she'd cleaned them upon inheriting them, and about the cases she'd originally had made to display them. Her favourite piece was a desk stand comprising a pen rack and two ink pots. The insides of the pots had been cleaned but were still ingrained with blue and black. The lids to the pots were silver and the corners to the stand had been carved with flying fishes.

'The whales they carved quite often bore little resemblance to the ones they hunted.' She showed me a plate of bone on which a stylised whale had been etched: the whale had two spouts and its eyes were enlarged and too close to the top of the head, making it look more like a cat than a whale. 'Whale fishes,' she said. 'You see the same on ancient maps. Mermaids and these. I remember the day we wrapped it all up and packed it away. "Hid" it away would be more accurate.' She showed me a rectangle of flat bone upon which a ship had been carved. The piece had been broken and then repaired. 'We thought about presenting it to a museum.'

I said I imagined that kind of philanthropy would have appealed to Colin.

'Something to commemorate the circumstances of our first meeting. I don't know why he felt it was important to keep on telling people.'

She unwrapped a comb and a hinged spectacle case. There was still pleasure to be gained in seeing them again. The name on the lid of the case was her great-grandfather's.

'Even then they must have had some idea of what they were worth. Not much else survived. Debts.'

I asked if the collection was still insured.

She said she supposed so. 'Someone who knows about them said we should wear gloves and not handle them too often.' She held the teeth of the comb to her face.

'Why not think again about presenting it to a museum?'

'Because it would only be a gesture – not what I really wanted. Besides which, there are better examples everywhere you look. The display cases are still somewhere in the house. Did you know that Colin had once filmed alongside a Norwegian whaler? He used to talk about it a lot. It was meant to be part of a film on endangered species but it was never used. The thing was, the endangered species was supposed to be the whalers and not the whales. It was one of the first films he ever made.' She fondled another of the carved figures. 'One of these pieces' – she searched through those still in the box – 'is two hundred years old.' She picked out the carved fish with the date inscribed. 'My family's involvement was only ever financial, you understand. I can't imagine any of us on the prow of the boat with anything as dirty as a harpoon in our hands. We came originally from the North East and I don't suppose these were anything more than a by-product of the fortune which brought us to London. It could have been anything, but it had to be whaling.'

I suggested it might have been worse – slavery, for instance.

'Don't even suggest it. I still don't know why I can't properly come to terms with all this yet. It shouldn't matter, it doesn't matter, and yet it still feels like a stain on an otherwise unblemished character. It's ridiculous.'

'Perhaps there's still too much of Colin in them.'

'Perhaps. It's why I'll sell this place in the end.'

And move out of London?

'Probably. No, I doubt it. Back to the North East, you mean? Listen to me, look at me: where else could I live? I was the one and only child. The Great White Hope, that was me. My parents were always old.'

She pushed her hand into the box of rolled newspaper wrappings, took several of them out, smoothed and read them.

'I sometimes wonder how complete the process is,' she said absently.

Which process?

'This, all this. From these to Colin to me – to what? I've only been back a week and I know less now than I did sitting in the tank with Valentine. I'm waiting for something to happen; I don't know what, but I'm still waiting for it. Or perhaps it *has* happened and I just don't know. Don't expect to make any sense of it.' She moved around the room switching on the lamps.

'There's a painting,' she said, and pulled it from beneath her chair. 'It was with the pieces.'

She handed me the small unframed painting of a whale and the men in rowing boats attached to it by the lines of their harpoons. It was a dirty and not particularly good painting.

'My great-grandfather wrote a letter to his wife – or she might have still been his sweetheart – telling her how six men had been drowned from one overturned boat. To read it you'd think he'd been with them, alongside, watching, instead of in his office up in Whitby or wherever. I suppose that was a kind of involvement as well. I wanted to have it framed but Colin thought otherwise. It's oil. It would never have been possible to protect it properly. I might still have it cleaned. What do you think?' She angled it to the dim light of one of the lamps but could not convince herself.

'Colin has a tape of whaling songs. He was going to use some of them as the soundtrack for the film, but everything gets cut down to seconds and would have become meaningless, background music. He'd calculated fifteen seconds for an opening and another fifteen to run over the closing credits. In his story of how we met he says he offered to buy me a model of the skeleton of the whale. He bought himself the kit; he bought me a record of the whales singing. My great-grandfather lived to ninety-six, and his wife survived him. Having come to London, they were then taken back to the North East to be buried.'

She said we didn't have to repack the pieces, but together we wrapped them and arranged them in the box. She considered the idea of making a catalogue of them.

'I don't know if I remember it accurately, but I'm almost certain that when I was a girl my father used to talk about a carved chess set, a centre-piece to the collection. I never saw it. One of those things you never had but always missed, like a nagging memory.'

Only the graves of her mother's sisters, all of whom were born in London, were within easy reach.

She sang a few lines of the only whaling song she remembered, and instead of packing the small painting she slid it back beneath her seat.

13

Colin sat with his face close to one of the screens ranged along the side of his room at Television Centre. Having slowed and then stopped the film on that screen, he pushed his chair along to the next, wound the second film on manually and moved on again. All these screens showed similar images.

His office was on the sixth floor. There were double blinds at the windows, most of which were drawn, and the light from the brighter side of the room barely penetrated the half in which he sat and studied the screens.

'I want you to look at this.'

He moved his chair to one side and pulled another close. I sat and looked at the screen with him. On it was a guillotine, surrounded on three sides by a crowd of almost motionless spectators, and a smaller group of people standing closer, one of whom was reading from an open book. The camera was in a fixed position high above the proceedings, looking down. The film had been badly cared for and flickered distractingly with clear circles like bubbles rising through water.

'Watch the small group.' He touched the heads of the people closer to the guillotine with a pencil. After a minute of nothing happening, three members of the group moved forward, a central figure held by a man on either side. 'It's a woman,' he said. The figure was indistinguishable from the two others. The guillotine stood on a low platform. The woman was guided up on to it and then helped to kneel, momentarily hidden by one of the upright supports.

'We estimate that the camera must be between forty and fifty feet above ground level. There's no indication that this was ever some kind of official record of the proceedings; probably the attempt of one of the warders or other workers in the prison.'

The original snuff movie?

One of them. It's obviously French, but that really is about all we know for certain.' He watched the screen intently as he spoke.

The two standing figures on the platform moved to either side of the kneeling – almost lying – woman.

60

'See how precise they are about everything.'

One of the figures shuffled back until he stood at the same distance as the other from the woman, and the man holding the book moved forward until he stood beside her head.

'We know he's speaking to her.'

'Last rites?'

'Or the finale of an official proclamation making certain she was fully aware of what was happening to her and why. They were very methodical about that kind of thing. Look.' He stopped the film and indicated the screens on either side. The picture on both was similar; only the angle and position of the camera varied. In each a figure lay ready in the wooden frame, the men beside it and the man with the book at its head.

'He's more likely to be the governor of the prison than a priest. We can identify him in one of the films. This one.' He tapped the screen with his pencil. 'It's even possible, judging by the film itself, that these two – the one we're watching and this one – were taken by the same cameraman. There are a few obvious similarities in technique, but I daresay the proceedings hardly varied. The chances are we'll never know. On with the show.' He let the film run on. The figure with the book took several paces back and drew a cross over his chest and face. Colin looked at his watch and started counting down from seven. At the last moment he stopped the film, studied it and then allowed it to move forward a frame at a time.

'There!' He indicated the blur of the falling blade, already a third of the way down. He ran the film on slowly and only the falling blur moved. The only faces discernible were those of the two men on the platform.

'Ready?'

The blade touched the body and he stopped the film again.

'From what we can see of the other executions, this one was clean and straightforward.' He wound the film back and let it repeat. There was a sack to catch the severed head. The image was confused, the only indication that something had happened being the response of the men in the small group nearby, all of whom took a step away from the body, or from where the head might have fallen had it missed the sack.

'Hole in one on this occasion. Sometimes they didn't get right through. Sometimes one of the two men on the platform would dash forward and raise the blade with a rope and let if fall again. Time now for a few more words.'

The man with the book moved back towards the decapitated

body, made another cross and read for a further few seconds. The two men on the platform above him stood to attention. When he'd finished he walked back into the small group, and they in turn moved back into the watching crowd, which began to file slowly from the courtyard through a single narrow doorway. When they'd gone, one of the men on the platform pulled the headless body from where it rested and the other fastened the sack and carried it to one side. Then they sat at the edge of the platform and lit pipes.

'The human touch,' Colin said.

'And your voyeuristic interest is purely professional.'

'What else? I wish we knew something more about whoever took the films. This one runs on for another twenty minutes. They cart the body and head off and then someone appears with a pail of water and a brush to clean the frame and blade. It's the same on the other film we think might have come from the same source.'

I asked him if he thought they'd been taken illegally.

'Almost certainly.'

He ran the film in the remaining monitors until the executions had been completed.

'We think – or, rather, we'd like to think – that the one of the woman was taken in 1928.'

'What's your interest?'

'Would you believe witchcraft? In France, believe it or not, the last person put to death for practising witchcraft was executed in 1928.'

'And you think it's her?'

'No, frankly, we don't. In addition to which, there was also the question of a more down-to-earth murder charge to answer. All we're interested in, as far as the film is concerned, is something to suggest how it might have been done. It isn't even my project, but I said I'd look at the film and offer my expert opinion.'

And my invitation to the beheading?

'Ah, that.' He occupied himself with rewinding all three spools of film. The task was hindered by the fact that his two broken fingers were still in splints, separate ones after their joint black sheath. I remarked on the length of time they were taking to heal. Instead of answering me he continued talking about the film and made only a passing reference to the small inconvenience they were causing him.

It was the fifth or sixth time I'd seen him since that first uncomfortable evening at the house, and the second time he'd invited me to a viewing in his room. The first occasion had been to show me a long propaganda film chronicling the architectural projections of the Third Reich. A documentary was being made and it was the first time that the film had been seen outside Germany in forty years. He'd asked me there to discuss the likelihood of the projects ever reaching fruition. Several of the projected buildings had been built and were still standing intact, others as museum pieces, and many had been destroyed during the war.

'We think the witchcraft story will tie in nicely with the guillotining of the woman. We'll make it very clear, of course, that this may not in fact be her. The trouble is, there's every chance it *is* her, and that's what's so frustrating. The husband of the woman who found the film had been with the British Expeditionary Force in France, and he'd told her that someone had told him that the woman being executed was a witch. He was probably sold it as a souvenir. Neither of them spoke French. It's all so very likely.'

'And so you asked me up here for my opinion as an architect?'

'If you have one to give. Everyone else in here has one. Everybody here has two good ideas in the same day and manages to stretch them out over an entire career.'

It was Sunday morning. The corridors and rooms around us were filled with people working. He took a bottle and two glasses from the top drawer of a filing cabinet.

'Cliché after cliché,' he said. 'It's all true: nothing here but the absolute and relative truth. I used to have a small sign saying something to the effect that never in the field of artistic endeavour had the willing – nay, the slavering – suspension of disbelief paid so many wages and for so long.'

'You're bitter and twisted.'

He held up his two broken fingers and then blinked at the pain of moving them apart.

'We had a surgeon in here a few days ago telling us about the pressure and striking force required to sever a head cleanly and completely. The guillotine, for all its symbolic connotations of dread, was not a particularly efficient means of dispatch. Efficient by French standards, that is. It was designed for public spectacle as much as anything. According to our surgeon friend a man with an axe or a length of cheese-wire is far more effective. Half the world still garrottes its convicted murderers and the other half – God bless its civilised heart – still wants to watch.'

I knew from the way he kept glancing at me that he was having difficulty with what he was trying to tell me.

63

He filled the two glasses and gave me one. He drank his own immediately and refilled it.

'We like to pad the clichés out wherever possible.' He smiled down at his desk. 'According to the latest multi-million-pound quackery, my tiny insignificant little bones are no nearer having mended now than they were five weeks ago when they were first broken.' He held up his fingers and turned them. 'And not only have the bones not set properly, but they show no signs whatsoever of making the slightest effort to do so. Ever since they told me that, I've felt every bone in my body crack up and powder. That, in essence, is my problem. Or perhaps only the beginning of my problem.'

He swallowed the rest of the drink.

I asked him how much more he knew.

'Only that the fact that they will not mend is probably an indication of something else being wrong. You'd never guess how many ways there are of being told that.'

'Is it a question of the breaks not being able to mend themselves because of where they're located?'

'You sound like a man in a yellow hat looking up at a centimetre-wide crack under a motorway bridge and trying to convince himself that a centimetre isn't very much. I'm sorry, I didn't mean to burden you with this. They think it's something to do with the bone rather than the break itself. I'm probably making it sound far worse than it is. I'm having some more tests done next week.'

He held up both hands and studied them. Then he flattened them as though he were about to slam them down.

I asked him how Rachel had responded to the news.

'I've only known for a week. It's not the end of the world. There's no suggestion whatsoever of me not surviving my alloted span.'

He hadn't told her.

'I used to bite my nails,' he said. 'I'm even scared to do that now.' He showed me. It was as much as he'd prepared himself to say on the subject. 'Someone was supposed to be sending us a film of a man being garrotted in Spain but it never arrived.'

I asked him if he would have been allowed to show it.

'You're joking!'

'How do they do it? Does he stand there and wait for someone to come up behind him?'

'I think he sits or stands against a wall with his hands tied to his sides.' He drew his thumb absently across his throat. 'I'd still like to have seen it.'

I asked him what he'd know as a result of the new tests.

'How much more scared to get before I enter my public, rational, not-the-end-of-the-world stage. I can't concentrate for thinking about it. It's starting to feel as certain as whatever it is they' – he indicated the screens – 'must have known when they were pushed down into position. You can be the first to tell me I'm overreacting.'

He poured himself a third large drink. I emptied my own glass and he refilled it.

I asked him when he was going to tell Rachel.

'When I know for certain what it is. She knows there's something wrong because of the length of time my fingers are taking to heal. She once broke both her ankles in a skiing accident; she knows about these things. Anyway – come and look at this. The televisual Cabinet of Horrors goes on and on.'

I followed him into a small, empty side-room in which there was a larger screen. He switched it on to reveal three bodies kneeling, with their heads lowered.

'Chinamen. You can always rely on the Chinese.'

The bodies were kneeling on sand and the shuffling feet of the crowd behind them could be seen.

'Notice anything unusual?'

Praying? Three more waiting for the chop?

'Count to three.'

I counted as the camera swung to one side to reveal the men's already severed heads arranged in a row beside them. Then the camera moved down to the faces until they filled the screen. The eyes of the three men were closed. One had a long, thin moustache, and another a shaved head except for a slender pony-tail, which had been smoothed and arranged beneath his chin.

'Chop chop Chinaman,' Colin said.

Looking at the heads, it was difficult to believe that they weren't still attached to three bodies buried up to their necks in the sand. None of the three faces looked in the least surprised or frightened. Or perhaps the eyes and mouth had been closed before the camera had been allowed near them.

14

'Before I went back to the clinic I went to Heathrow. I left here and went straight there. I walked up the hill and found a taxi.'

'Did you intend going anywhere?'

'I don't think so. It was just a nice ride out: quiet, clean, not too much traffic. I felt as though I'd become part of someone else's routine. "Heathrow, quick." I had all the time in the world and out of it I could create a sense of urgency; I could stay calm and pretend it didn't matter. It was how I used to be without trying. I just wanted to feel it again – knowing what I was about to do, that is.'

'You'd packed more than you needed for the clinic. You might have intended going somewhere.'

'Who knows? Perhaps sitting there and watching everybody else come and go might have helped me to make up my mind one way or another. It felt good just knowing that I could do it, that I could just wait for a destination to flicker into view and decide there and then to go. I could have ended up at the other end of the world on a whim. It was simply being in a position to do it that mattered. Not that I seriously believe I would have done. I think if I'm honest with myself, it was just another case of pretending.'

'And did anywhere appeal?'

She stopped drumming her fingers and looked at me.

'No. Practically every airport in the world flashed up and not one of them struck me as being somewhere worth visiting. It's pathetic. I just sat there and looked. I put my luggage away and tried to appear as though I was waiting for a flight or for someone to arrive. The place is full of people trying to occupy themselves. I suppose I should have felt at home. There's a scene at the end of *Billy Liar* – that was me: him on the platform, me in the starring role at Departures and Arrivals.'

'And then you went to the clinic?'

'No. I just waited. I stayed the night in the hotel. Extortionate, but I stayed. The point being, I felt relaxed and comfortable. Nobody belongs in places like that, but for the first time in a month I felt comfortable. No one looking at me would ever have known. Two men tried to pick me up – both very respectable – and one of them sat with me for an hour. He was flying to Zurich and bored me rigid with everything he knew about the place.'

She spoke quickly and when she hesitated she moved her fingers to suggest she was trying to remember something else, as though one thing led naturally to another.

The day was overcast and, although not particularly cold, the door into the garden was closed. 'I stayed there for the night, went back into the airport the next day and then back to the hotel for the second night. Two nights is a fortnight in a place like that. No one ever stays more than one.'

'And each day you just went out and sat and watched the planes coming and going.'

'Not so much the planes as the people. I very rarely used to go and meet Colin and I never went to see him off. Colin was a professional airport user. The way he moved through them always conferred a kind of status. He was good at it; he never seemed to have to do any waiting. On the second day I drank twenty cups of coffee – I counted them – and then I started composing an article on the comings and goings. I got the first sentence out nice and sharp. I wrote it down somewhere. Something else about an airport: it's a safe place to sit in public and write; anywhere else and there's always somebody looking over your shoulder. And when that came to nothing I just sat and watched. ''Sad Farewells and Fond Reunions''. There was a camera crew in one of the VIP lounges. I might even have had a walk-by part.'

She laughed at the thought. She was telling me all this to avoid having to come to the precise point at which she'd decided to leave and return to the clinic.

'I was once coming back from somewhere with Colin and we were rerouted because of fog or snow or an accident or something from London to the Midlands. I was asleep on the plane. It was two or three in the morning when we landed and nobody told me we weren't at Heathrow. There must have been a twenty-foot sign telling me where I was but I never saw it. I made an absolute bloody fool of myself by insisting to a stewardess that there'd been a mistake. Colin pretended not to have noticed. He said that perhaps it was a stop-over and tried to get me to turn round and stay on the plane.'

'And at the end of the second day?'

'I sat there for those two days, waiting and thinking about things, and when the time came I picked up my bags and left. Another taxi, another train . . . When I arrived they probably thought I'd walked. The truth is, they don't really listen to much because they think they already know it all. All they really needed to know was why *I* thought I needed to go back. I said if they didn't know, then there didn't seem much point in my staying. They like that kind of cleverness.'

She went to the door and looked out over the shrubs and brickwork.

'Had you expected something more exciting?' she said. 'Did you think I was wandering up and down the Embankment surviving on soup, dirty looks and good intentions? I did consider it.'

I hadn't even known about the two 'missing' days.

'I think the ride to the airport did me as much good as anything. If I could find that first sentence I might just be able to do something with it. It was on an envelope.'

Or it was in the margin of a newspaper, or on the back of a brochure, or on any one of a hundred scraps of paper she'd since destroyed.

'It took me practically all morning to get that one sentence right. Even that's a lie: it took me a minute, less, and then I spent the rest of the morning trying to come up with something to follow it.'

She circled the kitchen with her arms folded and sat back down.

'Now tell me what you've been doing,' she said.

I told her about a small office block.

'Will it be different from any other small office block?'

'The foyer will be good for plants. The receptionist will sit in an almost permanent shadow, but the tubs of plants they put in will thrive for a month before they die in the air conditioning.'

'You're good at irrelevancies, especially when they're called for. I think I might go out and you ought to come with me to celebrate my return.'

I told her I'd already made arrangements for the evening.

'I'll celebrate alone then. I invited Valentine to come and see me, but she won't. Did I tell you she now firmly believes that people have a good and an evil side to their character depending on where they are?'

'Is that why she won't go home?'

'I don't know. It's why she stays where she is. She says she's too good for her own good. She says she'll die of goodness.' She slapped the table with both hands. 'Right! Tonight, think about tonight. Food, drink, relaxation. If I don't do something, all the bits of nothing will begin to take over again.'

15

There was a small boy in the film. It may have been his first time in front of Colin's camera and he watched it apprehensively, uncertain of what was being asked of him. He stood in a neighbouring garden – his own – and his parents stood together to one side of him. He looked to them and they encouraged him to perform; he was no older than three or four. He wore only a pair of shorts and a toy watch. He ran on the spot and then stood still to recite a song or verse he knew, counting off its lines on his fingers. When he'd finished he applauded himself. His mother knelt beside him and whispered something. He nodded vigorously and began again, facing her instead of the camera. She stopped him and turned him and once again he became uncertain. She pointed to Colin and waved. The boy looked serious for a moment and then repeated his recitation.

Rachel appeared and knelt beside him. She gave him an ice-cream cone and he immediately ran over to show it to his parents. The camera stayed on Rachel as she watched him and then as she held out her arms for him to return to her, which he did. He sat in her lap and began to explain something to her, again using his fingers. She listened to him intently, nodding at everything he told her. She wiped the ice-cream from his cheeks and stroked his hair, and when he held out his hand she took it in her own, only to have him pull it free and continue with his explanation.

Someone threw a ball towards them and the boy was distracted. Rachel caught it and balanced it on his head. He knocked it off and laughed. She retrieved it and he ran in circles around her, falling frequently but not hurting himself. He became giddy, and instead of standing after a fall he began to roll on the grass. Rachel stretched out and lay alongside him. The camera was lowered until it looked across the lawn towards them. The feet and legs of the boy's parents were briefly in shot and then the camera moved to exclude them. Rachel still held the ball. She wanted the boy to stop rolling and to remain beside her. She tried to hold him but he pulled free and walked on his hands and knees towards the camera, growling and

69

barking. His ribs showed and he had the dark V of a tan around his neck. He stopped close to the camera and inspected it. He reached out to touch it and then drew back quickly. He sat, puzzled, for a moment. Rachel stood up and looked down at him.

The next piece of film showed Rachel with her arms out, calling for the boy to return to her, but by then he'd lost interest. He marched in a zig-zag path around her, deliberately avoiding her. She bounced the ball and then threw it into the air and caught it. He remained unimpressed. After a minute he sat within a few feet of her and occupied himself with something he'd found in the grass. Rachel moved to sit beside him.

Later, she sat on the lawn with the boy asleep in her lap. He looked much smaller. She arranged his hair with her fingers and cradled his head in her elbow. Colin walked around them, looking down and then lowering himself until he was level with both their faces. It was clear that they were now alone with the boy, who had his thumb in his mouth and his fist pressed into his cheek. Rachel pointed to it. The passage of time between this and the earlier film could be seen in the new shadows around them. Rachel closed her eyes and held her head forward until it touched the boy's. He flinched in his sleep and turned, removing and then replacing his thumb. Colin held their faces for a moment and then continued moving around them. A bird alighted a few yards from them and he filmed that instead. Everything about the film suggested stillness and silence. Then something disturbed the bird and Colin followed it into the trees, returning in the same smooth arc to the boy's bare feet, moving up his legs and body back to Rachel. Always back to Rachel. Her eyes were still closed and she was gently rocking the boy. His hand fell limply from his mouth and he woke up. He began to cry and Rachel stood him on the grass, supporting him. He was disorientated. He looked directly into the camera and then ran crying from the lawn towards the house. Colin followed him. The boy's mother appeared, lifted and swung him, and by the time Colin reached them he was laughing again. He pretended to punch the camera and the film jumped as Colin took a step backwards. The boy's mother wiped his eyes with a handkerchief and he struggled to be released.

Rachel arrived and Colin filmed the two women together. The boy's mother said something and they both laughed; they held each other's shoulders and danced in chorus. Then the boy's father appeared and they insisted that he stood between them and danced. Both women kissed him on the cheek and held the pose until the film ended.

PART TWO

1

Rachel insisted on having a radio playing whenever she was in the house; she said she simply wanted to be able to hear it. The noise emphasised something of the house's emptiness and of whatever she believed that emptiness might sooner or later reveal to her. She didn't want to be able to hear anything specific – music or voices – but simply to be aware of the noise. 'Whenever I'm working in the house,' she said.

'It bores me,' she freqently said of anything which was not pressing or did not in some way indicate the way ahead. She spoke about redecorating parts of the house, about replacing a broken bathroom window, about altering the arrangement of shrubs in the garden. She started talking again about taking a holiday.

'A holiday, we are all clearly decided, is what is needed.' She made it sound as though a committee of honest, straightforward and decent people had taken over the running of her life, and despite her previous reluctance to leave, I now detected a sense almost of urgency to get away. Or if not of urgency, of need, which she tried to disguise with her casual remarks and apparent indecision.

The radio played loudly on the kitchen table, and when the doors were open it could be heard to the top of the house. She had Radio Four days, Radio One days, days when she spoke enthusiastically of particular programmes, and days when she remembered nothing of what she might have heard.

I returned one evening to find she'd collected together all of Colin's mementoes and souvenirs of his foreign travels. She sat with a grey and scarlet handwoven rug folded across her knees, on top of which was perched an empty glass. She refilled it from a bottle of tonic water standing beside her.

'I'm making my abstemious good behaviour as painfully obvious as possible. I'm like a stopped smoker sitting with his chewed pencil or invisible cigarette just waiting for someone to ask him how long it's been.' She held up a corner of the rug. 'This came from Peru, or Bolivia, or Ecuador, or any one of those places I never cared enough about to find out exactly which. I was just tired of seeing them all

73

scattered around the house like trophies. They always meant more to him than to me. When I redecorate, everything will come down anyway, even the paintings.'

Few of which, I guessed, would be put back up.

She played on a small skin drum and held a pair of tusks mounted on a wooden shield to her forehead.

'I used to try and convince him to stop bringing it all back, that he was being conned into buying something that had been created purely for wealthy tourists, that he was a corrupting influence. He said he couldn't see why it mattered. I remember his mother used to collect round glass paperweights and pebbles painted with seaside scenes.' She pulled a face and sipped at her drink.

I asked her if she intended getting rid of it all.

'Perhaps I ought to fly round the world and sell it back to them. Paint "Greetings from Sunny London" over every piece and sell it back.' She laughed.

On the few occasions when the radio wasn't playing she always ensured that one of the televisions in the house was on. She talked about the ideas she'd had for new articles. She hid things badly, but because she herself was still uncertain of what she intended doing, it didn't matter.

It also became difficult to gauge the speed of her recovery. Neither of us ever used the word.

'The holiday is definitely on,' she announced one afternoon. The table was spread with brochures. 'Egypt, the pyramids, to start with.'

It seemed an unlikely choice.

'That's why I'm going. What would be the point in choosing somewhere you were determined to enjoy or somewhere you'd been before and enjoyed if enjoyment was not the reason for going?' There was a kind of logic in her argument. 'Perhaps I'll do the Seven Wonders – what are they? Are they all still standing or hanging?'

I told her I doubted it.

'So the place will be full of raggy Arabs, sandflies and camels. So what?'

'Have you actually booked?'

'This morning.' She slid her ticket out from beneath the brochures. 'Perhaps I'll meet a handsome, oil-rich Arab sheik and be carried off into the desert night. It is what we're talking about, isn't it?'

And after the pyramids?

74

'I'll come running home and promise never to do it again. I don't know, I haven't decided. Perhaps India or the far East. Perhaps Japan. Who knows? At least I'll get as far as the pyramids. I'll throw all Colin's junk out and fill the house with my own. Or perhaps I'll just travel hopefully and never actually arrive.'

I suggested she might use the holiday as the basis for some work.

She'd already considered the idea and the suggestion made her angry.

'That would defeat the object entirely, create a connection. What I need is to be cut adrift in as obvious a way as possible and then to see what happens. Perhaps I ought to get in touch with Valentine and ask her to come with me. She might be walking a more slippery rope just at present, but there's enough of her still unfocused and empty enough to absorb everything around her – myself included – if you see what I mean.'

I let her know that I did.

'It'd be using her to my own ends, but it's what makes her feel comfortable.' She hummed a sand-dance tune and swayed her arms and neck. 'Alternatively, of course, I might go back to the travel agent tomorrow and make him that much richer by cancelling everything and forfeiting my deposit.' She stood up and continued dancing.

She left without telling me three days later. Her note said simply that she'd gone. Colin's foreign mementoes still lay in a pile where she'd collected them. I took them out of the sitting-room and into his study.

The television was on in one of the first-floor rooms, suggesting to me more strongly her presence in the house than the note on the table which told me she'd gone. I looked into every room. In her bedroom half-empty drawers were still open and her dressing-table top was clear. Her bed was made and on it was the impression of a suitcase.

Five days later I received a postcard from Paris saying the pyramids were nowhere in sight. After that, cards came from Berne, Milan, Venice and Rome. They were ordinary, anonymous cards of famous views. They told me that she'd arrived and that the weather was good or the weather was bad. They listed the famous landmarks in four, five and six languages. She told me where she might or might not be going next. It was how she had chosen to temporarily disappear.

During her absence, several of the neighbours saw me in the garden and invited me into their homes, where we discussed what had happened to Rachel and Colin as indirectly as possible. They made a point of telling me how they thought she had been avoiding them since his death. I knew from Rachel that she had never been particularly close to any of them.

A week after the card from Rome came another. She'd stayed for six days and intended moving on to Athens to visit friends. She wrote 'Arrivederci'.

There was an address book in Colin's study and I searched it for the Athens address, but found nothing. There was the name of a hotel in Volos and the address of a news agency in Istanbul, but nothing else. I wondered how far she would move in one direction before turning round and moving in another. The fact that she was still travelling and making decisions for herself seemed to be enough.

After the second card from Rome nothing arrived for a week.

I worked longer hours and accepted an invitation to apply for a commission which meant a week's stay in Birmingham and a weekend afterwards in Wales. In the fortnight following, I visited Edinburgh, York and Cardiff.

More postcards came, but the trail they laid was a false one. She indicated she was at last going to Cairo and then a card arrived from Madrid, and after that from Grenada and Seville.

2

I'd been with them when Colin had reminisced about their honeymoon six months after the event.

'After the reception we drove north through the night to Scotland.'

'Scotland,' Rachel repeated derisively.

It was somewhere Colin had never been. An unbelievable admission from a man who had been at least three times around the world.

Colin always drove casually; always powerful cars, but with his hands barely touching the wheel.

'Scotland,' Rachel repeated. 'And "north through the night" makes it sound far more than it really was – Mercy Dash material.'

'Can you believe that? Three times round the world and I'd never been to Scotland. Carlisle, once, and Durham to cover something vaguely religious when I was still learning. But never Scotland. Not once.'

'Scotland the Brave . . . and wet,' Rachel said.

'It rained.'

My impression was of two people looking at each other; two distinctive voices coming back together after too long a time and from too great a distance apart.

The details of Scotland, the honeymoon, are perfect. Except that like the memories of the wedding, they are the memories of any honeymoon.

Except that they cannot have driven north during the night after the wedding.

'You're right: Colin was pissed. We were both pissed. We stayed the night at the hotel where we'd had the reception and left the following morning. We had to come back here first to collect the things we'd forgotten, and we didn't finally set off until mid-day. We were making for Inverness and stopped the night somewhere north of Glasgow.'

'North of Dumbarton, somewhere on Loch Lomond.'

So *some* of the driving was done at night?

'Very little,' Colin said. 'And none of it necessary. I'd misjudged the distances, the timing. I knew to the minute how long it took to get to Hong Kong, but Inverness beat me.'

Four days in a hotel in Inverness. Or perhaps five, or six. Five, definitely five. Arrive Monday morning – the Saturday wedding, Sunday night on Loch Lomond – depart Saturday morning. Monday night, Tuesday night, Wednesday night, Thursday night, Friday night. Five nights.

'Five nights. Definitely five.'

And the days?

'Touring.'

'Touring in the rain,' Rachel corrected. 'They're proud of it. They boast of it. They love their rain.'

'To Skye via the Kyle of Lochalsh, Elgin, Fraserburgh, and up to Caithness, Duncansby Head, John o'Groat's,' Colin said, speaking like someone who'd looked up the names afterwards. The itinerary, the details of every day mattered.

'John o'Groat's being a dump, and not actually the farthest point north.'

'Skye. You enjoyed Skye.'

'Perhaps it stopped raining for an hour. Perhaps that was it.'

'It didn't rain all that often. We did everything we intended doing, went everywhere we wanted to go.'

As far as Rachel was concerned there had been nothing to do, nowhere to go.

Rachel had wanted to leave after only one day. Rachel had never wanted to go there in the first place. Rachel had wanted to go to the Riviera. To the Riviera, where she had been once before – or since – and caught malaria. Or, if not the Riviera, somewhere close. What she had not wanted to do, she said, was to have to drive to Caithness to catch pneumonia.

Caithness – the tiniest, tiniest details. 'And *I* drove. *You* didn't do any of the driving. *I* drove everywhere.'

Castles, lochs, hotels, moors, twenty-mile-round journeys to move forward a mile –

'The hospitality, at least acknowledge the hospitality.'

'The French are hospitable, the Italians are hospitable – *would* have been hospitable given the chance.'

– the visit to a distillery, the forests, the salmon-fishermen, the stories of –

'You're beginning to sound like a brochure,' she told him. To me she said: 'We went to one castle and it was so cold that we daren't stand still. All Bloody Deeds in the Dark and Distant Past and a stuffed bear coming apart at the seams.'

'We were the only visitors. They opened up and showed us round.'

'For five pounds they opened up and showed us round. Bonnie Prince Charlie slept there – no doubt with Flora Macdonald or whoever, and – surprise, surprise – some of the Laird's ancestors had emigrated to America. Tourist-wise, that particular migration had been reaping the benefits ever since.'

Colin had cut a piece of lucky heather and wedged it into the radiator grille of the car. A month later, back in London, he'd miscalculated a small distance and run into a concrete bollard. He'd pulled out the heather and thrown it away. It was where the honeymoon ended. Details from beginning to end.

'"Memorable" is the word. Memorable, ineradicably memorable,' Rachel said.

'Why should it still matter?'

'You tell me. And it wasn't Loch Lomond, it was Loch Long.'

Colin was encouraged by the correction: 'That's right! We thought we were on Loch Lomond and all the time we were on Loch Long. We went for an early-morning walk to breathe in the Loch Lomond air, but we were on Loch Long. I don't know how we made the mistake, where we went wrong, but it was where we ended up.'

'Loch Long, Hong Kong. We should have taken the High Road, but instead we took the Low Road.' She made an attempt at the song.

'All that matters – '

'All that matters is that we should have done it properly.'

'By "properly" she means we should have done it as directed by the "Perfect Honeymoon" magazine articles. When it becomes fashionable to spend a wet week in Scotland, we'll have been the first to have done it.'

By the following Saturday evening they were back in London. A week had passed since the wedding. Colin said afterwards that it sometimes felt like a year, sometimes a day. Sometimes, Rachel said, it felt as though she had it all yet to come.

Alone with me, Colin said he didn't know why they'd had to go through it all again. He said there were different stories for different people, and I'd heard one of the worst.

It might not have mattered then, but none of it can ever have been lost. They saved the worst versions of all the stories for themselves.

Upon their return Rachel started arranging dinner parties. The invitations were reciprocated, and then there were lulls, long absences, the falling off of recent and shallow friendships. Comparisons of Before and After were made, were still being made.

Rachel stopped working as regularly as she had been doing.

Two days after their return Colin had gone to Oslo on the shortest notice. Often, as then, Rachel only learned of his departure hours after he'd already arrived wherever it was he'd been sent.

'If it hadn't rained so much . . .' he said. He made his fingers into rain and trickled them down between us. 'It wouldn't really have mattered it we hadn't found out about it being Loch Long and not Loch Lomond; we didn't walk all that far – just across the road from the hotel and down to the shore. We told everyone we were on our honeymoon.' It had come to exist for them in the smallest gestures. 'Nothing we did made anything of it; we depended entirely on other people knowing. Afterwards, I used to come back from having been away and make a point of telling people where I'd been. It never used to matter before, but suddenly it did. It was just a need. I felt it but I could never work out why. It has nothing to do with Scotland – except that for one night I sat looking out at Loch Lomond and it wasn't Loch Lomond.'

Except for that.

Photos of the views, the rivers, the hills, the skies.

'We parked directly in front of the hotel entrance and went in through a stone-flagged porch to a narrow corridor, at the end of which was a reception desk. Rachel rang the bell – I wanted to wait, but Rachel rang the bell. Beside the reception was a door leading to a dining-room with the tables already set for the next day's meals, sugar and butter already in the dishes. And at the end of the room there was a small bar – nobody sitting at it, but illuminated with concealed lighting and with music coming from a hidden speaker. Our room was on the first floor and looked across the road over the water. There was someone in the next room with children, a picture on the wall of a gamekeeper with the carcass of a deer. The people who ran it probably thought it was the finest hotel in the world. You can imagine the rest.'

Detail after detail. For him, a kind of encapsulated perfection; a kind of suppressed excitement at the thought of something so perfectly remembered; a kind of mystery at not understanding why it should have remained to the exclusion of a great deal else.

Rachel came back into the room. 'You think I'm ungrateful, don't deny it.' She held a presentation case of twelve miniature bottles of whisky. 'We visited a distillery.' She slid the bottles from the packet into her lap. 'Colin thinks we should save them. More mementoes. But would it be entirely honest? I know some people do save them, arranging them in prissy little lines, dusting them. I suppose they'd lose their value if I broke the seals.' After a few minutes she repacked the bottles into the moulded plastic case. Some of the bottles fitted several of the spaces and some would not fit at all without rearranging others already in place. She played with them as though they were an educational toy. 'Round peg in the round hole, you stupid child.' When she became impatient with the game she forced the bottles into any position and broke the plastic casing. This she then forced back into the box, tearing it in the process. 'There! Perfect!' She held up the box for our inspection.

'We bought it on Skye,' Colin said. He told me something about the decline in the number of small distilleries on the island over the previous half century.

'I'm sorry,' Rachel said. She held the broken box across her open palms.

'Drink them. That'd be the most honest thing to do. We should have drunk them there and then and brought a milk bottle full of Scottish rain back with us instead,' Colin said, still caring for her and everything she said and did.

'We spent an hour sitting beside Loch Ness waiting for the monster to show. The nearer you get the more you start believing it.' She folded her arm into the head and neck of the monster.

'And if it wasn't Loch Ness, it was almost certainly somewhere remarkably similar.'

'No – definitely Loch Ness. The monster paddled out and attacked the car.'

'That's right, I remember.'

'You fought it off with the lucky heather and I sat on the roof of the car and screamed. There hadn't been a scream like it since Glencoe.'

'And the hand-held was locked in the boot and we'd just finished the film in the Nikon.'

Where the memories became lies never mattered, and when it happened in reverse the distinction was even less clear.

Rachel sang a song to the Scottish rain and Colin broke the seal on each of the small bottles. He started to juggle with them and then dropped them.

3

Rachel returned from Europe a fortnight after her last postcard, during which time there had been no further communication from her. She'd spent the whole of the final two weeks in Rome. For a fortnight I'd imagined her to be sightseeing in Cairo and along the Nile. She was heavily tanned and looked healthy, the best she'd looked in the previous six months. She'd gained weight and had had her long hair cut short and dyed darker than its naturally dark colour.

She sat in the kitchen. She wore a broad straw hat, a tight white dress with a belted waist and a pair of sunglasses with tapered frames. Her feet were on the table, her flat white shoes on the floor.

'The Happy Wanderer returns,' she shouted. 'The bottles on the table are yours, the cartons of cigarettes mine.'

I told her she looked good, healthy.

'I always do.' She added something in Italian. 'Someone on the plane home told me I looked like Sophia Loren. *The Two Women of Rome*. I'd hoped she was going to say Audrey Hepburn – you know, something a little more gamine and a little less pasta brown. Still, it was good of him to say anything, considering he was travelling with his wife, who, needless to say, was temporarily absent.' She laughed and swung her legs from the table. 'I'm brown all over. I've done nothing but eat, sleep, sit around and soak up the sun. I feel recharged. Or at least I did until I came back to this.' It was raining lightly. 'I actually did get to see the pyramids on a two-day round trip.'

I told her I'd received her cards.

'They're not as spectacular as I'd expected, but then I was never entirely certain what I did expect.'

I told her that if I'd known she was coming back I would have straightened round in the house.

'Leave it. I prefer it un-straightened round. It's been straightened round for the past five years. I've come to the conclusion that in the rest of Europe tidiness is a sign of wealth, a means of conspicuous display. Or something. You lose touch, being away. You forget.

Anyhow, the cure has worked and I am delivered safely home. Flying makes me hungry. It's probably something to do with all that static. I've eaten three meals a day for the past three, no, four weeks – eighty-four meals, Italian mostly.' She held her stomach with both hands, trying to make it look larger; it looked no fuller than when she'd gone away. 'To be perfectly honest, Italian meals in London are better than Italian meals in Rome.'

She swung her feet back on to the table, took off her glasses, rubbed her eyes and replaced them.

'I still talk too much, and too fast. Perhaps that's also from being in Italy too long. I'm exhausted. I didn't let you know when I was coming back because it's all part of the new me. Don't say it: if I believe that I'll believe anything.'

I sat beside her and she immediately got up and went out into the garden. She crouched down and plucked at single blades of grass growing between the bricks. I'd neglected to carry out what little maintenance the garden needed, and it showed.

'I'm going to hire someone to come and do it for me. I've just decided – well, not just now, not this instant, but it's what I've decided. I've had a long hard look at things. I had intended to keep on travelling. Madrid was the nicest place I went. Everywhere else exhausted me, made demands. Do you want to hear my greatly improved Spanish? No, probably not. I left after three days and went back to Rome. I stayed a week on the outskirts in a small hotel and then moved into the centre to stay with friends. Friend, singular, male. Next question.'

I told her I wasn't making any kind of judgement.

'I know. Yes, friend, singular, a man. He might come to London in the near future on business. He probably won't, but he might. A month ago it might only have complicated matters, but not now. I've decided I'm going back to work. If I pretend I'm doing it for the money I might just be able to get something sorted out. What do you think about the garden? Two hours a week should be more than enough.'

I said I supposed so.

'Of course you do – you're a suppose-so man.' She stopped, took off her sunglasses again and apologised. She wiped the lenses. 'There's rain on them. Rain on sunglasses. Do you think I'm hiding behind them?' She put them back on. She skimmed water from a bench with her fingers. The seat was still wet but she sat on it, pulling a face as she felt the water soak through her dress to her legs. She asked me what I'd done with Colin's trophies. I told her, but she sat without really listening.

83

'I ought to start travelling more often,' she said. 'It broadens my hips.' Her manner had become more detached in the month she'd been away, but she was still uncertain of herself, and she still spoke quickly to fill the silences of her own making.

'I suppose appearances can be deceptive,' she said. I was uncertain whether she meant herself or the house or the garden. 'But in the end they're all that matter. Glib. I tried to stop smoking while I was away. *Sans succès, j'ai peur.* Smoking in all that heat used to make me feel sick. It was his flat in the centre of Rome. His father was English, his mother Italian, from the south. His father was in the army during the war, and his mother had grown into a mountain. He's funny. This dress was his choice, these shoes . . . I don't think he was in possession of a great deal of taste particularly, but I doubt if that was part of the attraction. I'm an attractive woman. No one here believes it, but I am. He used to say it to hear me deny it because of where he knew it would get him.' The memory caused her to pause. 'I was thinking, coming back, that I might go and visit Valentine.'

'Good idea.'

'It's an awful idea, like tunnelling into a prison.'

The fine soil beneath the shrubs and low bushes was dotted with weeds, and they grew in fine green arrowheads through the pattern of brickwork.

'London's full of reliable little men doing other people's gardens,' I said. 'Perhaps the man in the hothouse could recommend someone. Perhaps if you asked him nicely enough he'd come himself.'

She watched me from behind her glasses. Then she got up and walked back into the house. The wet stain on her thighs had soaked almost to her waist. She felt it as she walked and tried to pull the material from her legs. In the kitchen she slid the dress over her head and took something else from one of her cases.

'Welcome home, Rachel,' she said as I went in to her. 'Aren't you going to open your presents?'

I took the boxes from the airport bag and the bottles from the boxes. I thanked her and she presented her cheek to be kissed. She took off her glasses and threw them outside. 'Bloody awful things. I bought them at the airport coming home. He said I looked good in them. He said women began ageing through their eyes – typical Latin rubbish.'

I helped her carry her cases upstairs.

'Someone's calculated how long it will be before the pyramids are reduced to sand and lost forever. I can't remember how long it is – thousands of years. Does that sound like a long time to you?'

I told her it didn't.

'Perhaps I got it wrong – tens of thousands.' She walked ahead of me, trying not to struggle with her case.

4

Colin stood at the narrow window and looked down at the early evening traffic. The small room was filled with someone else's furniture and belongings, but at the centre of the floor were two of his bags; several of his shirts hung behind the door and there were the remains of a meal in foil trays beside one of the chairs.

'I've taken this room,' he said, going on quickly before I could ask him to explain. 'If I stand against this wall and look out sideways I can just about see the top of Broadcasting Temple. There she is.'

I told him he looked like someone in a bad film hiding from the police. He mimicked the voice of an American gangster and stood with a gun pressed to his cheek.

'Whose room is it?'

'It *was* his.' He pointed to a cluster of framed photographs of groups of men equipped for mountaineering. 'I knew him.' He picked out one photograph and handed it to me. 'I spent time with them filming. This was his London base, from where he did most of his sponsorship begging.'

What happened?

'A nice long, clean, unbroken fall is what happened, from the lip of a six-hundred-foot overhang. He was the best and most careful of the group. What was holding him should have held him, but when the time came it didn't.' He looked hard into the man's face. 'It wasn't a particularly important mountain and so his death never became news of any consequence. He used to let me have this place when he was out of town and I was working late.'

And now?

'A negotiated short-term lease from the trustees.' He turned back to look out over the traffic.

I asked him if Rachel knew about it.

'Not yet.' He looked at me pointedly and I drew a cross over my heart. 'She'll find out sooner or later, of course. She always does. There's even a film of him falling – not a particularly good film, but I imagine the subject more than compensates. Good, clear, blue sky behind him, a nice concave angle of rock . . . Have you ever seen film of people leaping from burning hotels? There's always some bastard ready with a camera, and usually it's me. He's been dead six weeks and you could fit what I've done since into one good working day. It's starting not to make as much sense as it used to. Usually it's me – the Philippines, Tokyo – ready and waiting, a small voice in my head shouting, 'Jump jump jump,' and my eyes and fingers plotting angles and trajectories before any of the poor fools have had the opportunity to weigh up their non-existent chances and launch themselves off a smoking balcony. If you look at some of them closely enough, they actually appear to swing or flap their arms as though they believe they might slow their fall or even start to fly and glide safely to the ground. *He* didn't bother with any of that, of course. When he first left the rock he turned himself, expecting to be held, bracing himself for the swing back to the face he'd just spent two hours climbing. But when he wasn't held, and when he knew exactly, precisely, down to the last sickening detail what was happening, he just let himself fall. The camera must have been on a nearby slope. He may have spread his arms and legs, but essentially he just fell and did nothing about it because there *was* nothing he could do about it. Six hundred feet in four or five seconds. I daresay it could be calculated more precisely.'

He stopped speaking and drew in his breath. He went back to the window and looked down.

'It's a miserable town. People are walking twice as fast as the traffic.'

So what?

'You're right. So what? His name was Ian and he was thirty-two. So what? He'd been climbing since he was sixteen and he had three brothers, all of whom were every bit as good as he was, if not better. So what? He'd been living with the same girl for nearly ten years. So what?'

I went to the room's other window and looked out. The pale, streaked stone of the buildings opposite was turning dark.

I'd known two months ago that the results from the more recent tests on his fingers had not been promising. They were no longer in their separate sheaths, but he held them stiffly, looked at them frequently and showed me how he'd been told to exercise them. He could bend them only into a slight curve.

'I used to scrub bits of dialogue like, "His worst fears were confirmed," because they sounded ridiculous and melodramatic. And now the received opinion is that clichés are an acceptable part of the language. What am I supposed to think? "Progressively worse

87

over an unspecified period." I've started to hear the bloody things creak every time I look at them. It might be decades. I'm not used to being on this side of disasters; I'm an after-the-events man. I like to get there with everything spread out around me before I start making decisions on what to do, what to include, what not to include. I like opinions. What options do I have with this? Rachel knows and soon everybody will know. Soon it's going to start making a difference. And then what do I do? Answers on a postcard...'

He drew the curtains and went back to the centre of the room. I asked how long it would be before he finished his documentary of disasters. 'I'll never finish it. It was meant to be a life's work. Instead, it's turning into a disaster of a documentary. It was only ever a personal project – something I thought I could piece together out of stock and archive – and as it stands, it now has every chance of being abandoned. Current Affairs pays all the bills. Even if I were to finish it and get it into a presentable shape, there's still no guarantee that it would be shown.'

I asked him if he intended going on with it.

'I suppose so. I suppose I'll go on adding it all up and piecing it all together until some kind of logical conclusion is reached. It shouldn't be too difficult; it's a very watchable film. No one really wants to know how the hotel fire started, or why the ship sank, or why the rope that should have held didn't. If I wasn't doing it, someone else would be.'

I suggested that we went out for an early meal, but he said he preferred to remain in the flat. He intended spending the night there, calling Rachel with an excuse an hour after she expected him home.

'There are never any problems with excuses in our line of work – mine and hers. Excuses, lies, whatever.'

He switched on the television news and watched it without any sound, switching from channel to channel. There were two portable sets side by side. He made remarks on the quality of the coverage, and when the news finished he swore because something of his own had not been included.

'Ian was trained as a geologist. In the bedroom he has a collection of primitive seismographic recorders, several of which he made himself. When his affairs are sorted out they're being given to some institute or other. I'll arrange them all in here one day and show you them.'

I asked him precisely what the doctors had told him. The silence which followed was broken only by the noise of the gathering traffic.

'Everything they said was imprecise. Precision was never a part of their guarantee. How precise are bones that won't heal without anyone really knowing why, or at least saying they don't know why because what they *really* don't know is how to cure them? There are still a few words in the language which, once said, can never be retracted.'

Bone cancer?

'You said it, not them. I daren't even think it. No, not cancer; I think they would have used the word before now.'

Would other bones also not mend if he broke them?

'"A strong possibility" is the best they can do so far. "Possible", "likely", even "probable".'

And treatment?

'They shine a magic light on me and give me a few magic injections. It's all guaranteed to be very painless.'

I asked him how Rachel had taken the news.

'My pain – real, or, as yet, imagined – is Rachel's pain. How can she respond? She might think she knows better than everyone else, but no one else believes it to be true. Rachel, despite appearances, lives a life governed by a very few resolute and immutable principles. Don't ask me what they are because you can work them out for yourself. It used to be part of her attraction; it still is, but there are times when what she is and what she does no longer counts for very much.'

With this, for instance?

'With this, and with a good many other self-evident truths she's chosen to ignore.' He stopped because he'd said too much, because he'd thought about it too much. It was why he'd started using the flat.

He looked slowly around the room and back to the photograph.

'He knew people who'd run – *run* – from one end of the Himalayas to the other. He was making plans for next year to walk across Australia and then to stay there climbing for another year. He made that kind of decision the way Rachel lays out her clothes in the morning and decides what to wear. He thought about it, he worked it out, he did it. No one ever told *him* about impossibilities or improbabilities. Christ, he didn't even want to write about it afterwards. All these photographs were taken by other people; he never took any, never wanted any, never needed any. Six hundred feet of nothing killed him. But the point is, he knew every inch of it –

it was his six hundred feet by virtue of the muscle he'd expended on climbing it. There wouldn't have been any other way in the world for him to have died.'

He showed me another picture of Ian beneath the Christ of the Andes, and another of him in a dinner jacket and black tie receiving an award.

'It makes this seem . . .' He held up his fingers, but was unable to finish.

I told him that any comparison would be ridiculous and he said he knew. He'd been drinking since before my arrival and we continued together.

'The fact is, there's nothing there any more,' he said. I thought at first that the reference was to Rachel. 'Nothing ahead. It only exists and appeals and draws us on because five or ten per cent of it's unknown, uncertain, with the chance of something big or important happening. Nothing that really matters is ever revealed to us in advance. But now I've got this.' He held up his hand. 'I *know*. It might be twenty years before it gets worse, or it might be fifty; it might be five or it might be one. The simple fact is, I *know*.' He looked at me. 'Does my being maudlin drunk make it any easier to listen to? In addition to which . . .' He paused and drained his glass. '. . .since I've known about this, since I've *really* known – the past month, say – I haven't had an erection. And before you feel obliged to try, there's nothing reassuring you can say in reply. It scares me. The more I think about it the more it scares me. Not once.' He forced a laugh. 'I suppose deep down . . . I'd say "psychosomatic" if there was the slightest possibility of being able to believe it, or if the word hadn't become an excuse for everything else. Rachel suggested it too, but she thought even less of it than I did.'

He invited me to stay at the flat for a meal, which he cooked in the cramped and untidy kitchen. He said he felt at home amid the disarray.

When I suggested it was time for me to leave he told me there was a fold-down bed and that I was welcome to stay. I declined and he didn't persist.

After several more drinks everything we said to each other became a joke and we laughed.

'When you get down there,' he said, indicating the street, 'look up and you'll see me looking down.'

In the street I looked up, but the curtains were drawn and there was no one at the window.

I found a taxi and the driver said it looked as though I'd had a good evening out. I told him he was right because the truth was unrepeatable to anyone who didn't already know it.

5

A week after her return from Europe, Rachel bought a car. She had a licence but had not driven regularly for several years. I accompanied her on several circuitous evening drives as she accustomed herself to it. She wanted us both to believe that it represented part of her new independence. A week after buying it she left it parked outside and resumed her few excursions by taxi.

Within a month she reported its first meticulously sought spots of rust. Upon finding them she rang the dealer from whom she'd bought the car and complained. He was off-hand with her and asked her what she expected him to do. She waved to me to remain with her in the room as she shouted at him over the telephone. She said he'd deceived her, and I heard his distant voice, its note of forced incredulity and the silences which followed.

'"Deceived" is what I said.' She began to spell it out to him. He would have felt easier with the word 'cheated'. Rachel's belief in the moral force of her argument overcame anything the man had to say. When he'd finished listening he asked her again what she expected him to do. She didn't know. Exchange. A refund. He told her he'd sold her the car in good faith. She told him the words made her laugh. He asked her to be a little more reasonable, more specific, to describe the exact location and extent of the rust. Not knowing the correct name for the part of the car on which the rust had appeared made her even angrier and weakened her attack on him. His voice became condescending. '"Well, is it on the front or back, left or right,"' she repeated, mimicking his voice, which had become more confident. Then she swore and shouted at him to stop patronising her. She told him where the rust was, and then said he'd known all along where it was because someone had tried to paint over it before the car was sold to her. I knew this not to be true. The man, uncertain now of how much he did know, could think of nothing to say. She hung up on him and sat by the phone breathing deeply with her eyes closed. When she opened them she applauded herself and began to laugh.

'I did it, I did it. He can't be sure, see. He can't be sure if he did or didn't do it.' She clapped again in her exhilaration.

'Achieving what?'

'This,' she said, and continued laughing.

'He won't ring back; it's the last you'll hear from him.'

'It's the last I want to hear from him.'

I still didn't know what she thought she'd achieved.

Later, still excited by her victory, she said she'd decided to visit Valentine. I agreed to accompany her. The car, she said, made everything much easier. Her defeat of the salesman made it easier still.

Arriving at the clinic, Valentine greeted us like long-lost relatives. She kissed me and then shook my hand. Her voice was louder than usual and everyone was made aware of our arrival to see her. She led us into the conservatory, where three of the more comfortable chairs had been reserved for us. She collected up the three pieces of card on which she'd written 'Keep Off. By Order'.

Rachel told her about the car and then related in detail the argument she'd had over the rust.

'He accused me of having hit something with it,' she lied. 'He suggested I might not know a piece of rust from a dirty weld.'

Valentine became outraged at each of the man's imaginary insults. She asked if we could see the car from where we sat. She and Rachel stood in the open doorway and looked across the lawn to the distant car park. Only the colour of the car would have been identifiable. Rachel thought she saw it and pointed it out. Valentine said that she could definitely see it and that it looked a smart car. They pretended to interest each other in a variety of technical details.

'My husbands knew cars.'

Surprise, surprise, Rachel said with her eyes.

Valentine let herself back down into her seat with a joint escape of air from herself and the cushions. One of her husbands had worked as a 'collision specialist' with his own pick-up fleet. The constant references to her husbands were made in an attempt to make me feel included in the conversation. She listed the cars she'd owned and asked me if I knew any of them.

'They're American cars,' Rachel said impatiently.

'So you don't know American cars?'

I told her that I recognised a few of the names. She said the place hadn't been the same since Rachel left.

'I'm sure you keep it lively enough,' Rachel said.

'I try, I try,' she said.

On the benches immediately outside the glass was a small group of women. They were less well dressed than those I had come to associate with the clinic and most of them looked genuinely ill. Valentine saw Rachel watching them.

'They only come to steal the magazines,' she said contemptuously.

'Who are they?' Rachel sounded threatened.

'That's the big joke. Anyone mobile from the rest of the hospital can now use the lawn in the afternoons. New rule. We complained, but where does complaining get you? You can say what you like – '

'What joke?'

'Them. They're the "Mothers and Babies". You see any babies? No, not one.' Having leaned forward and lowered her voice, Valentine sat smugly in her chair.

Several of the women outside looked in. Few of them spoke to each other. Rachel watched them. Valentine complained that no one was paying her any attention. I tried to divert her from Rachel by asking her about her plans for the future. She outlined them to me, constantly glancing at Rachel.

'No one cares,' Valentine said. 'You think we don't all feel for them? We're all women, aren't we?'

Rachel apologised and turned her seat away from the lawn.

'So tell me what's been happening. Are you involved in any midnight trysts with handsome young doctors yet?'

'"Trysts"! She's talking about trysts. I thought only I read that kind of crap.'

Valentine shouted for an orderly to bring us something to drink. The woman asked her what she wanted and Valentine told her to list what she had. The woman ran through half a dozen flavours and Valentine said, 'Is that all?'

'It's the same as yesterday, and the day before that, and the week before that. I recite that list fifty times a day. You all know perfectly well what there is. I wake up at night reciting that list.'

'You're lucky you can sleep,' Valentine told her.

'I don't sit around all day in here doing nothing, that's why I sleep,' the woman said.

Valentine didn't know what to say. The woman left us and returned a few minutes later with a jug of orange.

'Orange!' Valentine said. 'Again?' She told the woman that her remarks had not gone unnoticed.

'No, I don't suppose they have,' she said, and left us to attend to someone else.

'So it's "We Hate Valentine Day",' Valentine said.

94

Rachel told her not to take things so seriously and gave her a cigarette.

We drank the orange and then Valentine slapped her forehead and said she'd suddenly remembered. She took three postcards from her pocket. 'I got your postcards. Europe, ah, now there's a place.'

'"Yerp",' Rachel said.

'"Yerp"?

'Paris, France.'

'A beautiful, beautiful, *beau*tiful place.' Valentine's favourite place in the whole of Europe. She remembered her own visits there. Her second husband told her he'd been born in France, but she knew it to be a lie. 'He smoked French cigarettes, was all.'

'Perhaps he thought it conferred some kind of honorary membership. Things like that often do.'

'I like that — "honorary membership". Like that awful Greek wine, you mean?'

'Something like that.'

'But why would anyone want to lie about having been born in France?' She insisted on an answer from Rachel, and then confirmation from me.

I caught Rachel glancing to see if the women were still behind us on the lawn.

Valentine sipped at her diluted orange and pulled a face. 'You'd think they'd know better than to give us all the additives and colouring this stuff contains. People like us. If you pay for real orange juice, it's what you should get. So tell me about Paree.'

She gave me the postcards. They were all of well-known Parisian landmarks, but only one of the cards was postmarked from Paris, the other two from Rome. They were written with the same pen and in the same quick handwriting. All three might have been written within the space of a single minute.

'Was it where you stayed?'

'In the end,' Rachel said. 'I intended moving around, but in the end it was where I stayed.'

'We're the ones who do all the moving around, we Americans. I guess we're a restless race.' She looked momentarily solemn, and then said, 'You stay in a big Louis-the-something-or-other hotel, or what?'

'Big hotels, the biggest and the best, nothing but the best.'

'The Louvre, Notre Dame . . .' Valentine closed her eyes in her effort of memory. 'We once visited that place with all the painters. I was going to have a portrait painted but it would have meant

95

waiting for an hour. An hour was a long time in those days. Did you find yourself one of those amorous Frenchmen?'

'No, no amorous Frenchmen, Vee.'

'Good. They're lice. Take it from me. I've been there. What they're after is one thing.' She rubbed her fingers and thumb together to suggest money. She took the postcards from me, looked at them and returned them to her pocket.

Rachel became restless. She told Valentine that sitting in the heat beneath the glass was making her feel uncomfortable. We left the conservatory and followed the corridor into the large lounge and empty Day Room.

'You'd think that for the money we pay out to be here they'd come up with something better than "Day Room". Does that make it sound common, or what?'

'You are common, Vee.'

'Yeah, that's me: common. Some kind of second-hand-Rose character.'

'You never had anything second-hand in your life.'

'Perhaps not, but it feels like I did.'

Rachel said she felt better out of the heat.

Valentine asked her how many miles to the gallon her new car did. Rachel said she didn't know.

'She doesn't know.' Valentine said to me. 'You'll get us women a bad name. How on earth are we ever going to be taken seriously when you don't know a little thing like that?'

Rachel guessed.

'I shouldn't have asked. Now I've asked and offended you and you won't come back on another visit.'

Rachel assured her we would, but I knew from her voice that it was unlikely. Valentine saw it too.

'I wouldn't blame you,' she said.

'We'll come back, I promise we'll come back.'

'Maybe I should come and see you in London. Maybe I should arrange for that. Glass walls do not a prison make.'

'Whatever you like.'

After an hour Rachel said we ought to be leaving.

'You had a month in Paris,' Valentine said. 'You forget about places like this.'

'No melodramas, Vee.'

'Vee. It's what they all call me now. Four solid months I've been here. I'm one of the fittings. "Fixtures and fittings", that right?'

She walked with us back through the conservatory and across the lawn to the gate leading to the car park.

As we left the conservatory, Rachel looked for the group of women, but they had gone.

'Perhaps they went back to their babies,' Valentine said, angry that she was no longer the focus of our attention. 'Feeding time.'

She waved to us until we rounded the corner and were lost to her.

Rachel sat in the car and wound the window down. 'I should never have come.' she said. 'It still felt too easy, sitting up there with everything ready to catch you when you fall.' She watched her hands on the wheel and said she didn't want to drive. 'You must have been bored out of your mind. She's probably the most boring woman in the world.'

I asked her why she'd lied about Paris and Rome.

'Why should she know? Paris was what she wanted to hear about. If she'd ever spent a happy hour at the Vatican then I'd have told her I'd been there for a month. What she hears is what matters.' She pulled down the sun shield and studied her face in its small mirror.

As we left the hospital grounds she turned on the radio and searched the stations. Finding what she wanted, she turned it up until it became loud and distorted, leaving it for a minute before turning it down. She sat with her arm out of the window and her hand on the warm roof. She wore her Italian sunglasses again, tapped her fingers and sang the words of the songs she knew. She waved to the cars we overtook and then stuck up her fingers at those which overtook us. I slowed to the legal speed to pass a parked police car, and as we passed it she waved vigorously out at them. I told her to stop and she pulled in her arm.

'Are they following us?'

I checked the mirror.

'Shame.' She asked what speed the car was capable of, then turned up the radio and lost my answer.

We entered North London and were caught in queues of traffic. She spoke to people in the cars alongside. She used an American accent to ask someone if we were on the right road for Brighton. The man laughed at her and then began trying to give her directions. She waited until the traffic started moving and then told him to forget it. I saw him stationary behind us, the cars around him sounding their horns. Rachel continued laughing until long after.

The visit to the clinic had been a test, and her relief at returning home was obvious. It was something she regretted being unable to hide.

For Rachel, allowing herself to become what Valentine had allowed herself to become had been only one of the options on offer, one of her scenarios, and now, unexpectedly, that option no longer existed for her. For a time there had been something almost exciting in sitting back and allowing it to happen, a kind of daring, of edging to the brink and running back. For weeks afterwards she was careful not to mention Valentine's name. She'd made the choice and now needed to prove to herself that the choice had been the right one to make. There were still too many uncertainties, too many paths endlessly dividing ahead of her. 'I'm on automatic pilot,' she once said and I understood immediately what she meant. She moved from A to B and then from B to C, but any prior knowledge or preparation of her course would have been a cumbersome burden and might have slowed her down and then fixed her to the spot. It was why her small successes and achievements were so important. It was why she needed everything to be different in a world where, outwardly at least, everything stayed the same.

She was in high spirits for a week after this final visit to the clinic.

6

A fortnight later, she stood in the garden and shouted for me to go out to her. She drew two lines down the wall at the end of the garden with a stone, paced the distance between them and then moved them a foot further apart. There were other crude lines, horizontal as well as vertical, to suggest earlier miscalculations. I watched her from the kitchen doorway. She paced a rectangle four paces by six, stood at the centre of it and studied the sun and the shadows of the trees which overhung the walls on three sides. Seeing me, she beckoned me to her.

'Can I legally chop off all these overhangs?' she said.

I told her she'd be wise to ask nicely.

She concentrated on further, more precise measurements, moving heel to toe outwards from the wall towards the centre of the narrow garden.

'Okay, can I legally ask nicely for the branches to be chopped off? Can I get permission to do it myself?'

I asked her why.

'I'm building a conservatory. Right here. I've calculated sun, supporting wall, angle of shade, everything. The brochures are in the house. I'll have a brick wall up to knee height and then an aluminium frame to nine feet curving back to fix it to the wall. The door will be to one side to avoid having to do much to the path.' She drew everything with her arms as she spoke. 'You know about these things, what do you think?'

'If you get the branches down it sounds like a good idea. What for?'

'I can work here in the summer. If I get some kind of portable heating installed, perhaps in winter too.'

I commented on the fact that there were half a dozen rooms in the house she never used.

'Typical,' she said angrily. 'I'm trying to do this because it feels like the right thing to do.'

I told her I was only trying to be realistic.

'Well keep on trying,' she said. 'For you it's probably a good thing to be. I can bring a desk in, a couple of chairs and a filing cabinet or some sort of cupboard to keep things in. Damp might be a problem, but not if I do it properly.' She stood away from the wall and half closed her eyes, imagining the conservatory and its contents already in position.

'I have to say that something like this won't necessarily increase the value of the house if you are still thinking of selling,' I said.

'You don't *have* to say it.'

'I thought you were going to sell.'

'Was I? I've changed my mind. If I put the desk against that side then it should catch the morning sun, which is when I'll work, which is when all serious writers work, right? "Serious" in my case being anything more than a caption for a bowl of salad or some headscarved horsewoman posing with her dogs in front of the ancestral pile. I've let it be known that I'm about to resume. The conservatory is yet another indication of my good intentions. I had thought about adding it on to the kitchen wall with direct access through the door, but decided it would be too close. I'd need some kind of privacy. Do you think I'd be able to hear the phone from down here once I was inside with the door closed? I'll sit out here with my typewriter on my knee surrounded by all the birds and bees, like Saint Francis. Did I tell you that the woman two doors down said she'd seen a fox in her garden the other night? She's started leaving food out for it. She even asked me if I knew anything about the best way of setting up a camera which the fox could trigger itself. Having had a film maker for a husband, that was. All very tactfully done. I told her I didn't know. I'm not actually certain if I do know or not, but I imagine it would be simple enough to work out. She said she'd heard it barking in the night, and when she'd looked out there it was.'

I went into the house and returned with a retractable steel measure. Rachel read out the measurements from the brochure and I marked them out more accurately. I pressed sticks into the sand between the bricks to show her precisely how far the design she'd chosen would extend into the garden.

'The point being, I wouldn't lose any of the garden that I need,' she said. She was pleased with her ready answers. She'd made her decision and had then convinced herself of the reasons for it. She read out the names of the various designs. 'I should have done it years ago.'

I told her she would have to consider the noise people in other gardens might make if she intended working there, but my caution only made her angry again.

'You're getting me confused with Balzac,' she said. 'I can see you're impressed with my encyclopaedic knowledge of the literary world.'

I told her it was still a consideration if that was her prime motive for having the conservatory built.

'Which you don't entirely believe. Which you'll only believe when you see it.'

According to the brochure, the construction firm guaranteed delivery and completion within a fortnight. That was how long I would have to wait to find out.

I let the slack metal tape stiffen and then rewind. She crouched down against the wall on the warm bricks and looked up at the tall back of the house.

'Ought I to sell it? It feels just as right now to stay as it did then to go . . . Colin, I suppose. Still that.'

We listened to the hidden people in the gardens on either side. 'I had a letter from the great Latin lover this morning,' she said unexpectedly.

And?

'He says he's definitely coming to London. For a week, perhaps longer.'

I asked if he intended staying with her.

'It's what he'll expect. I should have had more sense than to stay with him in Rome.'

'You don't want to see him?'

'I don't think so. No. Not here. He doesn't really know the first thing about me — no Colin, no this, no nothing. He thinks I'm something big in advertising. It's a joke, but that's what I told him. I'm not even really sure what I hoped to achieve by it all. At the time, I was too busy staying ahead. Can we change the subject: is this back wall strong enough to build against?'

I told her it wouldn't be bearing any load.

'And dry enough?'

It would quickly dry out beneath the glass.

She held her palm against the wall. She was already expecting too much.

'I had a drink last night,' she said.

Only one?

'Only one. I didn't even finish it. An hour before you came in. I washed the glass out and put it away.'

And?

She relaxed and closed her eyes. 'And I didn't become a raving animal and drink everything in the house. I wasn't certain that I wouldn't, but in the event nothing happened. I survived.'

'No one suggested you should never drink again.'

'They might not have actually said it.' There was a long pause. 'If I did have this place built' – she traced the rectangular outline with her finger – 'how much of it do you think would be because I wanted it as a substitute for the conservatory at the clinic? Or is that being ridiculous?'

There was no safe answer to the question; it wasn't the conservatory that mattered.

'I enjoy it, sitting beneath the glass and feeling warm. In here I'd at least have the added bonus of a few plants. The point is, how do I know when a dependency on one thing becomes a dependency on something else?'

I said I didn't understand.

'No, me neither.' A harmless collision of lies. 'So the conservatory idea is a good idea.' She speculated on other fittings to avoid having to return to the drink she'd had. 'Or was it Proust who worked in a cork-lined room? One of them did. Dressed as a monk. I once went with Colin to Laugharne to see Dylan Thomas's boathouse. Something to do with a film he was working on. We visited other places. Gad's Hill. They all had their little sheds of one sort or another.' She stood up. 'So what do you think?'

I thought it was a good idea. Bad reasoning, but a good idea.

She was clearly relieved at having told me about the drink. Telling me had been harder than filling the glass.

'*The Bell Jar*,' she said. 'That's it: Sylvia Plath. She was another one, wasn't she?' She touched a finger into her throat and walked back to the house.

7

'What I *do* object to is the way half our private life ends up becoming a professional exercise.' Rachel picked pieces of salad from a shallow glass bowl. Her point, if not clearly made, was understood by everyone around the table. Only Colin wanted to disagree with her, not because he believed she was wrong, but because of what she was suggesting.

'Meaning what exactly?'

Rachel ignored him and concentrated on picking pieces of orange from the salad. The table became a cat's cradle of knowing glances as the three other men and three other women signalled their allegiances to either Colin or Rachel.

'What I mean, for instance,' she went on, still more concerned with the salad, 'is the way every camera angle in this house has been calculated down to the nearest millimetre. What is it – the setting for some sordid *Meisterwerk*? Some kind of day-in-the-life of a – ' She broke off to pick out the orange with her fingers. 'Forget I ever said anything.' She smiled at the three men and then at their wives.

One of the men spoke: 'What you have to remember, Rachel, is that all creative people are the same. Call it a failing, call it what you like, but it's why they are what they are. It's as simple as that. You may not like it, but that's the top and bottom of it.' The man held his glass in both hands an inch from his lips. The two others sitting opposite him nodded once. Everyone waited for Rachel's response.

'The Moguls closing ranks,' she said. 'And, please, let's not start on the "We're creative people" routine. You must be as sick of trying to convince yourselves of it as I am of hearing it. Technicians, that's what you are. And I don't have to believe it any more than you try not to believe it.'

The woman beside Rachel smiled with her; the two others agreed with their husbands.

'Rachel, I don't think – '

'Would any of you creative people like some salad?'

The woman beside her laughed.

Colin tried again to speak, but was stopped by the man who'd raised the subject. 'No, Colin, she's entitled to her say. I'm sure she's got something to add. We're all friends here. I'm sure we can take it. Fire away, Rachel. More wine?' His reference to the wine was deliberate and pointed.

Rachel passed him her glass and the man filled it to the brim.

'Perhaps when *we*'ve been stripped down to the bones we can begin on the wild and wonderful world of glossy magazines,' another of the men said. 'I'm sure there must be someone in that equally self-congratulatory little world who considers himself or herself to be of an equally creative bent.'

The man holding the wine laughed.

Rachel looked round at each of them. 'You all know what I'm talking about, so there seems little point going on about it. Why don't we just eat? This salad's the best I've ever made.' She looked to Colin for his confirmation.

The woman opposite her began to tell her about a new recipe she'd found. Rachel deliberately showed no interest. The woman's husband watched her from across the table, willing her to stop talking.

'Donald's the same,' one of the other women said. 'Forever framing things up.' She made her thumbs and forefingers into a square and looked at Donald through it.

'Oh, he does, does he? Strange that, Donald being a sound man – a man concerned with sound. Perhaps Donald has aspirations?'

Donald made sure he was the first to laugh.

To defuse the situation, Colin asked Donald if he'd seen anything interesting lately. Before he could answer, Rachel said to me, 'Donald's our expert on modern French cinema. He watches all the new films the instant they appear. He even goes to Paris to see them, all without subtitles.'

Donald bowed in acknowledgment.

'Which is a great shame,' Rachel went on, 'because it means he misses a great deal.' Both Rachel and the woman beside her laughed uncontrollably.

Donald's wife said Donald spoke perfect French, perfect French in several dialects. Donald regretted her dutiful defence of him; everyone at the table knew how perfect Donald's French was.

'*My* idea of speaking a foreign language,' Rachel continued, still unable to suppress her laughter, 'is to go to Boulogne and shout in English. I only ever got as far as survival French: *oui*, *plus*, and *je suis anglaise*. Fluidly.'

Only Donald's wife commented on the appropriateness of the pun.

'Rachel also speaks perfect French,' Colin said.

Rachel finished her wine, left the table and returned with a bottle in each hand.

It was Sunday lunchtime and the gatherings were organised on a rotational basis. This was the second of Colin's and Rachel's I'd been invited to. The arguments and topics of conversation seldom varied.

Rachel uncorked the bottles and drank a little from each.

'But do you accept, Rachel, that it's the kind of people we are? If we weren't committed to what we did – '

'Backtracking,' Rachel said dismissively. 'There's no need.' She told the woman beside her to use her fingers in the salad.

'We can't win. Rachel has an answer for everything. Why bother going on?'

'Because we always trade a good line in polite insults, that's why. It's dangerous but it's safe.'

'They're hardly insults,' Colin said.

'Colin says they're hardly insults,' Rachel said. 'Who agrees with him? I for one don't see anything wrong in it, but if you agree with him then say so.'

'Rachel ought to have been a diplomat,' said the man who'd encouraged the discussion. He raised his glass to her.

Colin watched Rachel drink. Other, private conversations began. People said complimentary things about the food.

'She was up until midnight getting most of it ready,' Colin said.

'Is midnight supposed to be late?'

'No, Rachel, midnight isn't late, but we're all very grateful anyhow. Why don't we tell her how grateful we all are? Or would that embarrass you?'

'Feel free. Coming from a creative person – perhaps we ought to tape all this for those unfortunate enough not to be here.' She then told a joke which everyone found in bad taste, but at which most of them laughed. She formed her own thumbs and forefingers into a square and spoke through it to each of them. 'Disconcerted?'

'Rachel, you've made your point. Somebody tell her she's made her point. Okay, we're all philistines, not a creative bone in our bodies. There, I've said it. Satisfied?'

'I do it without thinking half the time,' Colin said.

'Oh, well, then, everything is forgiven. Let's talk about something else.'

'You brought the subject up,' one of the men said.

'Perhaps Rachel misses the power involved. Perhaps her magazine work leaves her feeling unfulfilled. Is that it?' The man was deliberately provoking her and she knew it. 'I mean, we are talking about frocks and cheekbones and multiple orgasms, are we not? We're not exactly in the realm of *The Battleship Potemkin* or deconstructing the novel, or – or – Correct me if I'm wrong, Rachel, but that is what we're talking about, isn't it?' They were poor, easy examples and he regretted having chosen them; he'd used them before and they now weakened rather than strengthened his argument. Rachel understood this as well as any of them, but chose not to remark on it.

There was a silence of three or four seconds, broken eventually by another of the men who said he too had a joke to tell: 'On the question of multiple orgasms, when I married Ann I told her she could have as many as she wanted.'

Ann punched him and laughed the loudest of all the women. Like the argument, the joke was an old one.

'I think this might be getting personal and straying from the track,' the third woman said.

'God forbid that we should ever get personal,' Rachel said. Her drunkenness was becoming apparent to everyone but herself.

'If she hasn't the decency to apologise, I will,' Colin said.

'Decency? Apologise for what? Is there anything decent about feeling as though you've got a camera trained on you twenty-four hours a day?'

'She means an imaginary camera. You mean an imaginary camera.'

Rachel held an invisible camera, turning the handle as she moved it around the table. People froze and smiled as she focused on them. The motion of turning the handle prompted a discussion on recent advances in technology and the conversation once again became unfocused.

'I meant a camera,' Rachel said, lifting pieces of food from her plate and letting them fall.

Colin filled people's glasses and then stood the bottles away from her.

'I don't complain ordinarily,' she said. 'Ordinarily I keep my big mouth shut. No, that's a lie, I keep it open when it ought to be shut.'

'Okay, Rachel, we think you've made your point.'

'Shall *I* see to dessert?' Colin said.

'He means he thinks I'm incapable,' Rachel said to the equally incapable woman beside her. She lit a cigarette and tilted her head back to blow the smoke high above the table. One of the other women watched it spread outwards over the ceiling and then fall.

106

'What are you working on, Rachel?' someone asked seriously.

'I've given up multiple orgasms as a lost cause – professionally that is. Always professionally. I don't know. I went to Dublin last week to look at a women's co-operative textile works.'

'Were they any good?'

'As women perhaps. The textiles were awful. They gave me a blouse. There were twelve of us. They gave us all a blouse. I went as a favour to someone else.' She reached across the cluttered table and knocked over an empty bottle. 'That's always a good sign,' she said. 'Tendency to knock things over, clumsiness, starting to ramble. You'll have to stop me before I become embarrassing.'

'It's all within these four walls, Rachel, you know that.'

'If you believe that you'll believe anything,' someone added.

'I don't believe it so it doesn't matter. You need more drink.' Rachel took the man's glass and filled it. 'Colin's taking his time with the trifle. You don't suppose he's filming it? He's been watching a lot of Polish films lately.'

'I'll go and see if he needs a hand.' One of the women left the table and another went with her.

A discussion began on the merits of different types of film. When it ended, Rachel said, 'Is that it?'

'You weren't even listening, Rachel.'

'I've heard it all before.' She flicked her fingers at a fly which hovered above the table.

'You've heard everything before,' the man said.

'In that case tell me something new.'

Colin's absence gave a new edge to their remarks.

'Let's have some music.' Rachel went to the stereo, slid out a record and put it on without looking at it. She turned down the sound until it was barely audible, kicked off her shoes and danced barefoot across the room. She closed her eyes and held her arms as though she were holding someone. When she bumped into the table she laughed and the men laughed with her. One, whose wife was out of the room, stood and held her and danced with her. She rested her chin on his shoulder and tried to sing the words to the song. After a minute the music stopped. The man released her and told her she'd exhausted him. She kissed him on the cheek and walked her fingers up his face. She resumed dancing alone as he returned to the table.

Colin and the two women came in from the kitchen. He looked surprised at hearing the music and seeing Rachel dancing.

'Light entertainment,' the man said.

'The dance of the seven veils,' Rachel said. She held her arms out from her shoulders and turned in a circle. Colin and the women each held three plates. Rachel shouted that she didn't want any dessert. She came to the table, took one of the bottles and continued dancing with it. When the music stopped she bowed and almost fell, laughing at herself as she returned to her seat. She looked at the food in front of her and mashed it with a spoon.

'Delicious,' one of the women said. Others repeated the word.

'Next you'll be asking me for the recipe,' Rachel said, and continued reducing the contents of her plate to a liquid.

'Well, I like it,' the man who'd danced said. 'In fact, I like Rachel. Full stop.'

'And I like you. Why do you like me full stop?'

The man told her why he liked her. Rachel repeated everything he said to Colin. The man's wife told everyone he'd been drunk the previous evening, as though this had some bearing on his present behaviour.

'Stinking, roaring, filthy drunk,' the man said proudly.

'Just drunk,' his wife said.

He pretended to be contrite and tried to kiss her.

'Kissing at the table,' Rachel said, and then, 'I think I'm probably drunk now.'

'She thinks – '

'Praise the Lord – '

'Action! Take One! A sunny Sunday lunch. Rachel, me, the so-called hostess, is once again drunk. Her mostest as the hostess is nowhere in sight. Seated around her – ' One of the men turned a camera, another held a microphone.

'And?'

'And the drama unfolds,' Rachel went on. 'Rachel, this once proud ace reporter, is enjoying a quiet meal with close friends – '

'Quiet?'

'Close friends! She does this to us every Sunday. Quality friends is what we are – what we must be.'

'I can't think what happens next,' Rachel said.

'Perhaps if you were a little more creative . . .'

Rachel considered them all drunkenly. 'At least I keep you all amused. What else would you have to talk about? Who else – ?'

'We'd find somebody. Somebody who'd been invited but couldn't come.'

'Who couldn't come because he was off being creative in some far-flung corner of the world.'

108

'If you say so.'

'And we'd take him apart behind his back. Just as we do with any of you when you don't turn up,' Rachel concluded.

The record on the stereo ended and Colin replaced it with another. Rachel played the trumpet on an empty bottle. From being drunk enough to have slurred her words, she now seemed almost perfectly sober. She said she wanted to dance again and pulled up the man who'd danced with her before. He rose and held her, but not the way he'd held her when his wife and Colin had been out of the room.

Rachel waved at us with her fingers over his shoulder, and when it was the man's turn to face us he shrugged apologetically.

'You're a good dancer,' Rachel told him when they stopped. He held her hand up and bowed to the others as she curtsied. They returned to the table and she told Colin to fetch more bottles, that the others were all empty. Two of the women said they'd had enough to drink. Colin hesitated and she asked him what he was waiting for.

'I've written a piece on a new jewellery designer in Milan,' she said. 'It's probably a scoop. The world may not fall at my feet for introducing it to this genius, but it ought to. He makes everything out of glass and clear plastic. To tell you the truth, most of it looks like boiled sweets strung together, but who am I to judge?'

Colin returned.

'Rachel is telling us about her jewellery genius in Milan.'

'That was three months ago. They still haven't printed it. She must have mentioned it before. The man's a genius but no one knows who he is and no one buys his jewellery. That's how much of a genius he is.'

'They will.'

'Perhaps.'

'Male jewellery,' Rachel said. 'Colin can't bring himself to agree with the concept of necklaces and brooches for men.'

'I can see exactly why they might appeal,' Colin said.

'No you can't. No he can't.' She was hostile again.

Someone else spoke: 'I remember last year, Rachel. You were telling us we were all going to be wearing frocks. Frocks, for Christ's sake.' The man looked around the table for support.

'They were not frocks. They were – '

'You still said we were all going to be wearing them. And what happens? Anyone here seen a man in a frock? ''Frock'', Rachel,

109

despite what you might want to call them. Or perhaps I don't get out and about to the right places any more.'

'If you ever did.'

'Okay. If I ever did. So where are the frocks? Have you got any of this jewellery?' He looked around the table to ensure the others were still participating in the joke. 'If you've got any get it out and let me try it on. Or perhaps this is what you expected. I know, you could publish the article under the title "Pearls before Swine" and have a picture of me with a couple of earrings in. That's the sort of title you go in for, isn't it? Everything's a gimmick these days – the titles, the jewellery, the necklaces, the frocks, everything.' It seemed a natural end to the conversation.

Colin filled our glasses and brought in cheese. Eight different types. Rachel told us about those she could remember. People told her they were delicious.

From the dining-room table we spread ourselves around the house and out into the garden. The drink and the heat sent the man who'd danced to sleep in a deckchair. Two of the three women insisted on washing the dishes. The third was drunker than Rachel had been. Food was thrown out for the birds and we watched them descend to eat it.

The first couple left at seven. The others an hour after that.

Rachel had gone upstairs and fallen asleep at five.

As we left, Colin said he hoped she hadn't said anything to offend anyone and we all vigorously denied it.

Rachel told me long afterwards that when she'd woken and gone back downstairs the house was empty. It was six the following morning and Colin had gone. A note telling her of his departure and the expected date of return was taped to one of the empty bottles. The others had been salvaged and formed into the letter 'R' on the kitchen table. He was gone for three days, and during that time she hadn't the faintest idea where he was. He'd told her afterwards, but for some reason she'd forgotten.

8

The angle of the camera now is such that Rachel's eyes are on a line with the double blue horizon of sea and sky. She is standing on the promenade above the beach, leaning against the railings. The sea around her head is free of waders and swimmers, but to one side of her the shallower water is filled with splashing forms. The camera moves from her head to her feet and then back to the receding line of the railings, following them first to her left and then moving more quickly in the opposite direction. As the camera moves past her, her impatience with it becomes apparent.

A few yards away from her stands a small group of holidaymakers waiting for a bus, or perhaps a tram (there are cables in the air above them), or perhaps a horse-drawn carriage. They are clearly holiday-makers, and when they see they are being filmed they become predictably self-conscious. One of the women in the group straightens her hair, and several men, having looked quickly into the camera, look away. Two younger girls begin to pose, and the youths with whom they are standing gesticulate and push themselves forward.

The camera leaves them and returns to Rachel. She turns to look into it as it arrives at her face. She looks somehow threatened. It is closer to her than previously. She smiles unexpectedly. She holds her face in her hands and then leans further back against the railings. She sits on them and then raises her legs until they are horizontal, supporting herself like a gymnast on a bar. The absence of any connecting middle distance and the size of the people beneath her on the sand and in the sea suggest that she might be twenty or thirty feet above the beach, at the edge of a sheer drop. She presents both profiles to the camera and is unable to avoid a glimpse of the distance she might fall if she released her grip and overbalanced. To hold herself more securely she bends her knees around the middle bar of the railings. When she has finished she jumps down and takes a step away from the drop towards the camera. A couple pass between it and her, turning to face it as their blurred image fills the screen, only the outline of their two heads discernible.

The promenade around the small watching crowd looks busy, suggesting that Colin has asked people to walk behind him. Perhaps there is an even larger crowd already gathering to watch; perhaps their inquisitive and resentful presence has something to do with Rachel's expression and the way she is responding to his obvious directions to strike different poses.

Having passed out of the range of the camera, the man of the blurred couple steps back into it and waves. Laughter, perhaps; or calls of encouragement; or an embarrassed wife pulling him forward again and out of the line between Colin and Rachel.

Watching the films, there are times when that line seems as tangible and as dangerous as a tautly drawn wire.

The blurred image moves forward and the film freezes. Rachel is looking towards where the man and woman might be standing, or to where they might be walking away from her having said or shouted something at the camera. For the others – the crowd gathering behind Colin, the crowd turning Rachel into a seaside spectacle – the novelty of the camera is enough to hold them. Some will be asking the purpose of his filming; others will be suggesting that they too might be included.

It is still easier to consider the films as the individual pieces of a much larger, overall design. They are more than a record; they have become a substitute for something. There is seldom any dialogue, sound or any other indication of the purpose of the films. They are intended to speak for themselves.

The perfectly level line of the horizon and the two distinct blues give Rachel's head and the expression on her frozen face an unnatural, abstract appearance.

The film begins to move again. She smiles, she frowns, she opens and closes her eyes; she turns one way and then the other, she looks up and then down. All suddenly, all with an expectant pause in between, all as directed. It might not be a film of someone standing at railings against the beach and the sea, but a choice of a thousand or a hundred thousand fixed images, any one of which might be picked out as perfect. Whatever, it is intended to say more about what is happening *privately* than what might be more directly revealed. I expect the camera to turn and reveal the crowd – something of Colin's style I have identified, a statement about the watchers as well as the watched, the fact that he is not alone and all that this might suggest.

The remainder of the film is of the sea and the beach and the outside town – Blackpool, the tower, *the* seaside town – and with

112

Rachel as an almost incidental feature – standing in shop doorways, eating an ice-cream, moving with the crowd, their briefly turning heads, her own eyes carefully avoiding the camera. A shot of her standing with her legs astride and with the tower apparently supported on her shoulders. A shot of her looking down into the sand with her skirt bunched around her knees as a line of donkeys with children on their backs passes slowly behind her, led by one man and followed by another. A shot of Rachel's hands holding a giant stick of pink-and-white-striped rock perhaps three or four inches in diameter, turning its spiralling outer pattern until the word '*Blackpool*' is revealed through it. Night-time shots of the illuminations, the lights made to look sharper and the darkness blacker by the camera. Outlines dancing above the road and amusement arcades, a clown juggling a half-circle of balls, a parrot flapping its wings, Rachel standing beneath them, completely unaware. Colin reminding her why they were there – why, specifically, Blackpool, what it represented, what he thought about it, how he felt.

Lies, half-truths, elements still hidden within the overall design.

Rachel speaking into the camera, describing something with her hands. A nod of agreement from the camera.

Then Rachel standing with a candyfloss, being told to raise it and hold it in front of her face, then to move it towards the camera until her head is completely hidden and she becomes a surreal joke. Candyfloss with Woman.

Another shot (suggested by the candyfloss?): Rachel throwing pieces of bread into the air above her and then shielding herself against the gulls which arrive to catch it, or which descend to the ground around her. A variation on the theme of Trafalgar Square. Some of the birds fly close to her head and any one might be frozen into a smudge of black and white against her sharply focused arms or summer dress.

A shot taken from a moving car of street after street of almost identical boarding houses, people standing in open doorways, the small paved gardens, waiting for others, slabs of sunlit interior.

A shot from the top of the tower following the line of the coast and then moving around the outskirts of the town and into the undistinguished countryside beyond, congested lines of traffic, the crowds on the beach, the same crowd moving imperceptibly along the endless promenade. The promenade where Rachel posed and people watched her. The details of which were Rachel herself, the pavement, the railings, and the detached backcloth of sand, sea and sky – orange, blue, blue, the colours of Rachel's dress.

A shot of Rachel in a hotel bedroom, sitting on the bed beside the pillows, pointing to the window and explaining something, reading from the leaflet in her lap. Talking about Blackpool. The rest of the room is seen, and then the view along the street outside, the net curtains drawn back by an invisible cord as the camera approaches. More hotels, a street of hotels, and between them guest houses. More holidaymakers, the same sky. More traffic, another shot of the top of the distant tower. Shots of sandcastles on the beach being destroyed by the returning tide, being rubbed slowly smooth and worn down (half an hour, an hour?), some waves coming faster than others. Desert islands, and then nothing but the sea. An appropriate ending which does not include Rachel. Because Rachel is still back in the hotel bedroom, still on the bed, considering the view from the window, the view which for once does not include the sea. In the hotel, away from the window, on the bed.

9

'Colin called me once from New York, said he was coming home and wanted me to go and pick him up at the airport. He gave me the flight number, arrival time, everything. He said he'd been up for the past two nights covering something or other and that he hadn't slept. You can hear Colin rubbing his face over the phone, even long distance, to suggest tiredness. Drop everything, Rachel, and come and get me. I must have only known him for about six months, but at times like that it felt as though we'd grown up and old together.'

And you said?

'What does anyone ever say to Colin? Of course, Colin; I'll be right there, Colin; count on me, Colin. He was due in at something like three in the morning, which meant an hour's drive beforehand. We weren't living here then. Night driving used to scare me. I'd had an accident one night not long after I'd passed my test. With me, driving at night is a bit like playing a computer video game: all bright lights and moving lines, especially on motorways and dual carriageways. On the night I went to meet him, I had another accident. I ran into the back of someone at a set of lights. You see that?' She showed me the faintest line of an inch-long scar on her forearm. 'Arm straight through the windscreen. Trying to protect myself, I suppose. Ten miles an hour and I end up scarred for life.'

She showed me how she'd held up her arm to cover her face, how it had gone through the glass.

'I told the guy in front that his rear lights were out. He was driving on side-lights at two – no, three in the morning! He said he'd take care of everything himself, very concerned. All I could think of at the time was what Colin was going to say. Both my headlights were smashed and the bumper had come loose and there was a pool of dirty water from the radiator on the road. Me bleeding to death and this guy's more concerned about pushing the cars off the road. All he was worried about was having the police turn up. To be perfectly honest, I didn't know then that I'd cut myself. We heard a siren and he jumped a foot and looked ready to run. I told him he smelled of drink and he jumped again. I told him I was on my way to the airport and he offered to pay for a taxi. And the trip back? I asked him. He paid for that too. All very efficient, level-headed, a drunk being sober and indignant. Anyhow, we got the cars off the road and he gave me his card, telephone numbers, addresses, everything. It was only when I got into the taxi that I saw the blood. I told the driver what had happened and he got out some antiseptic and a bandage and made a good job of it. I tipped him with the money for the return journey. I still arrived at the airport an hour early, and it was there that I realised I couldn't remember exactly where I'd left the car. All the time I was one jump ahead of thinking about what had happened. I knew roughly, of course, but not the name of the side-street. I worried about the broken windscreen. The man said he'd wait with both cars until he could find someone to come and tow them somewhere safe. He had my number, he'd ring me. Then I started worrying about him ringing first thing in the morning and waking Colin. All this was still for him, you understand.'

She stopped speaking and began pacing the room, surprised and pleased by the vividness with which the details of the night had returned.

Is it important?

'Important! It's a litany of fucking disasters. You ask me – Colin calls up, says he's in New York and I set off on a trail of fucking disasters all across London. I couldn't even be sure if I'd locked the fucking front door. The speed, the way one thing came straight after another, that's what threw me. I'm sitting there in the middle of the night with a bleeding arm waiting for a flight which, when it finally arrives half an hour late, is practically empty. No Colin, no film crew. What am I supposed to do? What *can* I do? I check the passenger list: Colin's name, but no Colin. The next flight arrives in an hour. I wait. Nothing. By that time I can see pink showing through the taxi driver's bandage. All I can buy are Elastoplasts, so I buy some and try to tidy things up. It's obviously not a lot of blood – I wasn't likely to pass out or anything – but it's still blood. I sat there with an eye on the arrivals until it started to get light. This was autumn or late winter, seven, perhaps eight o'clock, and all the time I can imagine the phone ringing at home ready to tell me why he hadn't come. Finally, I decided enough was enough and went home. I rang his office to find out if they knew anything. They're pathetic; they tell you everything as though they were giving away state secrets. They thought he was still in New York, someone else thought he'd been back two days, someone else thought he'd gone to Berlin. They treat you like some kind of idiot. Two hours later

116

Colin rings me to tell me he won't be on the flight, makes a joke of it. He's coming back via Berlin and thinks he'll be home the day after tomorrow. I told him nobody knew where he was and he behaved as though I'd been spying on him, asking me who I'd called, what they'd said. I asked him how I could be sure he was even in Berlin and he started speaking German. Big joke; all is forgiven; everyone can relax. I told him about the car and he said, 'So what?' I told him about my arm and he told me to see a doctor. The doctor took one look and said he promised never to take up taxi driving – something smart – and put in two tiny stitches to teach me a lesson. Scarred for life. He told me there would have been no need if I'd gone directly to him. Two o'clock in the morning? Who are you supposed to trust? Who are you really supposed to trust?'

And had she contacted the other driver?

'Eventually. Some time in the afternoon. You can imagine how stupid I felt having to ask him where the cars were. He said he'd had a verbal estimate for my headlights and radiator and that he'd send me a cheque for the amount if I wanted to have the car fixed myself. It sounded suspiciously low, and when I questioned it he said it seemed high to him. He started getting technical and I told him I wasn't about to enter into a debate over it. I asked him about a replacement windscreen and he said he hadn't included the cost in his calculations. Can you believe it? He was actually trying to suggest that I'd put my arm through it unnecessarily! I reminded him that I had his home number and that unless he paid up *after* everything had been repaired I'd ring him ten times a day until it was. Should I have done that, do you think? Hysterical woman?'

I told her that having run into him from behind, technically speaking the accident had been her fault. It wasn't what she wanted to hear.

'I'm talking about five years ago. Having to resort to that kind of threat just made everything pointless. Colin said I should have looked for some compensation for my arm. He was keen on that kind of thing. I think he was even angry with me for having left if for so long before doing anything about it. The car came back a day after he did, and by the time he'd talked me into even considering doing anything about my arm it was too late. I might have been good at some things, but that kind of efficiency was never my strong point.' She showed me the pale line again. 'It shows up more the browner I get.'

And Colin came back from Paris. Or wherever.

'He came back. Paris, New York, China for all I knew. The point is, I *didn't* know, not for certain.'

117

I asked her what difference it would have made. The accident had been simply that. One thing had led to another.

'One thing led to another because Colin had shouted jump from the other side of the world and I'd jumped. It wasn't the first time and it wasn't the last.' She held up her hands to stop me. 'I know, I know – I'm being unreasonable, overreacting. I'm making something out of nothing. I'm a stupid woman standing beside a car with a smashed windscreen in the middle of the night with a strange man trying to tell me how it happened. It's beginning to feel as though that's how it's always been. That's what I'm trying to say, that's the point I'm trying to make. I never used to be like that before I met Colin. For the first time in years, the accident with the car and then his non-appearance at the airport left me feeling helpless. It wasn't something I was used to feeling and I resented it. I resented him for it and I resented myself for having allowed it to happen. You see what I'm saying?'

And you've felt the same since his death.

'I think so. But beforehand there was always some kind of justification for it – call it an indulgence. I indulged myself almost to the point of letting him take over completely. Even his death didn't really resolve anything. That probably doesn't make much sense.'

It was why she'd abandoned everything for the clinic, and why she'd fought against it for two months beforehand. She'd been looking for something she'd never found, and something she knew was unlikely to exist in the first place.

'It's still happening. Everything, here, now, this: it's still how I am, *what* I am.'

And the car came back as good as new: problem solved. One problem solved.

'You know what I couldn't stop thinking? All the time he'd been away and I thought I'd known where he was, all the time I couldn't get it out of my head that he was with another woman. You see how easy it would have been for him – doing what he did, being Colin. The Colin-ness of being Colin. I still don't know, can't know for certain. If I'd asked him it would all have been my fault again. I would have been that same panicky woman back beside the car with a shattered windscreen in the dark. Perhaps there might even have been a small crowd gathering round to tell me how lucky I'd been. The world's full of small crowds waiting for something to look at, and recently it feels as though it's always been me.'

She left the room and returned with two glasses.

Since her confession of having had a drink a week previously, she'd had another every night. Raising the subject, pouring and drinking had become another part of the ritual. Initially she behaved like a child in front of adults testing an act of adolescence before committing it, a little more than half certain of acceptance and then encouragement.

Her decision to build the conservatory had marked a high point, and since then she had become progressively less certain of herself. Everything she did and said continued to suggest a kind of restlessness.

Colin's illness and death were two unconnected events, one gradual, one sudden, but it was still not how she saw them, and the events of five years ago still had a greater bearing on what she felt now than the days and weeks immediately beforehand. The resolution, when it came, had been illogical and unexpected, and as a consequence she had been adrift ever since. It was why she returned to the events of five, three and two years ago to make sense of the immediate future, which, for her, remained uncertain. Her accident in the car had been no more than a detail by which she was able to recapture how she had once felt, and the details of the present continued to be important only insofar as they created other such links: it was why her trip to Rome had mattered; it was why the conservatory mattered; it was why her determination to return to work mattered.

'Have you ever wondered how many glasses there are in this house?' she said. 'I counted them: a hundred and sixty. A hundred and sixty glasses and I keep using and washing out the same one. Colin could have had fifty international love affairs and I might never have found out.'

I told her that as far as I knew there had never been any other women.

She emptied her glass and said she knew.

'That kind of detail never mattered to Colin – the headlamps, the bumper, the radiator. All that mattered to him was what they signified. I'd have looked good, on film, standing with the car and not even knowing where the fuck I was. Faces mattered to Colin, expressions, the faces of people caught up in something they hadn't the faintest idea about. When you see faces like that you realise exactly how much every other kind of face is telling you. Most of it's in the eyes, but the faces matter. Look at the faces of the crowd watching the space shuttle blow apart.'

We'd watched it together on the news the previous day, seen it on every news broadcast since.

'They don't even know what they're looking at. "Is this happening? Is this a film? Is this what we're seeing?" Ka-boom. One and a half minutes up and there's suddenly nothing left. What they're seeing is something spectacular. All they know is that it's something they shouldn't miss, something they have a right to see, an entitlement. Colin never had to convince anybody that what he was giving them was what they wanted. They did it all for him.'

She switched on the lamps and poured herself a second drink.

'What do you imagine the man smelling of drink and with only his side-lights on at two in the morning told his wife about what had happened?'

Always assuming he had a wife.

'He might have been on a dash from his mistress back to her. Is "mistress" still a good word?' She said it as someone who had suffered might say it. 'There's this American television quiz show where, for some reward or other, a man's wife is introduced to his mistress. She knows nothing whatsoever about this other woman, she's not even sure why she's there in the first place. She's sitting with her husband, holding hands, and not two feet away from her, behind a screen, is this other woman, glamorous, necklaces, nice dress, cleavage, all smiles, waving out at the camera and enjoying every minute of it. The compère starts to quiz her and you can see the man's face go – drop, try to smile, try not to believe what's happening to him. Good old wifey, meanwhile, is still sitting, stupid and ignorant and happy, grinning out and then tugging his sleeve when she sees that something's wrong. This other woman's talking about the necklace he bought her, about the fur coat he bought her, about where they'd been at weekends when he was supposedly away on business. And then the compère asks dear little wifey what he bought *her* for Christmas, and nothing comes out. She just sits there with her mouth open. Then she finds her voice and starts saying that everything's a big joke, that it must be, that he's never bought a fur coat in his life, that he's morally against the killing of animals to make fur coats, that he works hard and that whenever he's away she knows exactly where he is. *That* was a face to see, *there* was a disaster, *there* was fifteen years, home and kids and future being flushed away in the name of entertainment. We've got it on a video somewhere; I'll look it out for you. The man's holding his face in his hands, wanting everything else to be as dark and quiet, and his wife's still tugging his sleeve and wanting to be told that a big mistake's been made. And then they pull away the screen and he's sitting there between these two women. You can see the way they

120

look at each other. One of them's practically dead and the other one's doing the killing. Three faces, and there wasn't anything they didn't have between them. That bit of film to Colin was like someone else's favourite joke – the one they always end up telling, the only one they ever really get more than one laugh out of. He loved that piece of film. "All television is here," he used to say.'

She stopped talking, made another remark about her drink, something about the restfulness of the room.

One way or another, everything she said was about Colin and her stories were all the same story.

Once upon a time, Colin . . .

It was what had defeated her once and what was defeating her now.

10

'No one's taken Colin's project on; it's been scrapped.'

I asked her how she knew. There was no suggestion of surprise or indignation in her voice.

'I phoned up and asked them. You usually get shunted from one office to another until you're worn down and give up hope. No one knew anything about it. Did he tell you who might take it over from him?' She went on without waiting for my answer. 'Everyone in that place has heard about everything else. Likewise, everyone is interested in what everyone else is doing. It's part of the job – they mistake it for commitment. I should never have believed him in the first place.'

'Colin?'

'He had no intention of finishing it, of passing it on. He hadn't even had official clearance himself to be doing it. Why should he have told me anything? He knew how I felt about all that.' She gestured with both hands to suggest everything he'd done. 'The film was supposed to be about how people perceived what was happening to them, how they responded, and how those events were reported, right? He thought he knew. He thought he had a nice simple theory to hold it all together. Don't ask me what it was, I was never privy. But the fact is, *he thought he knew*, and with Colin that was enough. And then, when it happened to him, everything he thought he knew, he suddenly didn't know. It stopped being other people somewhere else – some poor sods watching a mountain come down on them – and became him. Can you see how simple and clear-cut that made everything? The truth was, he never did know. Because if he had known, then he would also have known about what was happening to him, and that was something he could never admit to. Did he ever suggest to you that there was someone waiting in the wings ready to catch the baton and run on with it? No. He'd known for too long that the film was never going to amount to anything other than a personal obsession.'

'Did you try to find out if there was anyone willing to consider – ?'

'*Me, me, me.* Didn't *I* try?'

'All I meant was – '

'I know what you meant. Colin, Colin, Colin. What do you think I'm doing now, with myself? Don't tell me. Perhaps if he'd been famous and respected then I would have become his famous and respected widow, spreading the word of his good works. These people don't exist any longer. One or two, perhaps, but that's all. The fact is, people who spend their lives reducing everything to thirty-second news reports will be lucky to become one themselves. Take it from me: words of wisdom from one who knows.' She pointed between her eyes.

The fact is, the facts are, the facts were –

'Pithy epigraphs. Even *he* knew that much.'

'But if the film was as good as he said it was . . .'

'How good? Just as good as he said it was? How much of it have you seen? There's nothing there. Somebody told him it would have made a decent video nasty. Not a very popular suggestion, as you might imagine. If nothing else, Colin needed to be seen to be suffering for his so-called art. Do I need to make the point any more clearly? He once made a film on Goya – one of his heroes, don't ask me why. You wouldn't believe it, would you, looking at some of the crap he brought home to hang around the house. Another thing: when I first knew him, he had a wall of framed certificates hung where everyone could see them. Did he ever strike you as a framed-certificates man?'

No.

'Said with such conviction.'

I never saw them.

'But you've seen them since in his study. He still had them framed and hung. Hidden away and yet not hidden away. They may not be for public consumption any longer, but they're still all there. He was given an award posthumously and I had it framed and hung it with all the others. A kind of momentum, a rite of passage, easing things from one state into another. I talk too much. Think too much.' She laughed coldly at the suggestion.

Her anger and derisive remarks were another attempt to shed a skin of her own. It was mid-morning and there was an empty glass beneath her chair.

And so that was it – the end of the project.

'I hope so. When he died I had letters from the people he'd worked with. You know, you were here, you saw them. His "colleagues". All telling me how much they'd learned from him, how great an influence he'd been on the way they themselves worked. What they were really saying was that I'd still be seeing him in ten- or twenty- or thirty-second snatches every time I turned on a news report or watched a documentary. They obviously thought they were telling me something I wanted to hear. I know why they said it, and I suppose it might even have made some of *them* feel better – about what they carried on doing, I mean. It must be a nice lever when it comes to pay negotiations to be able to point out how dangerous the job is. It wouldn't be too difficult to confuse the issue and for them to convince themselves that he'd died in the line of duty.'

It is still what happened. The likelihood –

'Talk to bookmakers about likelihoods, not me. If *you* want to believe it, fine, but keep it to yourself. As far as I'm concerned – ' She rose and stood with her elbows on the marble mantelpiece. 'Tell me, what would happen if you fell from the unfinished twentieth floor of an office block you were building? I suppose there would be too much at stake for it not to be completed.'

Instead of an answer, I told her that on some sites rope netting was strung around the building.

'Would they save you?'

'I doubt it. The people who work above them don't believe in them. The people who put them up don't believe in them. Too little faith all round for them to be able to work properly.'

'They'd still be there.'

She slid her hands to each end of the mantelpiece and held it.

'We never had a real fire in here. Coal-dust, smuts. When Colin died, when I went through the house from top to bottom, it looked as clean then as when we first moved into it. Nothing seemed to have changed. I remember feeling sick at seeing it like that. I went round shifting furniture and pictures just to reveal where the carpets and wallpaper had faded. It mattered to me to be able to see that those years had passed. Some people believe you can feel human suffering in a house – I don't, but some do. I went to see a writer who lived by the Thames in Richmond. She was convinced that the house into which she'd recently moved had suffered as a result of some previous human tragedy in it. That was as precise as she could bring herself to be. She sells millions. "The Way We Live Now". "Homes for the Eighties". Good idea? The worst idea you ever heard? I've a projected list of six interviewees.'

I told her it sounded like a good start and asked if she thought it would work.

'I'm still at the projecting stage. Yesterday I projected five; today I prefer nice round numbers instead. The editor I showed it to thought it was awful. She didn't exactly say as much, but she was holding her nose all the same. "Do one and see how it works out. Find a photographer. All expenses claimable, within reason." What she was saying was that the idea had been done to death. Then she had the nerve to suggest that our Dear Readers might be interested in a series on coping with bereavement. Can you believe it? Of course you can – it's that kind of magazine. First find six recently widowed women. Women with well-known husbands, of course, and "recently" meaning anything from yesterday to ten years ago. Apparently, she thought I'd have a sympathetic ear for that kind of thing. She's been married and divorced twice. Her ex-husbands visit her regularly each month. She's written about it. "An Arrangement of some Convenience", or something. One of them's a barrister and the other's a stockbroker. I suppose you can afford to be casual with that kind of ex-husband.'

She moved from the mantelpiece to the drinks cabinet, took out all the bottles it contained and arranged them along the top, where they had originally stood. She made no attempt to pour another drink; instead she stood back and admired the arrangement. Then she went back to the mantelpiece.

I asked her when she'd first known about the end of Colin's project.

'When he started saying too often that something worthwhile was going to come of it: when *he* knew.'

Then I asked her if he ever spoke to her about his illness. The word was wrong, but neither of us needed to be any more specific.

'Rarely. But I think *he* knew everything there was to know about it. I think he knew ten times more than he ever thought he'd find out. He was always very professional in his application to the task in hand. I think the truth was that the film had become some kind of diversionary tactic: surrounding himself with the suffering of others. Did he ever talk to you about titles?'

If he had, I didn't remember.

'He always waited until he'd finished. I used to think up half of them for him, and vice versa. Most of them were rejected in favour of something more catchy or punning. He never liked that, neither of us did, but we accepted it. You can lose yourself in little things like that, lose control, lose any feeling for the piece. I suppose you see your buildings finished right down to the doorknobs.'

'Right down to the greenfly on the potted plants. I try to interest clients in paintings or pieces of sculpture, investments. But plants

125

are living, breathing things, and supposedly create a certain ambience. We once experimented in some hotels with tapes of running water in summer. People said they felt better and cooler. No tapes in the bars and they drink more. It's no longer deception, but the Art of Deception. All legal and above board.'

'He once told me that if he hadn't broken those first two fingers, none of it would have happened.' She'd been waiting for me to finish and she hesitated before going on. 'Can you believe that? *He* did. Or at least he believed it until he stopped believing it. Those two fingers were his blue touch-paper. Light, retire, wait, bang.' She made a firework with her hands. 'I feel more comfortable standing than sitting in this room. It's a standing-room.' She stood back at the mantelpiece and let her hands feel for its edges until she was once again positioned at its centre.

The previous day, two men had arrived with the components of her conservatory and had erected it in outline. When they'd gone she went out and stood beneath the unglazed frame and convinced herself that the decision had been the right one. The men were due back in two days' time to complete the task.

11

'Enzo's here, in London. He called two hours ago from the airport.'

'So where is he?'

'I haven't moved since he called. He's coming here, *here*.' She stood in a corner of the kitchen, her arms folded, holding her elbows. 'I don't want him to come, I don't want him here. He's a creep. He should be here by now. I thought you were him. Three nights.' She held up three fingers. 'Three nights I spent with him. The rest of the time I stayed in a hotel. I didn't think that kind of thing was supposed to be any big deal to an Italian. He's making it into something it's not, wasn't. I told you, he's a creep. I might have given you the wrong impression. What did you expect me to say? That I'd had three grubby nights with an Italian businessman? He's married, with kids. He knew this address when he rang up. He thinks I'm standing here panting for him. Look at this place: it's ten times what he expects. He lied to me, I lied to him. He'll already be making up stories to tell for when he gets back. He works in his father's business; he hasn't an ounce of business sense in his body.' She was afraid to stop talking for fear of hearing the doorbell. 'You could answer the door and say you'd never heard of me.'

'He can't be all that stupid.'

She unfolded her arms and slapped her hands against the tiled wall. 'Big help.'

'I really think –'

'Don't tell me what you really think, because deep down you're enjoying all this. What you really think is that I'm getting exactly what I deserve.'

'All I know – '

'Creep is all you need to know.'

And the fact that you're behaving like a sacrificial virgin being roped to an altar.

'Very funny. Ha ha ha.'

I asked her how long he was in London for.

'I don't know. He said a week to a fortnight.'

127

'Perhaps he'll turn out to have as bad a memory for these things as you seem to have.'

She picked up a cup, looked to see if it was empty, and held it as though she was about to throw it.

'If you mean "liar" say "liar". It's a better word all round.'

Liar.

She put down the cup. 'Perhaps he *is* lost. Two hours is a long time from there to here.' She held her palms together and said, 'Dear God, let him be lost. On the Underground. For a fortnight.'

I asked her to tell me exactly what happened in Rome. She took it as a sign that I was willing to help her and told me.

'Three nights, four at the very most. We were in a flat which wasn't even his, and less than an hour after I'd met him he was flashing me photos of the bambini and mama. I still don't know if it was his wife or mother. He left first thing each morning and came home late each afternoon complaining of how hard he'd been working and with armfuls of dramatic gestures. I honestly thought it was what I needed. There was half a day when I was stuck waiting for some cash to be transferred. I'd been in too many places, overspent. He introduced himself and helped me out. I'd spoken to no one except tourist guides, waiters and hotel receptionists for a fortnight and under those circumstances he was a civilised conversationalist.'

And now he was a creep.

'And now he's a creep.' She was impatient to continue before he arrived. 'He doesn't even speak that much English. He always kissed my hand before starting on anything more substantial. I don't know what I expected, but it was either too much or too little. It just felt right at the time. I came back a week earlier than I'd intended, and without telling him. That's it.'

She walked to the far end of the kitchen and then back to the corner. I told her that all we could do was wait.

'Please, dear God, the Underground. Or let him be hijacked. I deserve to be struck down by lightning. I'll die and go straight to hell, no hesitation.' She jabbed downwards, and as she did so, the doorbell rang. She looked at me, drew in her breath and ran her hands down her sides. 'Let him in. Just don't tell him who you are. Oh, Christ – '

I answered the door.

Enzo was short and stocky, like a footballer two years out of training. He had short black hair and a day's growth of moustache which would be a full moustache in five. He introduced himself, shook my hand and said in poor English that the house was much larger than he'd been led to expect. He spoke with a faint, boyish lisp, which was lost when he lapsed back into Italian.

'While I am here I should speak only English.' It sounded like the start of a comic routine. He had only one medium-sized case with him and he tried to explain to me that he'd bought it specifically for the journey. He looked beyond me into the cool half-light of the hallway. Rachel waited in the kitchen. I heard her trying to sound busy. I let him in.

Inside, he said that the house was much more impressively furnished than he'd imagined. Rachel appeared in the kitchen doorway and he walked quickly towards her with his arms out. She let him hold and kiss her, but kept her arms by her side. She told him she hadn't expected to see him.

'She hadn't expected to see me. I let her know, I telephone from the airport . . .' He held up his hands.

I carried his case into the kitchen and stood it on the table, hoping to suggest to her its smallness. He thanked me and gave her a present of scent. He took it from the box for her and insisted she sprayed some on her wrist. She did so, but pulled away as he leaned forward to kiss it.

'Tea?' she said, and then did nothing as we agreed with her.

'Your house . . .' Enzo began, again raising his hands.

'It isn't all mine. I own part of it, share it with some other people. They're away.'

He looked disappointed – whether at the revelation or the lie, it was hard to tell. 'It is still a beautiful house.'

I began to prepare the tea and he took a bottle of gin from his case and stood it on the table.

'Do you also own part of the house?' he asked me. I told him I didn't. Behind him, Rachel bared her teeth. Enzo pulled his tie lower and tugged at the sleeves of his jacket to reveal small sweat-stains. He looked even shorter and fatter when he took off his jacket. 'That damn airport and their searching into everything,' he said. 'In Italy we have respect for businessmen. They are important people.'

'Rachel told me you were a businessman. What is it you do?'

He held a hand to his chest. 'I represent. I am here in London on business.'

Important business?

He fluttered his hand. All business was important.

Rachel asked again if we wanted tea and I indicated the tray I'd prepared. Enzo touched the cap of the bottle on the table. It told me Rachel had started drinking while she'd been away.

'Outside,' she said, and went into the garden. Enzo waited until she'd gone before turning to me for an explanation.

'She means shall we have the tea outside,' I said.

His look changed; he'd understood perfectly. 'Perhaps it will be warmer,' he said. 'Join us.' He picked up the bottle and I gave him some glasses. He followed Rachel out and began a discussion on the garden. Rachel gave him a tour, listing the names of the plants. The closer she came to the kitchen the louder she raised her voice.

'Lady's Mantle, periwinkle, London Pride, clematis, honeysuckle, camomile, Silver Queen, skimmias, charity.'

'Tea is served,' I announced. Only Enzo appreciated the gesture and applauded.

Rachel poured us all gin.

We sat at a table and Enzo smoked Italian cigarettes in that particularly casual continental manner, as though it were a natural bodily function, careless of both the smoke and ash. Rachel copied him. In addition to the obvious physical differences, he was as unlike Colin as it was possible to be, and I saw what his real attraction had been for her.

After each mouthful from her glass, Enzo topped it up. He rubbed his face as though he'd already had a busy day.

Rachel peeled three peaches with a small knife and he watched closely as she discarded the skin, seeing something he'd seen before, almost an intimacy.

'How long was the flight?' she asked him.

'These things are always too long. For any businessman, time is money.' He wore a short-sleeved shirt, rubbed his arms and seemed perfectly relaxed. Rachel wanted to ask him how long he intended staying in London. She would emphasise 'in London'. She would want that point to be clearly made and clearly understood.

'I forget the name of this plant,' Enzo snapped the full, flowering head from its stem beside his chair.

Rachel didn't know. She told him a name.

'Ah, of course.' He cupped it in his hand and sniffed it before throwing it down.

And that one? And that?

Rachel saying she would shortly have to leave London to make a promised visit to friends,

— to start work on something she'd been planning for weeks
— to look at a new house she was thinking of buying

– to discuss a business proposition with the editor of a magazine on which she'd been promised work.

Except 'business proposition' would be too close to Enzo's own deceptions. Except to him they were never that.

The next time I spoke, Rachel held my arm and agreed with me. She laughed and asked me if I remembered something which had never happened. Enzo looked at her hand and then at her knees. He wanted to talk about Rome to the woman he had known in Rome.

'Do you have the pictures of your children? Can I see them again? Can we both see them?'

'Ah, no pictures.' He patted his breast-pockets and thighs, making it clear that he did not intend showing them to us.

'What were their names? I remember most of them, but . . .'

Enzo listed their names. His proudest possessions.

He asked me what I did and then repeated the word 'architect' until he'd assessed its position on the shifting scale of the business world. He fluttered his hand again. 'Architect . . . okay.'

I thanked him and he took it seriously.

'You build,' he said. 'You draw houses and then you build.' The insult was a deliberate one. He spoke for a minute in Italian, watching Rachel, who caught some of the words and nodded in a wasted effort to let him know she understood.

He was telling her he had never imagined she owned such a large and beautiful house, or such a well-planned and relaxing garden, that he would never have guessed that she took an interest in such things, that she was considerably more than he'd ever expected or than she'd ever suggested to him in Rome. He was telling her how much he was enjoying himself, despite my presence; how nice she looked, her dress, her hair, her scent. He was offering her more drink, more cigarettes, anything she wanted. He was asking her in the politest and most respectful way he knew why his visit wasn't progressing as he'd expected; why they weren't already together on top of one of the beds in one of the beautiful rooms in her beautiful house.

As it had been; as she might have promised him it would be.

He was asking her why she'd left him without telling him she was going.

He was telling her that he knew precisely what was happening, what she was allowing to happen, causing to happen.

He tapped his teeth with his finger.

Rachel poured the tea and alternated drinking it with the gin.

He asked me if it was how tea was drunk. I said perhaps.

Rachel understood exactly what he meant.

He said he liked the mixture of hot and cold. He turned a ring on his finger.

The gin was warm from having been in his case all day.

He pointed to a nearby sparrow and told us the Italian name for sparrow. He made his hand into a gun and shot it. Then he pretended to be eating the tiny carcass and laughed at our revulsion.

'A delicacy,' Rachel said.

'You remember. One must have some appreciation of the finer things. Money is not everything, am I right? Perhaps I should not say it. For many people, to talk about money is an insult. But not here. Here you only pretend it is.' He refilled our glasses until the bottle stood only half full.

He'd been there an hour. There were events ahead, events the afternoon around the table in the garden were leading to, which Rachel was not even allowing herself to consider.

She left us and went indoors. A minute later she shouted me in to her. A full silent minute of gin and tea and observed niceties.

Inside, I told her she was making everything too obvious, that he knew.

'Too right I'm making it obvious. I'm making it as obvious as I know how short of walking out there with a sandwich board or waving a banner. He's a creep. I told you he was a creep.'

Look upon him as a stranger in a strange land.

'Which is precisely what I was, remember? You'll have me crying for him next. Short of births, deaths and marriages, this is the worst day of my life.'

I looked out to where Enzo was sitting with his back to us.

'What are we going to do? They have this idea that no matter how badly they might treat you or you might treat them, they still get to sleep with you at the end of the day.'

'He's whistling to the sparrows,' I said.

'They'd better not get too close to him.'

'What you want me to do is to go back out there and insist that he stays for a meal with us and see how he reacts. You want me to ask him which hotel he's staying at.'

'Tell him all important businessmen are supposed to stay in big hotels overlooking Hyde Park. See if he understands the word "escort".'

Enzo turned and looked in at us and Rachel waved.

I went back out and told him something about the meal she was

132

preparing. He said he hadn't eaten since leaving Rome. He looked down at his stomach.

'Is she a good cook?'

'Not particularly. It doesn't matter to Rachel.'

He turned to the house with a look of undisguised scorn and told me what a marvellous cook and mother his wife was. When his English became once again inadequate, he continued in Italian. I told him I understood little of what he was saying, but he dismissed the remark with a shrug. He said I didn't have to know to understand what he was saying. 'Will we eat outside or in?'

'In, probably. The evenings aren't yet particularly cold, but – '

'In Rome they are still warm. I am not so much of a businessman that I cannot be at home early enough to play with my sons and daughters.'

I knew by his tone of voice that he had finally accepted what had happened between Rome and now, and that when the time came for him to leave, he would go. He repeated the names of his six children. He asked me if I thought six was a large number for such a young man. He was thirty-six and disclosed his age as though it were an achievement. In another year he would have gained a stone in weight, and a stone every year after that. He said he was hungry again. I went to the house and took out some cheese and bread and wine, which we ate and drank with the gin. He asked me if I'd ever been to Rome, and when I said I hadn't he began to describe it for me.

In the kitchen I told Rachel that I thought he'd finally got the message.

She said, 'Thank Christ for that,' and made me feel like the perpetrator of a cruel trick.

'I didn't actually lure him all the way here just to let him know,' she said. 'He came because he was following his prick. He's going to finish that bottle. He'll probably ask for the scent back to give to Maria or Gina or whoever. She's probably already carrying his tenth child.'

Seventh.

'Do you think it makes a difference?' The knowledge that he finally understood had given her strength.

Rachel is in the kitchen preparing us a meal. She told me about the meals you shared in Rome.

Had she told me about the drink or their beds, or the rooms they'd shared, the pattern of sun on the walls? I tried to imagine him naked. Black hair showed above his open collar. Colin's body had been almost hairless.

He lifted his feet on to Rachel's empty chair and let his shoes fall off. They were patent leather with a buckle. He pulled them to him and stood them neatly together beneath the table.

Rachel returned and said, 'Half an hour.' She filled her glass. Enzo swung his feet from her chair. She asked us what we were talking about.

'Rome,' I said.

'You've never been.'

No, but you have.

'The Eternal City,' Enzo said. 'Eternally there. My father helped liberate it.' He spoke as though he resented that part of his ancestry. Nothing else he did or said suggested it. 'I doubt if I will stay for your meal,' he said. 'I have promised to visit some of his relatives. He has not been back to England since 1952. I was two years old. Apart from which, it is never wise to mix business with pleasure.'

Rachel knew enough to apologise, but enough also to make it only a slight and indirect apology.

Enzo retrieved his jacket and took out another packet of cigarettes. He said that people were watching us from the windows of neighbouring houses. Rachel told him to ignore them and he said he was used to being watched in that way.

I wondered then if she'd told him anything at all about Colin.

Rachel had this husband, Colin, and after his death – since long before his death, to be precise – she began to – she let herself – everyone but Rachel could see exactly what – she went to Europe in an attempt to – And in Europe she met you. End of equation. You can be reduced to a point along a short line of cause and effect, act and consequence. And by coming here you've diverted from the main path and closed a circle. A big mistake. I'm telling you all this because Rachel herself does not yet understand it. Just between us, between men. Understand? *Ha capito?*

'They can look as much as they like,' Rachel said. 'They never see anything worth waiting for.'

Enzo looked at me in a way which deliberately excluded her. He asked if I'd been born in London. He told Rachel to make another pot of tea, and when she hesitated he told her again almost angrily. She collected the cups from the table and pretended to be a maid, bowing and touching her forehead.

'Like in Rome,' Enzo said, watching her go.

When she returned he told her to pour the tea before it was properly infused and then to fill up our glasses with what remained of the gin, most of which he'd drunk himself.

'A man on the plane said London was very awful at this time of the year. He was an Italian, like myself, and I agreed with him. I told him I came three times a year to London and three times a year to New York. He said New York was even worse and so I agreed with him.'

He indicated the recently completed conservatory and said he supposed it was where Rachel worked.

'It's where I plan our advertising campaigns,' Rachel said quickly, reminding me.

'Rachel is very important in the world of advertising,' Enzo said. He proposed a toast and drank to her: 'To important Rachel.'

Rachel drained her glass and started laughing.

'Rachel thinks this is funny.'

She stopped and looked down at her feet.

'Everything Rachel says and does is funny,' he said.

She looked from her feet up into the sky.

He rolled his glass between his palms. Then he rose from his seat and apologised for leaving so soon. Rachel said she understood.

I went with him back into the house and through to the front. He walked into the street with his case like an unsuccessful salesman. I gave him directions to which he hardly listened.

'I understand perfectly your part in all this,' he said as he went.

I watched him go and then I left the house and walked up the hill and on to the Heath to one of the benches overlooking the city. I saw the ten thousand places in which he might lose himself. I watched aircraft climbing through the haze.

I went back to the house two hours later. Rachel was still sitting in the garden. She'd arranged the food she'd prepared on three plates and set them at the kitchen table. There were pieces of broken crockery on the floor and the overpowering smell of the perfume Enzo had brought. I traced it to the plates of food, over which she'd emptied the entire bottle. Flies crawled across the table and food.

'Before you say it, yes, everything was entirely necessary.' She was standing in the doorway. 'You weren't hungry, were you? Has the miserable Latin cretin gone? He'll probably fuck off home to Rome on the first flight he can get – if he can find his way back to the airport. I know why you're looking at me like that.' She held her head.

'Insisting that he stayed and had something to eat wouldn't have made that much difference, would it?'

'I don't know. You tell me. Or perhaps you want to tell me that I've got no feelings whatsoever. Well if that's the case, let me tell you: it's a good way to be. In fact, it's the only way to be. Here, and now, there's no other way I'd rather be.' She came forward, moving unsteadily from the light into the shade. 'I feel ill.' She sat at the table, caught the smell of the spoiled food and began to heave. She was sick into her lap and then on to the floor. She leaned forward until her forehead rested on the edge of the table. She sat back gasping for air and with saliva on her chin. 'Mia fucking bambini, how about that, eh? Mia own fucking bambini, bambino, bambina.' She let her head fall forward again and began to cry.

She cried for an hour. She cried herself sober.

Later, she threw the plates complete with their contents into the bin because she couldn't bring herself to scrape them clean.

12

In the middle distance, a small pack of wolves ran from left to right across the screen. Between them and the camera were several unfocused, indistinguishable objects, trees and people, one of whom I knew would shortly be revealed to be Rachel. The film was titled simply *A Day at the Zoo*.

The wolves ran in their characteristically casual, loping stride, losing and gaining speed as a single animal, and then stopping suddenly and looking around them as though they were surprised that their short journey had ended. They dispersed, most of them walking only a few paces before circling and dropping down into the long grass of their enclosure, their pack instinct gone, looking listless and tame, and waiting for the signal which would have them all up and running again a few minutes later.

A solitary animal moved in the direction of the camera, was focused upon and then lost as the double mesh fencing surrounding the enclosure materialised across the entire screen. The wolf turned and walked away.

Two nuns appeared in focus, standing together at the fencing and looking at the animals. Rachel arrived beside them, her back to the wolves, facing directly into the camera. She smiled and then looked puzzled. I imagined Colin urging her to turn the nuns to face him, perhaps even for her to stand between them with her arms around their shoulders. I could imagine the significance of a shot containing Rachel, the nuns and the wolves. Not its real significance, perhaps, but the private joke it might have become.

The nuns moved off, both turning briefly in the direction of Colin, who, judging by Rachel's reaction, had called out to them in the hope that they might acknowledge his presence, his role in the proceedings. They both smiled before passing out of the shot in a single movement as smooth and as synchronised as the wolves' had been.

Rachel was speaking to him, reprimanding him and laughing, shielding her eyes, first from the sun and then from everyone around her. She lifted her face, turned her hands into ears, and silently howled at the sun. By the time Colin had refocused on the distant wolves, most had looked at the howling woman and looked away again.

Then Rachel came towards him, her hands held out in front of her in a less than serious attempt to block the lens. Colin sidestepped her and went on filming.

The film ended, was blank for a second, and then resumed with Rachel carefully positioned in front of the tigers' enclosure, holding out her hand, upon which one of the animals sat and groomed itself. Then she moved slightly and the effect was lost. Colin called out to her. She raised her hand, complained that her arm ached and then lost patience with him. She was separated from the animals by a wide moat and concrete wall, again topped with mesh.

It was a hot day, and in her other hand she held an ice-cream cone. She leaned back against the enclosure and Colin swung the camera to look at the people around her, many of whom responded to him. A group of small children waved and the film shook as he waved back. When he returned to where Rachel had been standing, she wasn't there. The camera swung from side to side, blurring everything, until he finally located her again walking away from the tigers. She stopped, waited a few seconds and then turned. She was grinning, her lips pursed and ready to kiss the lens as Colin ran towards her.

A foot from her face the film ended and the screen burst into light.

13

Three months after he'd broken his fingers, Colin injured his wrist of the same hand. He'd fallen and held out his arm to protect himself. He'd been holding a small camera in his other hand and had fallen badly, with his free arm at an awkward angle. The immediate damage was confined to his wrist, but he said he felt the pain jar to his elbow and then up to his shoulder and down his spine. As he told me, his arm was in a light sling. His fingers were still stiff and it was painful for him to fold his hand halfway into a fist. He'd been told to imagine he was gripping a tennis ball, but the effect was dispiritingly claw-like.

We were in his Shepherd's Bush flat. When he finished telling me, I tried to think of something to say.

'I fell as I did because all I could think of when I went over was how expensive the camera was. It was a new model and I'd been on and on at them to buy it for six months. And then the first time out with it, this happens. Do you know what did it – what I was so keen to get out and shoot?'

I didn't.

Guess.

What?

'I said guess!' He shouted and then stopped, surprised by the sudden severity of his voice.

Guesses:

– A hijacking somewhere.

– Police with megaphones and dogs surrounding a house.

– Pieces of bodies being drawn up out of the sewers and drains.

– A tug-of-love siege and a crying child being held to a window.

– A bomb ready to explode unspectacularly into an ordinary street.

– None of those things.

'Prince William going to school. Oh, not his first day – nothing so common – but Prince William going to school. I was like a kid with a new toy. When you want something to happen, nothing does; and so we settled for a royal. The only reason they let me do it was because it was supposed to be my day off. The beauty of the new camera is that it's fitted to a harness which allows you to run and yet still film in a relatively smooth line. They've been around some time, but this one was the very latest, the best.'

– Eliminate the shudder of the exploding bomb,
' – the run across a street to crouch behind a car,
– the jostle of a crowd trying to reach a man being escorted beneath a blanket.

'I was running alongside the royal car, focusing on him on the back seat. Good shot, good film. Completely unusable, but it proved a point.'

And then you fell.

'I shouldn't have shouted. I'm sorry, there's no excuse.'

I asked him if anyone knew that he still occasionally stayed at the flat. Occasionally, regularly.

'Rachel, you mean? Or in the case of an emergency?'

Whatever.

'A couple of people from the office have the number.'

I asked him if there was any real need to keep it and he looked around the room uncertainly.

Originally his wrist had been bandaged, and when that was removed it was held in a device of rods connected to two padded leather straps, one of which fastened over his forearm, the other over the back of his hand. It was intended to hold the small bones rigid and in position in the hope that they might partially reset themselves. It made him look like a falconer awaiting the return of the hawk. In a month it would come off and be replaced by a short inflatable sleeve. His belief that whatever was preventing his bones from healing properly was now spreading was unshakeable and ridiculous in equal measure.

'I said I'd show you Ian's collection of seismographs.' He left me and returned with a glass case of delicate machinery. He cleared a surface and set it down, ensuring it was level with a spirit gauge. He opened the glass door and made some adjustments. 'Watch.' He gently closed the door and inserted a slender key through a hole in the glass, turning it once. A slim roll of paper began to move between two small rollers. He told me to keep perfectly still, explaining what was happening in a whisper.

We watched the stub of a pencil against the paper. There was a tremble in the line caused by the vibration of the traffic outside, and I saw the corresponding jump when something heavier than usual passed beneath us.

140

'It's very primitive. According to Ian's records, it was most likely the work of an amateur naturalist. It was made in North Wales and was probably used to register quarry explosions. There were still some of the original rolls with it when he bought it, but I can't find any of them now. Watch.' He picked up a paperback and let it fall to the floor beside the table on which the seismograph stood. The pencil shook and the line on the paper faded in a series of waves.

He watched it intently. 'There's very little accurate indication of the scale or extent of the tremor, simply that one has taken place. It wasn't built to be used in situations like this.' He indicated the window and the traffic. He tapped a finger of his injured hand against the case and watched the line jump. 'Most of the others need to be more carefully set up, but I'll clear some space in here and set them out. I've offered to buy some of them from the trustees.'

'Successfully?'

'I shouldn't think so. They're more valuable as a collection, and that's more valuable in public hands.'

He continued to experiment with the simple recorder until the roll of paper stopped turning. He unwound it from the mechanism and held it in a strip for me to see.

'How did Rachel respond to your wrist?'

He thought about the question before answering. 'What mattered to her was how it had happened. The camera, my eagerness to try it out, the subject . . . My wrist seemed almost inconsequential by comparison.'

I asked him if it would affect his work.

'I doubt it; there's always someone else to hold the things.'

I'd been with them in the house when he'd told her the final verdict on his broken fingers. They'd argued until my departure and presumably for long afterwards. Rachel's tactic seemed at first to be to try and shock him into not believing what he'd been told, largely because she could not bring herself to believe it. At the time, a second opinion had seemed to suggest an almost fatal desperation. She'd argued that they were only his fingers.

'His fingers, *his* fingers, *my* fingers!' he'd shouted.

The next time I saw Rachel she accused me of having known before she did. I was staying with them and Colin was away. I told her I only knew as much as he'd told me.

Increasingly, whenever Colin was out of the country she made arrangements to stay with friends, often returning to the house with them the following day. If I was there she would make a point of introducing me as Colin's friend. My presence, intended initially by

141

Colin to have some conciliatory effect, was indirectly the cause of other arguments: ones I was not intended to hear, but which I could not avoid overhearing.

'You heard, I suppose,' Rachel would casually say to me afterwards. Colin would sit with a look on his face which said that none of this was happening to him. He would say, 'We've decided – ' and Rachel would interrupt, saying, 'You've decided, *you*.' Colin's face would hold the same look and the cracks between them grew to reveal a darkness.

'You exasperate me deliberately,' he once told her.

'I ex-as-per-ate him deliberately. Is that exasperate as in mind-of-my-own, think-for-myself exasperate?' She asked for my opinion. She called me an impartial observer. 'United Nations,' she said.

'Two fingers, two fingers,' Colin shouted. 'There are people walking round with every bone in their body crippled, and all this is what might or might not be happening to me as a result of – ' He held up his black sheath, still vaguely ridiculous and obscene.

'Then they'd hardly be walking around, would they?' Rachel said.

'You can't resist, can you? You just can't resist.'

'I'll have to think about that one.' She slammed out of the room.

Colin apologised and sat at the table with his elbows on the morning's mound of newspapers. I suggested moving out but he insisted I should stay.

'She thinks I ought to get a second opinion. And then she'd insist on a third and a fourth until she heard what she wanted to hear.'

The problem then seemed nowhere near as serious as it might yet become.

'It's the beginning of the end as far as Rachel's concerned,' he said.

Rachel returned and sat with us. She said she'd been a cunt to talk about other people that way.

'You're a cunt to most people you meet, Rachel,' he said fondly.

'I learn it all from you.' There was a great deal of affection in the exchange and she held his injured hand. Then she apologised to me and said we ought to make plans for the day, which was a Bank Holiday. Colin disappointed her by saying he had to leave in an hour.

Later, Rachel went out and didn't return until early evening. Two other women came back with her and filled the house with their noise and shouting. The three of them had a small private party and the women stayed the night in one of the spare bedrooms.

I saw them the following morning, when Colin returned, and as they came downstairs with their hands against the walls. Rachel told Colin how they'd spent the evening. The two women managed to look guilty and unrepentant at the same time. They were wearing Rachel's clothes, and both glanced continually at Colin's hand.

A joke: a man has two of his fingers encased in a black phallic sheath. His wife says to him –

Have you heard about Colin's sex life since he was told about his bones? No? Well, apparently –

What do you call a man without any bones on his wedding night? I don't know. A –

Colin kissed the women and told them individually how long it had been since he'd last seen them.

'Colin has this memory,' Rachel said.

All three women sat in the kitchen with their eyes shielded. Seeing how they felt, Colin began to sing.

'Colin thinks he has this singing voice,' Rachel said. 'His father was half Welsh. It's a common failing. They can all sing, they're all singers.'

The women dropped tablets into glasses of water.

Rachel asked me if I had anything to say on the subject.

It was hearing Colin talk about the Welsh origin of the crude seismograph that reminded me of Rachel's remark and I asked him about his father.

He lifted the glass case from the table and returned it to the bedroom.

He told me about his father – nothing memorable – a clerk in an office, whose own father had worked as a labourer building roads, whose own father had never existed in Colin's memory. His father had died when Colin was sixteen.

'He thought I was going to be a clerk, a better-qualified and better-paid clerk than he was, but a clerk all the same. I don't even think he would have been particularly proud of what I became, except when he was talking about it to other clerks. I only really started to know him when he was dead. His mother was Welsh, and she probably encouraged him to sing.'

Colin's own mother had died ten years after her husband. Both were buried two hundred miles away in a cemetery they had been able to overlook from their home.

'When Rachel found out about my wrist I lost every argument I'd ever had with her. She was right and I was wrong. She'd been right all along, and if I'd listened to her in the first place none of this would ever have happened.'

143

'You don't believe that.'

'Why don't I? I believe what *they're* telling me. Why shouldn't I believe her? I doubt if Prince William ever even knew what was happening. Funny man falling over with his camera. Big deal. Funny man on the pavement and all the funny man can think about is the six months he's spent trying to get the bloody thing in the first place.'

'Was it damaged?'

'What do you think? Not a scratch. Well done, what a relief, he's saved the camera. Three cheers. I didn't tell them about my arm being on fire. Like the stupid cunt I was, I stood there bowing and encouraging their applause. I knew then, as clearly as I've ever known anything in my entire life, what was happening.'

He picked up the strip of paper from the floor and wrapped it in a boxer's bandage around his good hand.

14

Rachel began work in her new conservatory; in the new conservatory where her unfulfilled creative talents were waiting to be reborn; in the new conservatory where she would achieve everything she deserved to achieve.

Or Rachel went through the motions of working in her new conservatory, the building of which had been invested with considerably more than the fragile-looking structure could ever possibly bear.

Or Rachel went out there at ten each morning and returned to the house at one.

Or that, in essence, was what she said she did. The alternatives were endless depending on how much you were prepared to believe or hope.

She even told me one day that Rachel was not her first name – her second, or perhaps even her third: something Rachel something.

Conservatory. Or conservatoire, she said. Conserva*toire*.

'I've decided on conserva*toire*. Let's be honest about it: I should never have had it built in the first place. But at least I can sit in here and wait for something to hatch. Listen to this: "It was the best of times, it was the worst of times . . ." A famous beginning. Guess.'

'Are you serious?'

'Do you know it?'

'*A Tale of Two Cities*.'

She sagged, then revived. 'Ah, but if you were more interested in making the perfect baked Alaska or constructing macramé plant-holders, would you know it?'

Or, to put it another way . . .

'"Call me Ishmael,"' I said.

'A commission is a commission.'

'Why do you need them – the beginnings?'

'Don't ask. A competition. Two weeks in Brussels, would you believe. And *I* ought to get that for setting the questions. It's a long way from where I used to be. How the mighty are falling.'

She was in a better frame of mind than I'd seen her for a week, since Enzo's abrupt arrival and departure, during which time she'd drunk very little and had crossed her heart and spit into her palm to prove it.

'How many more do you know? Famous beginnings. Let's not restrict ourselves. Books, films, Patience Strong.'

'Who?'

'She goes very well with baked Alaska. If I get this one right, it might lead to "Dressing From a Catalogue", "Authentic Italian Cookery" – I know, don't remind me.'

The top of the sloping conservatory roof was filled with the smoke from her cigarette. She turned a handle beside her desk and two small panes slanted to release it.

'*Voilà*! You said, "Call me Ishmael."'

'*Moby Dick*.'

'Ah, now that I think not. Spotted dick, perhaps . . .'

'"It is a truth universally acknowledged, that a single man in possession of a good fortune, must be in want of a wife." *Pride and Prejudice*.'

'I'll use that one. It's bound to strike a chord.'

'As you say, it might lead to something else.'

'No doubt about it. ". . .universally acknowledged that a single man . . ."'

I repeated the line for her.

There were several insects inside the glass and she swatted at them as she wrote. She'd bought plants and arranged them around a narrow glass shelf. The scent of them was overpowering.

'Would *you* want to have to spend a fortnight in Brussels?'

I told her I'd never been.

'Believe me, you wouldn't. Prizes generously donated by the Belgian Tourist Board. Logo on the cover, the name of the place repeated as many times as the copy can bear. A day, perhaps a weekend . . . And to top it all, they're going to ask the lucky couple to relate their memories of this marvellous fortnight and then run it a month later. Ghost-written by yours truly, no doubt. Explain in no less than two thousand words what you enjoyed most about your Belgian experience. To me. I can imagine it now.'

'It's still a start,' I suggested.

'The impression I got was that it was a chance I didn't deserve, that I was taking the bread out of someone else's mouth. Someone more needy, someone still on the up and up. Name one export for which Belgium is famous world-wide. Don't think about it too hard, there aren't any. What we have to suggest to the people who enter the competition is that there are thousands of others who *do* know. The Belgian Tourist Board will no doubt have the answer in a sealed envelope. I once almost reviewed a book on the Flemish textile industry for the *TLS*.'

Almost?

'I wrote it but they never used it. Someone who supposedly knew said they were interested in a review, and so, like the alert and willing young hack I was, I sent one off – after, incidentally, forking out for the book in the first place.'

And?

'And nothing. I think there might have been a paper slip of *Thank you*, but, essentially, nothing.'

I asked her if she'd tried again and she looked at me and blew smoke over my shoulder towards the open door.

'From now on, I'll stick to this. We'll pretend it's a stepping-stone back to where I used to be, but I personally won't try too hard to believe it. ''We loved Brussels because everything was free, paid for. We went in September because it was less crowded. It's one of the most beautiful capitals of Europe. Its architecture and relaxed, friendly pace of life came as a complete surprise to us.'' I ought to write it now and simply get them to sign their names to it like a confession of guilt. No doubt someone from the magazine will accompany them to keep a gushing record of this trip of a lifetime. I think we already have the photographs. All we'd need would be one of the happy couple posing with a flower-seller, or cast in reflection in one of the city's many beautiful and tranquil canals.'

'Perhaps you could superimpose them over something you've already got.'

'Perhaps we could, but there are limits to what people will believe. Brussels they might believe, but the photograph they would not. Everyone else who'd entered would be looking very closely at it, seeing the good time *they* might have been having. It hardly seems an adequate challenge for all my many skills.'

Or, one deception led to another, and then another.

Or, she was now ready to believe it.

Or, there was little else she could do, and she *had* to start believing it.

Or, she had learned to ignore it completely.

'I'm talking about it rather than doing it. A bad sign. I'd hoped to be able to impress people with my working routine. I used to know people who did this kind of thing in taxis on the way to real assignments. *I* used to do it in taxis. So why is it such a big deal now?

147

She tore a page from the brochure from which she was working and stuck the point of her pencil through it. 'It might be one way of getting back to where I once was, but the more of it I do, the more obvious it's going to become – to me and everyone watching – exactly where I am *now*. You – see – my – point.' She jabbed the pencil with each word. 'If I was unlucky enough to accompany the winners, I'd talk them into swapping the tickets for four or five days in Paris. We'd go to Brussels for the photographs and then get on a train for somewhere civilised.'

'The Belgian Tourist Board wouldn't be too pleased.'

'They'd get what they wanted.'

'They'd still know.'

'What does that have to do with anything? You might already think you know how to make the perfect baked Alaska, but it won't stop us from telling you every year how to do it that little bit better. Nor will it stop you from trying. We search around for a status quo and then look for a way of cementing it in. It's all very well done and no one would ever really want it any other way. It's why, when you're in, you're in.'

We were distracted by birds walking across the glass roof.

'I didn't bargain on that,' she said.

I told her I'd known people keep them off by siting a pot or plastic crouching cat somewhere prominent. The deceptions – if that is what they were – grew outwards like crystals, beautifully constructed, but ready to shatter at a touch.

She looked up at the roof, considering where the cat might be placed.

'I suppose something in terracotta might be acceptable. This isn't Islington, yet.' She threw up her pencil to scare off the birds.

'Life into art,' she said. 'Lifelessness into artlessness.'

'"There was no possibility of taking a walk that day." *Jane Eyre*.'

'"Reader, I married him."'

'"Stately, plump Buck Mulligan came from the stairhead – "'

'Where he came across some delightful outdoor markets, quite beyond anything he'd expected.'

'"April is the cruellest month."'

'"We particularly enjoyed our many sightseeing visits into the beautiful Flemish countryside with which Brussels is surrounded."'

'"Now the leaves are falling fast."'

'Our problem is that we know too much.'

Or, everyone else's problem was that they knew too little.

Or, could things ever be that simple?

148

She pointed out to me precisely where she thought the terracotta cat ought to be placed. 'The toms can come round and practise on it.' She threw another pencil at the birds.

15

A routine was established. Or, rather, one routine replaced another. A routine, in the house, for Rachel, lasting anywhere between a day and a month. Each routine being yet another counterfeit, composed of the details and irrelevancies of her day-to-day existence – a substitute for what was important and what she needed to happen.

She worked, she cleaned the house, she visited friends. She visited the cinema, visited museums, visited the theatre. All of which maintained a kind of forward momentum. She was running and falling at the same time. She made plans and then discarded them. On the few occasions we were together in the company of others I felt them watching her. They encouraged her in her plans and commiserated with her over work which had never materialised. Everything was someone else's fault.

She resumed drinking more regularly, but never to the point of even early drunkenness.

There were still small successes but even greater failures.

She spoke again about selling the house, but not seriously, only out of uncertainty, of needing to maintain some control over what happened next.

She wrote to Enzo apologising for her behaviour and then destroyed the letter. She prepared detailed outlines of the work she proposed to undertake and then read and reread them until their flaws were big enough to convince her of their uselessness. She retrieved the less objectionable of Colin's mementoes and returned them to the sitting-room. She hung the small oil painting of the whale and whalers between the two larger paintings above the mantelpiece and repositioned their spotlights to include it. She bought an expensive new book on whales full of colour photographs, tore a page from it and pinned it to the kitchen wall. She bought a PLEASE DO NOT DISTURB sign and hung it on the conservatory door. On the reverse, she printed DISTURB, PLEASE DISTURB. She said she was relieved not to have lost her sense of humour. She needed tablets to help her sleep. Her unimportant needs were always the most easily fulfilled.

The model aircraft reappeared above the garden, and after a disappointing day's work she went out and cursed up into the sky at it. The disappointing days ran into each other. She threw a handful of soil up at the plane and then shook the powder from her hair.

I waited a fortnight before asking her about Brussels.

'I don't want to talk about Brussels.'

'I assume – '

'Then you assume right. An earthquake; Brussels was destroyed. The whole of Belgium has been lost beneath a tidal wave.'

'They didn't like the idea?'

'Why should they? It was an awful idea. I didn't like it; the magazine didn't like it; the Belgian Tourist Board didn't like it. And who am I to argue with the Belgian Tourist Board? The brief suggested something with a cultural bias; they'd expected something about national costume. Do you know what the Belgian national – do you even know what the Belgian flag looks like?'

I asked her if they'd suggested anything else she might do.

'Surely you can come up with something kinder than that. How about an enquiry into my "Homes for the Eighties" series, projection. "Projection" being the operative word. Projected right out the window.'

No go?

'The idea and what little bit I did has been paid for in full. No further obligation. I tore up their cheque, but I still don't feel that marvellous.' She arranged the objects on her desk into another symmetrical pattern. 'I have a very tidy mind. I have the tidiest mind of everyone I know.' Then she swept everything from her desk on to the floor of the conservatory in a single violent action. 'In the eyes of the world, I've been and gone. A small draught in passing, perhaps, but not much more.' She spun in a full circle in her chair. She'd bought it at an auction specifically for use in the conservatory, and a week later had had it re-upholstered at ten times its original cost. 'It's a good chair,' she said. She'd dragged it from the house, and in doing so had dislodged several bricks from the pattern on the ground. 'The chair isn't entirely at fault for my failings,' she said.

She'd also taken a bottle and glass from the house and kept them in the bottom drawer of the desk.

I suggested she might try the same idea elsewhere.

'Where for instance? They're all the same magazine. Why don't people realise that? The covers are all the same; why can't people see?' She formed her hands into fists and banged them on the desk. She lost control, and only when she knocked over and smashed a

151

jug of water did she stop. She stared down at the shattered pieces and the stain on the warm floor. 'You shouldn't be seeing any of this,' she said, avoiding my eyes and covering her own with her hand. 'To answer your question: no, no one else is interested in the ideas. I'm about to start work on a masterpiece: a history of the baked Alaska, with an index on how to make it that Little Bit Special. At least the prospect of a fortnight in Brussels with Mr and Mrs X no longer hangs over me. Do you know what a *tsunami* is? T, s, u, n . . . A type of tidal wave. I came across it and looked it up. It'll probably make a good title. I'll sell it to someone more needy.' She began picking up the pieces of the jug and the scattered contents of her desk. She lifted several sheets of wet paper by their corners and pressed them to the glass, where they stuck.

'What do you think I should do?' she said eventually. 'Complain to the Society of Authors?'

Few of the sheets contained anything.

'I'm going to have another holiday. I need it. I can afford it. What do you think?' My reluctance to respond made her angry and she formed her hands into fists again. The chair rose and fell as she spun in it. Even at its lowest it looked at an uncomfortable height for the low desk. 'A few days. Somewhere in the country. Norfolk, Cambridge. Country living. I'll write something about high-rise tower blocks in depressed city centres and sell it to people living in thatched cottages. The tide's bound to turn.' She blew at the ash and cigarette ends from her spilled ashtray. 'I'm supposed to be working. This is my time for working.'

It was three o'clock, Saturday afternoon.

'What difference does that make? We writers are free spirits, we live on our wits, and living on your wits is not a nine to fiver; I wish to Christ it was.'

The paper against the warm glass dried and came away in crinkled sheets. She took them down and returned them to her desk.

'And *that's* beginning to get on my nerves.' She indicated the stone cat I'd bought her and which she'd positioned against the wall on the conservatory roof. 'The birds sit on it. Apart from which, it's not terracotta; it looks cheap.'

I told her I could easily take it down.

'And then what? In a sack and into the canal? No, leave it. Wherever I was, there'd be something wrong.'

She left the conservatory and sat on one of the seats at the centre of the garden.

'I might have guessed it was Saturday. Listen.' She held a finger to

152

her ear. 'The sound of Saturday.' A lawnmower, children, traffic, sport on television through an open window, a woman's voice, an electric saw or drill.

She complained of having lost weight again. She had a habit of feeling her cheeks and the line of her jaw, lifting it until the slack of her neck tightened. There were rings of weight-loss around her neck like threads of white cotton, and the outline of her collar bone showed clearly against her shoulders.

At the bottom of the garden, the reflection from the panes of glass lay in strips across the brick. It was warm, but she began to shiver, rubbing her arms.

'*Tsunami* is a Japanese word. If anyone knows about earthquakes and tidal waves, they do. The Japanese take earthquakes in their stride. They even work through them.'

I left her and went into the house. She went back to the conservatory and sat in it for an hour. I heard her typewriter, its clicking amplified by the glass.

Later, someone called and invited her out for the evening. She told the woman she was working to a deadline and couldn't possibly come.

'Next time anyone rings hold the phone to the door so they can hear me at work. I'll have an answering tape made up, saying "Rachel is at work right now, but don't worry it can't last." I'm going out.' She put on her sunglasses. She frequently wore them now when she left the house. Not the ones she'd bought in Rome, the ones she wanted to believe she looked like Audrey Hepburn in, but a larger pair, with white frames and green lenses. 'How do I look?'

You look perfect, presentable, thin, awful, a woman just going out for the last few hours of the afternoon.

She glanced at her watch as though to suggest she was already late for an appointment.

Later, when she still hadn't returned, I went out to close the conservatory door and windows. Her typewriter contained a page of gibberish, typed on one of the crinkled sheets. The rhythm with which it had been produced had been that of an accomplished typist.

I went out until mid-evening and when I returned I saw that she'd been back. A note on the table said she'd decided to go out for the evening after all. Love, Rachel.

She hadn't returned by three in the morning, and then by midday the following day. She was away for that night and the two following nights.

She returned after three days.

She sat in the sitting-room in a chair drawn close to the empty hearth and behaved as though nothing had happened. Her bag lay unopened at the centre of the room. She'd been drinking, and started telling me what a wonderful time she'd had. Invigorating, relaxing, refreshing.

I asked her where.

'Oh, here, there, everywhere.' She searched her pockets and waved a receipt at me for a hotel in Chelmsford and another in Colchester. 'I took the train,' she said. 'Same line. Next on the list would have been Ipswich, but I never got that far. First class. Nothing but the best for hard-working little Rachel. I had little drinks from their little bottles. Definitely no drinking and driving.' She pushed herself away from the hearth with her feet. 'Now you can tell me how worried you were. It will only make the entire fucking exercise pointless, but go ahead. Feel free. I suppose you rang all the hospitals and police.'

On the second day of her absence, the unidentified body of a woman had been found in the Thames. There was a description of her, but no photograph. The description was of the woman's clothes – of what little she'd still been wearing – and I immediately saw the loose white dress she'd worn in the garden, and how easily it might have been pulled from her by the river, and how she might look, her near-naked thinness, once it had gone. The report said the body might have been in the water anywhere between twenty-four and forty-eight hours. There was a photograph of the mudbank on which it had been found: the kind of mudbank broken by channels of muddy water and the mud and brick of disused wharves; the kind of mudbank on which women's bodies were always found.

'You should learn not to worry,' she said. 'The fact is, if I did disappear, you'd be their most likely suspect.' Her laughter, from being natural, became forced and then stopped. 'I went away for a few days, that's all. Let's forget it. Millions of people go away for a few days.' She refilled her glass, spilling more than she caught. 'Did anyone call?'

No one.

'So you see – ' She waved her glass. 'I may even do it again. The trains are very cheap, even first class. And you get to sit practically alone.' She put down her glass, sat back in her seat and covered her face with both hands. 'I'm tired. I'm just tired.'

There might come a point when all I would recognise of her would be the self-inflicted wounds of her excuses.

154

I left her and she fell asleep where she sat.

The following morning the room still smelled of drink. She'd switched on the electric fire and had scorched the corner of the rug. When she woke and I pointed it out to her she said she could have been burned alive.

'Can you imagine anyone less like Joan of Arc than me? "Hampstead Woman in Human Torch Drama". No, I suppose not.'

I told her about the body that had been washed up and she nodded in tired agreement.

16

I'd watched the film in her absence, half convinced she'd drowned and that the last anyone would see of her would be her mud-stained body, and that only then would the double tragedy be revealed and perfectly understood.

It appeared to be a continuation of the film in which she'd posed against the bedroom wall wearing different outfits. She wore a blue dress to her knees and was dancing with her eyes closed. She was pivoting from the hips and moving her arms in a dance of the sixties. Except that it cannot have been the sixties because Rachel was only thirteen in 1965.

Her hair was much shorter and she looked younger than in the previous film.

I watched her closed eyes, waiting for them to open, and tried to decide whether they were closed through embarrassment or because she was genuinely engrossed in what she was doing.

Between Rachel and the camera was a thread of smoke, the almost liquid smoke of incense rather than that of a cigarette. Rachel dancing belonged in another age. She wore a headband which pulled her hair in and then forced it to bunch out beneath. Her hair was lighter, dyed, and she wore dark make-up around her eyes. She danced well, recreating the rhythm of the music out of the silence. There were times when she almost stopped, holding her arms on either side of her as though she were yawning. She opened her eyes, but only momentarily. The dance lasted fifteen minutes.

She responded to the smoke and began to move more violently. She spun herself until she looked about to fall. She was wearing no shoes and her toes were splayed. Occasionally her finger would flick at the non-existent hair on her shoulder, as though she'd only recently had it cut.

The film ended abruptly. When it returned a few seconds later, she was wearing the same dress but with a pair of white, knee-length boots covering her legs. Her movements in the boots were less graceful, and her eyes opened more frequently. She took off the headband and shook her head until her hair regained its natural shape. The smoke in front of her caught the eddies of her movement and was dispersed around her. When she paused she breathed deeply and held out her arms to steady herself. She moved from side to side and the camera followed her to include the familiar terrain of the bedroom.

She began to undress, her eyes still lightly closed. She started with the headband and by swinging the points of her hair over her eyes. She continued by slipping down the shoulders of her dress until the tops of her arms were exposed and she stood bound by it. She turned and continued dancing with her back to the camera. She lifted one shoulder and then the other until the dress was worked down and the shape of her back was revealed: the curve of her arm, the prominent ridge of her spine. She held the edge of one of the short sleeves and flapped it up and down, laughing at herself. Raising her arms out of the constricted sleeves was difficult and she moved more slowly for the few seconds it took to pull herself free; having released the first, her second arm came out more easily. She held down the bodice of the dress. She held out her arms to show that it would not fall of its own accord, or that it would only fall slowly and then only to a certain point. Her style of dancing changed: she began to twist, bending and then shooting out her arms as she moved up and down to maintain the rhythm. She pulled the dress down further to reveal the white bra beneath. Then she let it hang, its looseness catching her movements. She cupped a hand over each breast and held out her forefingers to the camera. Her eyes were open and she was laughing again. The dress fell to her waist and stopped on her hips, making a pouch, which she lifted and flapped as she had done with her sleeve. She kicked her legs, moved back to the wall and held herself steady. The camera moved closer to her and concentrated on the flatness above her breasts and that beneath them to her waist. She pressed out her stomach. She pressed the dress down to the widest part of her hips and then continued dancing until it fell of its own accord to the ground, slowly at first and then in a sudden concertina over her knees and boots. She lifted it on one foot and kicked it into the air, where it filled out before falling back to the ground.

She moved more slowly in only her underwear and the boots. The line of her hips joining her stomach was as prominent and as sensual as a man's and she traced it with her finger.

She danced along the wall towards the bed, passing through the outline of light cast by the window. She moved in and out of the shade until it split her from between her legs to her forehead. She stood with her feet apart and moved her arms, bunching her fingers and then flexing them open, drawing her open hands, palm outwards across her face.

I stopped the film. To one side of where it had been projected was the same outline of light from the window, the curtains drawn except for the crease of sunlight at their centre. By opening one of the curtains and shifting the projector it would have been perfectly possible to superimpose the image on to the reality. Except that by opening even one of the curtains the room would become lighter and Rachel would fade to a trick ghost. There was a carpet in the room which was not on the film. By lowering the angle of the projector, it too might have been included. A soundtrack of traffic and birds, and of music from downstairs played at loud volume through open doors.

I wound the film back to maintain continuity and restarted it. From being divided by the shadow of the curtain, Rachel moved into the deeper shade until the edge of the bed came into view. She turned her back to the camera and unfastened the clasp of her bra. Its straps fell but she held the cups and made her breasts look larger with her hands. She opened her fingers slowly until all that remained hidden were the centres of her nipples, pressed in by her thumbs.

Her leg touched the edge of the bed and she fell forward on to it, kneeling and moving her arms over it as though she were swimming. The camera moved down to look into her face. Her arms moved more slowly and then stopped, and she turned her head to one side and listened. She pushed herself up from the bed and then fell forward again. She held one of her arms to her side and the camera followed it from her shoulder to her hand, and from her hand across the leg it held. There was more shadow away from the natural light of the window, and the camera came close and reduced the tops of her legs and the small of her back to barren landscapes.

When she'd fallen forward the second time, it would not have been difficult to believe that she'd been pushed.

The camera followed her spine and then lost its curve as she turned and faced it. Her eyes were still closed, but not as they'd been closed when she was dancing. This time they were held shut and creased. She swung her arm until it rested across her neck. Her entire body became stiff, and sensing something was wrong, the camera withdrew. Her face lay buried in the bed and both her arms were folded around her neck.

17

A week later I returned to the house to find her clothes scattered along the landing and down the stairs. She'd thrown a bundle of them over the banister and had knocked over the bamboo table on which the hall phone stood. She heard me arrive and shouted down from her bedroom, where she was sitting on the bed amid more clothes. She wore a thick sweater over black tights. She took a delicate blouse from beside her, held it up for inspection and then tore it almost in half. She'd been crying.

'The nothing-to-wear syndrome,' she said calmly, defeated by a seam in the blouse which would not give. 'We're supposed to be famous for it, women.'

The full-length mirror had been taken from inside one of the wardrobe doors and propped against the wall, and the mirror on the other door angled to face into it, repeating that part of the room caught in between them into the far distance.

She lifted handfuls of the scattered clothes from the bed, clearing a space with her hands and feet. 'A moment of weakness,' she said; it was how her days now progressed. She reached under the neck of her sweater and pulled out a rope of tangled necklaces. 'This is every necklace I own. They're all knotted and I don't think I can get them off. We might have to use a pair of scissors to cut me free.'

The skin of her neck was red where some of the tighter braids had twisted. She turned her head to indicate the full extent of the problem.

On the dressing-table her jewellery cases had been tipped out and their contents scooped into mounds. The photograph of Colin and herself taken three months before his death stood propped beside them. Another award ceremony. Colin was doing his utmost not to smile and Rachel had been caught as she turned her head, her necklace between her lips.

'It's all junk, mostly,' she said.

I imagined Colin standing in the bedroom doorway telling her what he thought she should wear, telling her how late they already were, how late she was making them. He was wearing a dinner jacket and black tie.

I asked her if she wanted me to collect the clothes and bring them back into the bedroom.

'I don't know why I bother; I never wear half this stuff. Every year I try and do something charitable with it, and every year I manage to convince myself that my need is greater than theirs, whoever they might be, wherever they are.' She pulled the sweater over her folded knees and tried to push back her hair. 'I've been up here all day, trying to do something about it. I was going to be methodical – drawer by drawer, hanger by hanger – but it all became too much. I've come across stuff that's ten years old and that I haven't worn for nine and won't ever wear again.'

The clothes lay around her like the torn and scattered months of a calendar.

I went out and retrieved the pieces strewn along the landing and down the stairs.

'When it came down to it, I usually ended up wearing what he wanted me to wear,' she said. 'He used to buy me things without asking and I wore them and pretended to like them. This – ' She picked up the torn blouse and held it to her chest. The pattern of her sweater showed through the double layer of almost transparent material. She held the blouse in her mouth and pressed her fingers through it. She pointed to a drawer of lace and straps which hung to the floor in shreds. She continued trying to tear the blouse along its seams. But the material still defeated her and she threw it down. 'If you hadn't come back I might have started on the sheets and curtains.'

There were still shoes on the stairs, and more in a heap by the wall against which she had thrown them.

'I just don't want any of it.' She smoothed a piece of the torn blouse over her shin.

I occupied myself by collecting together and pairing up the shoes. She said she'd chosen them all herself except for several pairs of high-heels and a pair of boots still in the bottom of the wardrobe. She asked me to take them out and let her see them. I recognised the boots immediately as those she'd worn in the film. She told me to throw them back inside.

'Colin's taste in fashionable tart. Embarrassing.'

I picked up the few remaining pieces of clothing and laid them over the chairs and on the bed. She shook her bracelets and watched herself in the telescoping distance of the mirrors. She raised and lowered her legs. She pulled the pieces of the torn blouse in strips through her hands. She'd spilled talcum on the dressing-table and

160

written her name in it. I picked up a string of imitation pearls and it disintegrated in my hands. She told me how many times it had been broken in the past; another of Colin's unwanted gifts. She told me to leave them where they'd fallen. She lay back on the bed and pulled the clothes I'd collected in a bundle over her.

'The invisible woman. You *shall* go to the ball, Cinders.'

In the film, all she'd finally worn had been the boots. She'd knelt beside the bed and prayed, and the camera had moved to her closed eyes and followed her body down to the boots' pointed heels.

The mound of clothes trembled and she lifted her arms from it and sat slowly upright like someone rising from the dead through a shallow grave. She held out her arms and moaned like a ghost. Then she pushed herself free and swung her legs to the floor.

'Leave it,' she said, and left the room. She stopped on the landing for a moment and then came back in, tugging at her rope of necklaces. She sat with her head bowed as I tried to untangle them for her. She said she intended holding a party in the house, but sounded unenthusiastic and unconvinced that it was what she really wanted. I was able to remove some of the larger necklaces without unfastening them, but the finer ones were so caught up in each other that the only way of getting them free was to cut them. She tried to catch the beads and links which came loose, but after a few minutes she became impatient and pulled at those still caught, breaking them. She moulded the lengths of bead and chain into a ball in her palm and then threw it towards the dressing-table, where it hit the mirror and fell apart, scattering in small pieces across the already littered surface.

18

'I once filmed an almost total eclipse of the sun in the early afternoon in Regent's Park.' Colin drew two intersecting arcs in the air.

'Successfully?'

'Not particularly. Human interest, filler. Can you imagine the problems with the light on that kind of job? We're looking straight up into a pale, bright sky, trying to catch something that's impossible to look at unaided in the first place and which is slowly disappearing. We were saved by the fact that as the moon covered it, the sun became at least watchable and spectacular. We only needed the final few seconds of blackout, and then the moment when it started to light up again from the other side. We had all kinds of filters and spent half the time trying to stop people staring directly up at what we were shooting. It wasn't actually total, of course, because of their respective sizes: it's known as an annular eclipse. I'll blind you with science – or at least terminology – umbra, penumbra, crescent and gibbous. I'd forgotten about it until today. Someone's going to Norway to film a lunar eclipse this evening. It shouldn't be too difficult.' He made his fingers and thumbs into circles and moved them one in front of the other in a quick calculation.

The sleeve of rods and straps had been taken from his arm and he now wore the less-intrusive inflatable cuff which cushioned his wrist against being knocked. He visited the hospital at regular intervals, but there had been nothing new to report. 'Progressing steadily,' he said when anyone asked.

'They have more time with the moon because of the relatively larger shadow of the earth.'

Then he saw that I wasn't particularly interested and changed the subject.

Afterwards, we went out and walked the short distance through the traffic between two bars.

In the second we sat in a quiet booth and he told me he was going to Africa in ten days' time.

'Apparently, I'm no longer a two-hours-notice-man. I've become

162

part of the planning-ahead process. And after Africa it's been suggested that I might be in line for promotion which would more or less restrict me to working in Europe.'

'"Promotion" as in "promotion"?'

'As in "think of a job and then slip him into it". I'm the victim of a conspiracy of concern. I wouldn't even be going to Africa except for the fact that someone who should have been going will be on a month's exchange in Australia. See how internationally interconnected and inescapable these things are?'

'Do you think it's because of your wrist?'

'Is that "wrist" as in "expensive hand-held equipment", or "wrist" as in "uncertainty, unpredictability and unreliability for the future"?'

It was a bar where he was known, and still empty enough for the woman collecting the few glasses to bring our refills to the table. He joked with her and she asked him about his wrist. He showed her the plastic cuff and invited her to squeeze it, which she did, but only very gently, and with her face screwed in anticipation of his pain.

'That's all the concern I need,' he said when she'd gone.

'So what's in Africa?'

'Unrest, what else? They're starting to use Africa – the real Africa, that is, the bit in the middle – like they used to use the eclipses or the birth of quins, or the long walks home of family pets left behind by removal men.' He caught my look. 'Yes, these aren't my first drinks of the day, and yes, my wrist is only the tip of the proverbial iceberg.'

A couple came and sat in the booth beside us and he lowered his voice.

'The doctor sees neither improvement nor deterioration. After all, I'm not a racing driver or middle-weight boxer.' His exasperation returned. 'You ought to try sitting and listening to someone talking about a "perfectly normal healthy life" when it's yours they're talking about – yours specifically.' He pointed his finger as though he were about to jab me in the chest. He sat back and sighed.

'I'm boring you,' he said. 'I ought to go to Africa and then abscond and begin a one-man journey into the interior. There's still a heart of darkness in there somewhere. It'll probably belong to a mining company by now, but it's still there, beating like a drum. The trouble with the White Man's Burden is that it's all of his own making: he throws it off and it's all still there. The drink philosophising. Perhaps I'll lose myself for twenty years and return to civilisation a hero, cured and strong. The snows of Kilimanjaro, prehistoric creatures, lost tribes, that kind of thing. Last year I wanted to go to the

Philippines to take a look at a Japanese soldier draped in a Rising Sun after forty years in the jungle, surrounded by microphones and cameramen and trying to explain something everybody else in the world had understood for a generation. I wanted to see how many minutes it would take for those forty years to be reduced to something less than novelty value. He'd been cleaning a radio which hadn't worked for thirty-nine years for want of a single valve, and a rifle which was still in perfect working order. He fired it using blanks for the cameras.'

I saw the three women behind the bar watching us. The one who'd held his cuff smiled at me. The others watched us as though we were doing something distasteful.

'Take Rachel with you,' I suggested.

'To Africa? I don't think so. She used to accompany me on decent assignments, but it was never because they were places she wanted to visit. I don't think Africa would be very appealing at this point in the proceedings. Rachel has fixed and unshakeable images of these places and, from what I've seen, she's better off staying away and hanging on to them. Africa for Rachel is still bold colours and stark, simple prints, breeze blocks, dogs instead of lions, and people walking round with no shoes on. There's nothing you can tell Rachel about Africa. West Africa, Nigeria, Benin, Togo, Ghana. About as big as your little-fingernail on the map. I've been to Freetown, Abidjan, Accra and Lagos. Always keep the sea within your sight.'

A television was switched on above the bar and he shouted for someone to turn it down.

'I don't think Rachel's entirely happy in any environment other than that completely of her own making. Now, whenever we're invited out, she's always the first to start itching to leave. She'd much rather invite people to come and see us. It gives her a big advantage, being in her own home; it never used to, but I've noticed it over the past year or so. When I first knew her, her idea of hospitality was trying to make visitors feel at home while wishing they actually were.' He laughed at his rediscovery of the joke.

I went to the bar for more drinks. The woman said she would have brought them over, but the bar was filling up. She asked me if Colin was all right; she meant drunk. 'He's going to Africa,' I told her, and she briefly closed her eyes to imagine Africa. 'He's been before,' I added, and made his forthcoming visit seem unfair.

'We'll go home together,' he said when I returned with the drinks. 'And when Rachel asks us where we've been, you can lie for

164

me and I can lie for you.' He lifted his glass in his weak hand and watched his cuff as he drank.

It was the end of November, and the daylight had faded several hours before we'd gone into the bar.

'I'll be away for a fortnight,' he said. 'Which means I'll probably be stuck there over Christmas. Being heathens, they have no respect for that kind of commercially rampant tradition. I was away last Christmas, and the one three years before that. I got to where I am today by allowing myself to be sent away at Christmas. The first Christmas I knew Rachel we spent it in Brazil at someone else's expense. I made her coming with me a condition of going. Rio, Vitória, Belo Horizonte. For the fortnight we were there I called her Belo Horizonte. It translated well.'

'It can't be anything unexpected in Africa if you've been given ten days' notice,' I said.

'No, I don't suppose it can be. They did tell me, but I've forgotten.' He waved his hand to cover the lie. His disillusionment seemed almost complete. 'I don't actually have to pay that much attention to whatever it is until I get there. It all ends up by making perfect sense even if it starts out as a balls-up. The people in the Department of Perfect Sense are the last people to get their hands on everything before it's dished up to the paying public.'

I suggested that we leave and he agreed. He shouted, 'Taxi!' as we left the booth. Then he shouted his farewells to the women behind the bar.

When we arrived at the house, Rachel was out. He looked for a note, but found nothing. He said that he was starving, and then that he was dying of thirst.

After we'd eaten, we sat and watched television until Rachel's return. He told her about Africa.

'I always lose weight in Africa,' he said to me. 'She's jealous because the two things are permanently linked in her mind.' He repeated the word 'permanently', surprised that he was still able to pronounce it. Rachel had gone through to the kitchen but he spoke loudly enough for her to hear.

She returned to sit with us and told us what a successful day she'd had and how much more work she was likely to gain as a result of it. She wore a woollen suit with a brooch at her throat which reflected the glow of a lamp and shone like a gimmick.

'The truth is, Colin thinks I'm racist,' she said. 'He thinks that because I don't want to go to these places – primarily because they stink and I don't see why I should – he thinks I'm a racist. In fact, the

165

opposite is probably true: Colin's a Rider Haggard man.' She smiled at him and Colin nodded contritely. 'He'll tell you about Africa and South America and the Far East, but basically it's all the same dull description brightened up and made bearable by death and mayhem. Theirs, that is.'

He told her about the suggestion of promotion and the consequent restrictions on his travelling, about his uncertainty for the future upon his return.

19

On the day when a rainless August became September in the midst of a torrential downpour, I returned to the house to find a van from the Electricity Board parked outside and the front door open. I heard Rachel inside shouting.

'If there's anything electrical you need, use it now,' she said as I entered. 'We're about to be cut off.' She shouted the last two words in the direction of the basement.

I shook the water from my clothes and went through to her.

'Why?'

'How should I know why? Why does it matter? Why should I care, why should anyone care? *They* don't care.'

I heard men's voices in the basement.

'They don't deem to tell mere mortals these things, but as far as I can make it out, they have a hat full of the names of defenceless women and when they've got nothing better to do they draw one out at random, whip round and cut you off. Simple. Effective. Clean. Like they say in the adverts.'

I went down to the basement and she shouted after me.

Two men knelt beside the electricity meter. After Rachel's abuse, one of them didn't want to tell me anything, but the other showed me the paper which empowered them to carry out the disconnection. He'd tried to show it to Rachel but she'd refused to look at it. He'd left it on the table and she'd screwed it into a ball and thrown it down the stairs after them.

'She must have known,' he said. If there was any concern in his voice it was only because of what he'd already seen of her. 'She must have been written to at least three times since the final demand.'

I told him I thought I knew what had happened and asked them to stop what they were doing for a few minutes. They considered my request with glances and agreed.

I went back up to Rachel and asked her why she hadn't responded to any of their demands.

'What demands?' she said. 'All that was Colin's business. We had standing orders. Why should they think this one hasn't been paid?

167

The phone people haven't come to take out the phones; the gas people haven't cut us off; the Water Board — Why them? What makes *them* think they can force their way in here and threaten me with this? Put me in a white wig and a rocking chair and they wouldn't come within five fucking miles of the place.'

I asked her again what she'd done with their reminders.

'They never sent any. That's what I'm trying to tell you.' Then she sighed, opened a drawer in the table and pulled from it a wad of unopened envelopes. Judging by the postmarks there was mail from the past six months.

I asked her if she'd read any of it.

'X-ray vision. I don't need to read it. They're only out to intimidate people. Let them do it to somebody else. Let them go and cut off somebody who's already socially deprived, somebody who won't miss it. There must be hundreds of people who expect this kind of thing. Tell them to come back here when they've finished with that lot.' She pushed past me into the hallway and shouted out into the street that the electricity was being cut off. Then she came back in, sat down and said she knew how ridiculous she was being. She'd collected seven discarded cigarette packets from around the house, four of which still held two or three cigarettes.

I went through the letters until I found those with the Electricity Board logo. I called down to the men that I was sorting things out. Neither they nor I believed it.

'Five minutes, you said,' one of them shouted back.

I invited them back up into the kitchen, but they refused to come. Rachel ran upstairs and into the room above me. I heard her open the window overlooking the garden. She hadn't worked in the conservatory since her 'holiday' in Essex.

I went back down to the men and tried to explain the situation. They said they were sorry for her but that they were bound to carry out the disconnection. I said I supposed they didn't get to this part of the city very often. They shared a look and shrugged. I showed them the reminders Rachel had left unpaid. I told them that she thought someone else was taking care of it for her. I found the most recent reminder and the sum matched that on their docket. I looked down the list of people whom they had yet to visit.

'Light, light,' Rachel shouted above us. 'Let there be light. Lo and behold, there *was* light. There *is* light.'

The lights in the basement flicked off, on, and off again. Both the men switched on torches. Nothing was going to stop them now from doing what they'd come to do, and telling them she was putting on an act would only have sounded like an excuse.

When I offered to pay the amount owed they began a detailed explanation of how simply paying would not be enough. There was a charge for disconnection and another for reconnection. I offered to pay these in addition to the bill, but that too, apparently, would have disrupted the procedure.

Rachel returned to the top of the stairs. 'Bribe them,' she shouted down. 'Give them some money, but be careful to pretend you're *not* giving them any money. That way they'll be able to pretend they're not taking it. Do what you like, just get them out.'

One of the men told me that in the past they'd been told to report cases of attempted bribery to the police.

Rachel came halfway down the stairs. 'They're threatening me,' she said. 'You heard them; they're deliberately trying to intimidate me.' She asked for the number of their head office, the name of their superior. One of them reached up and gave her a slip of paper. She read it and tore it in half. 'They're all in it together,' she said, and went back up into the kitchen. 'I'm putting the e-lec-tric kettle on,' she shouted. 'And later I might want to use the e-lec-tric blender.'

I asked the men how long it would take to reconnect the supply if I paid and applied for it now. They told me I couldn't do it through them and that the details were on the piece of paper Rachel had torn in half. I picked up the pieces and went back up to her. The men took my departure as a victory and turned their attention back to the meter.

Rachel sat watching the light above her, and when it went off, she applauded. She'd covered the surface of the table with the unopened letters, half brown, half variously coloured.

'I just couldn't stand any more condolences,' she said. 'You'd better open the brown ones, the rest can wait. Forever.'

Most of them were bills, but *For Information* only, and related to the other charges which were paid by standing order. I couldn't find out why the Electricity Board had stopped being paid.

'All this is Colin's fault,' she said. 'He kept a ledger with records of all this kind of crap – money received, money spent.' She made instant coffee with warm water. 'How long will we be without?'

Ten days; a week if we were lucky.

I suggested she might stay with friends, tell them she was having some rewiring or something else done to the house.

'"Or something else"? And how long would that big secret last? Apart from which, I don't intend leaving the house. I know people who'd die if something like this happened to them. Or at least they'd have the good sense to go round telling everybody they'd want to die if it ever *did* happen. But it never does happen to them, does it? Only me.'

We heard the men at the bottom of the stairs.

'They're probably frightened to come up,' she said. She left the table and went to the basement door. I heard her apologise, and then insist when the men told her to forget it. They said they knew how distressing something like that could be.

'But there's still no excuse for my behaviour,' she said. 'For my language. You're doing your job and I respect that, I understand that. The last thing you need is some hysterical stupid woman making it harder for you.'

The two men relaxed, but still half suspected they were about to become the victims of another of her outbursts.

'I want to give you this,' she said, taking a five-pound note from her pocket. One of them said they couldn't; the other watched the money in her hand. 'For my rudeness. Unforgivable. If you don't take it, I'll never forgive myself.' She pushed the money into the pocket of the man who'd watched it. 'I would, of course, like to offer you a cup of tea – and please don't think I'm being sarcastic – but . . .'

They said they understood. Both wanted to leave.

'Have we sorted out the details concerning reconnection?' she asked, and said, 'Good, good, good,' as I began to explain the procedure to her. 'Where next?' she asked the men. 'Somewhere nice? Up the road in Golders Green? I assume they're all electric.'

The men laughed and agreed with her because they hadn't really understood.

She looked at me and said, 'Well, if we have all the details, I'm sure . . .'

It was a signal for the men to leave.

'So, here we are back in the Dark Ages,' she said when she returned from letting them out. 'It's a hard life.'

I reminded her that it was September and getting cooler. It was still raining outside.

'Is it? I hadn't noticed. I don't notice these things. I have a friend who's a professional Earth Mother. She's in touch with these things. In fact, she's in touch with most things – body cycles, the comings and goings of the tides. She's been pregnant every other year for the past eight years because she says she feels more in touch with her real true self – whatever that is. None of which helps me with my particular problem.'

170

In two of the unopened brown envelopes there were cheques amounting to almost five hundred pounds. She looked at them without interest and made no effort to remember when I asked what work they were for.

'They're for a long time ago,' she said. 'Work it out for yourself. I suppose you've already calculated how many times over they would have paid the bill, and how easily this little one-act tragedy might have been avoided. Tragedy, farce, whatever.'

She emptied the last of the lukewarm water from the kettle and then went round the kitchen unplugging all the appliances. She asked me to check that nothing else had been plugged in and working when the power was disconnected. 'It was the first thing they asked me after they'd told me what they were here for. I should have asked them what difference it would have made.'

We spent six days without electricity, and during that time she made no further comment on the fact. Her only real surprise came when the light she'd had wired along the garden wall into the conservatory didn't work; she said she'd always considered it as being something separate.

Afterwards, the house was filled with the scent of the candles we used. She'd wanted plain white ones but had ended up buying thick red ones with ribbed surfaces and printed designs.

She gave the man who came to reconnect the power another five pounds, and tried to explain to him how the mistake had been made in the first place. He told her he believed her and they celebrated together with tea. She told me he'd been surprised to hear that two men had been to disconnect her instead of just one. She said she knew by the way he responded to her that they'd already warned him about her.

She destroyed rather than read the remaining unopened letters. They'd served their purpose, but now their value had been destroyed and something else had been lost to her.

She left the house and returned with a bottle of whisky and a block of coffee ice-cream and served both as though they were a celebration. She said she'd read in her new book that the peak of the whaling industry in terms of tonnage and killing had been between 1945 and 1960, and that in the forty years prior to 1960 a million whales had been killed. She said she'd always assumed the moral responsibility for the slaughter to have been her grandfather's or even her great-grandfather's; she seemed surprised that it might now, however indirectly, turn out to be hers.

Because the ice-cream would not refreeze properly she ate most of the carton at a single sitting until her gluttony made her feel sick.

She spoke again about holding a party in the house.

Previously, she had spoken of things having gone wrong for her as a means of avoiding the real issues; now, even as she came to terms with the extent to which events were beyond her control, there was a feeling of once again being overtaken by them. Planning and preparing for the party would prove to her, temporarily at least, that she was still capable of reimposing some of that control.

PART THREE

1

Rachel spent a day on the phone calling people to invite them to her party, undeterred by the succession of answering machines and new numbers she was given in her attempts to make direct contact. People asked her what she was celebrating, and when she said 'nothing' they insisted she needed an excuse. She decided eventually on the conservatory, which few of them had yet seen. After a number of them said they were busy on the weekend she proposed, she changed it to the one following and then had to phone again those she'd already contacted. She didn't keep a check-list and called some people twice. She left messages asking to be called back; she left no explanation and made her calls seem urgent.

'Of course, what they're saying,' she told me, the mouthpiece cupped in her hand, 'is: "Here's Rachel in the middle of the day ringing round about a party no one wants to come to. Here *we* are, working, and here's Rachel wanting to stop and chat about her party. A con*ser*vatory, for Christ's sake."'

Two days after her first round of calls she rang again all the people who hadn't answered her messages and told them everyone else she'd contacted had promised to come. Most said they'd be there. 'Such enthusiasm,' she said.

When the arrival of forty people was guaranteed she said the party sounded like another of her bad ideas.

She asked if I knew anyone from whom she might hire several barbecues, and then if I could find some way of lighting and filling the conservatory with a display of plants for the occasion. I arranged both for her. For an all-inclusive price, a 'chef' would arrive with the barbecues and undertake the catering, and I filled the conservatory for the weekend with plants grown to survive in hotel foyers and office receptions. Rachel described it as spectacular. Then she said she was having second thoughts about the barbecues, but only to be convinced by me that her decision had been the right one.

She bought the drink and the additional food a week early, and for a week she sat and thought about what might go wrong. The permutations of disaster became endless.

She made a dozen lists, from the names of people who were definitely coming, to the variety of food she wanted to be able to offer them. She bought a new outfit and then on the night of the party wore something she'd owned for five years.

The first arrivals congregated in the kitchen. The barbecues had been burning an hour and the chef stood singing in a white apron and an oversize chef's hat. He gave a xeroxed sheet of his services and prices to everyone who spoke to him. The name of the business and its telephone number were stitched in a panel across his back. He splashed wine and spirits over the glowing charcoal for effect and dropped in excessive amounts of various herbs to scent the air around him. It was a warm evening and there were outdoor tapers stuck into the flower beds to be lit later.

For two hours Rachel drank nothing, greeting new arrivals, introducing them among the growing crowd, accepting compliments. She made an announcement when the first of the food was ready, and then another when too few people went out to collect it and the chef complained to her that he needed more space to continue with a second batch.

She showed people the conservatory, and when they commented on the plants she told them she was green-fingered.

She flirted with the husbands of her friends. For many of them it was the first time they'd been in the house since Colin's death.

She'd hung a speaker from a tree and music from the house played over the garden.

Many of those she'd invited had clearly come out of a sense of duty, an obligation to the past. Also obvious was the fact that they had come not expecting to enjoy themselves. But for the first few hours it was a good, well-organised party.

When the music was loud, Rachel encouraged the women to dance with her as they might all have danced ten or twenty years ago. She'd laid sheets of smooth hardboard over the bricks and many of them danced in their stockinged feet. When the music was slow she made couples hold each other and dance together. I heard her telling the story of the men who'd arrived to disconnect the electricity. She hid nothing, but at the same time made it sound as though it had all happened to someone else, and that she in turn had been told about it. When the woman to whom she was telling the story laughed, Rachel laughed with her, encouraging her to repeat the tale to others.

People in the neighbouring houses watched us from darkened windows. Rachel had invited them, but few had come.

As it became cooler people moved indoors.

Later, I saw her alone in the conservatory with the husband of a woman who'd spent the evening inside because she suffered from hay fever. Rachel was standing with her back to the wall and the man was supporting himself against it with his hand above her shoulder. There was a gap between their faces, but the light was fading and from where I stood it looked as though they were kissing. I was listening to more complaints about uneaten food from the chef. Rachel returned to the house alone and had her first drink of the evening. The man came out of the conservatory a few minutes later and told me he'd accidentally dropped his glass and that it had smashed on the floor.

He spoke to me again an hour later in one of the first-floor rooms in which people were sitting rather than dancing. He was asking me about the plants when we were interrupted by Rachel.

'They're plastic,' she told him, surprised and angry at finding him there. 'What else do you want to know?'

'What's she talking about? They're real plants; I've seen them,' he said.

The man's wife joined us and held his arm. 'They're lovely plants,' she said. 'It's just a pity I can't – ' She held out her handkerchief in explanation.

'Rachel says they're plastic,' her husband said contemptuously. 'So you can go out and sit among them without any need to worry. Why don't you try it?'

There was a pause in the music downstairs and he stopped speaking. Rachel asked him how much he'd eaten. The man looked at his stomach before answering her. 'I'll tell you,' he said. 'One small steak and four so-called sausages.'

'He told me they were delicious,' his wife said.

'I told *you* they were delicious.'

'No one's forcing you to eat,' Rachel said. 'No, that's wrong: *I* was forcing you to eat. My fault.' She smiled at him over her glass. 'He spilled his drink,' she told his wife, and wiped at a non-existent stain on the man's shirt. He tried to stop her hand, but she was too quick for him. His wife stopped him from saying anything more by insisting that he dance with her in the next room.

Downstairs, the doorbell rang and Rachel left us to welcome the late arrivals.

After that she started drinking more quickly, and in the kitchen she apologised to the chef for the uneaten food. There were foil parcels in the oven, and outside the barbecues were already being

177

allowed to cool down. The chef said he expected his partner to return in a van and help him load up. Rachel asked him if she'd paid him and he said she had. She asked him what he did with the uneaten food and he told her that if he was allowed to take it home with him he lived off it until the following weekend. He said his diet consisted almost totally of meat. She took the foil parcels from the oven and gave them to him. Afterwards, when people came into the kitchen for something more to eat, he gave them sausages rather than steaks. Rachel told him he looked more like a clown in his tight apron and hat. It was not yet midnight and he explained that he frequently had to wait until two or three in the morning for his partner and the van. He explained about the charcoal, went outside and poured water over it.

'What did happen in the conservatory?' I asked Rachel.

'What do you think happened? He dropped his glass.' She began to sing the words of the song coming from the speaker beside her. At the centre of the room people waved their arms in the air at each chorus. 'Vee would have liked this,' she said. 'I should have invited her. Except she'd have eaten everything in sight and then shaken the place to its foundations with her flapper impersonation. She said she wanted to have lived in a gilded age, but wasn't sure what it meant, or even if it was the right word.' She looked around the room, said, 'Some of them still want to say how sorry they are about Colin,' and left.

I next saw her sitting on the stairs with the two women who'd stayed the night during one of Colin's absences. By then all three of them were drunk. They were smoking and held bottles between their knees.

'Tell them how green-fingered I am,' Rachel shouted down to me. The women laughed. Rachel waggled her fingers. 'Tell them how wonderfully wonderfully accomplished I am in matters horticultural.'

'Gilbert and Sullivan,' one of the women said.

'I am the very model of a model model something.'

They drank from their bottles in unison and the wine ran down their chins.

'No one approves,' Rachel said. 'They've all come, and they've all seen, and no one approves.'

The women put their arms around her shoulders and she shook them off.

'Go and tell that bloody idiot in the kitchen to get out of the house,' she shouted. 'Van or no van. He's moaning and spoiling everything. He's ruining the whole fucking thing.'

178

People started to leave around one in the morning. They sang and shouted in the street. Even people who hadn't sung or shouted in the house did it in the street. Rachel tried to persuade them to stay longer, and when the few who refused had gone she told everyone else that they were miserable and that she was glad to see the back of them. For an hour afterwards people were afraid to leave.

She told me she intended spending the night with the two women because they were her only friends. She returned to sit between them on the stairs, and when her hair fell out of place they let their own down in sympathy.

'Three wise monkeys.'

One of the women covered her mouth. The other covered her ears. Rachel covered her eyes. When the other two lowered their hands, Rachel kept hers in place and started to cry. She dropped her bottle, but it was empty and rolled slowly down the stairs. The women offered theirs but she took neither. They held her again and tried to coax her hands from her face.

People began to leave more rapidly. Only the music suggested any real momentum. In the garden, someone lit the tapers.

The man with whom Rachel had been in the conservatory came into the hallway with his wife and stood by the door. He looked up at Rachel and shook his head.

'What is it this time?' he shouted up to her.

His wife told him he spoiled everything they did together, and went outside to wait for him.

'Don't forget the broken glass,' he said to me. 'And it was hers, not mine.'

Rachel still held her hands to her face.

The man was having difficulty getting his arms into his coat sleeves.

His wife shouted to him from outside.

'I'm going, Rachel,' he said. 'Make sure you sleep tight. You and your . . . your *friends*.' He turned to me. 'She – ' He pointed to the open doorway. 'She thinks *I* spoil everything, but compared to her' – he indicated Rachel – 'I'm an amateur. Look at her. She's ridiculous. What are you going to do, Rachel? Walk round with your hands over your eyes for the rest of the year? Take them away and let's all see.'

Rachel pulled herself free of the women and shouted down to him. Her hands left her face and searched for something to throw. The women quickly restrained her.

The man held up his hands in surrender and said, 'I'm going, I'm going, I'm going,' until he was out of the door.

In several of the rooms there were still people sitting in small groups, overtaken by the night and then the early hours. The doors had been open and the house was growing cold. People switched on the fires. There was the sound of a man and woman arguing in the kitchen; one moment the woman was crying, the next laughing. People stood in their coats waiting for taxis to arrive. They told me for a second and third time how much they'd enjoyed themselves. They asked in their indirect ways about Rachel and then provided their own answers. They supposed it had all been too much for her – exhausting – emotional – Colin –

People moving up and down the stairs stepped over the three women without speaking to them, trying to pretend they were asleep.

The chef's van arrived and I helped him to gather together his equipment. He said every Saturday night was exactly the same. The man who helped him carry out the barbecues looked as though he'd just woken up. He pointed out the moon and stars reflected in the conservatory roof.

Rachel came downstairs with the women on either side of her. She saw who remained and then danced with one of the men with her arms hung loosely over his shoulders. He spoke to her and she let him kiss her cheek. The two women danced together. Rachel released the man halfway through the song and said she'd had enough. Her face, despite the attention of the women, was still streaked and there were damp patches on her blouse where she'd spilled the wine and cried. She went into the kitchen and returned with another bottle, which she shared with the women, all three of them now dancing together.

In the garden someone told me that the man who'd stood in the hallway and provoked Rachel had known her since before she'd married Colin.

Inside, Rachel and the women had stopped dancing and were sitting on the sofa looking up at the copy of Wood's *American Gothic*. They were trying unsuccessfully to imitate the looks on the faces of the man and his sister. Rachel had been crying again and shouting for the people who had already gone to come back. One of the women was trying to convince her that this was how all good parties were supposed to end.

'They all end like this. This, all this, is the way they end. A party cannot be ended by someone ringing a bell, ding-a-ling-a-ling.

180

Some parties don't even end in the same places they started. This, by comparison with some parties, was – is – a very respectable party.' The woman's speech slowed and she pronounced each word carefully.

Rachel didn't believe a word she said.

'Believe me, I know,' the woman insisted. 'I'm an expert on these things.'

The other woman told her to shut up.

Rachel pushed herself up from the sofa and left them. She went first into the kitchen and then upstairs. The woman who knew about parties said loudly that someone ought to go with her, but no one made the effort.

A short while later, everyone had gone.

Rachel fell asleep on top of one of the beds. The two women fell asleep on the sofa, woke and went up to her.

As it grew light I heard Rachel crying, and then nothing for six hours until she and the two women rose. I heard them talking and laughing in the room together before they came down.

'Do people really forget the nights before?' one of them said, half jokingly.

'Well, I do,' the other lied. 'It's an in-built survival mechanism. *Nil memorandum.* Apart from which, what's the point of making the effort to remember when there's always somebody else ready and willing to do it for you?'

Rachel banged her head on the table. 'What is there to remember?' she said.

'Hypothetical, Rachel. Hypothetical.'

Earlier, I'd gone out into the conservatory and cleared up the broken glass. I'd brought in the other glasses and bottles and tried to brush away the stain left by the water being poured through the charcoal. The chef had said it was a common complaint and that the rain would take care of it. When he'd had too much free drink he said the rain would eventually take care of everything. He said his ambition in life had been to become a great chef and run his own restaurant. He asked me what Rachel did and I told him she was big in advertising. He told me how much his own printed advertisements had cost. He said it paid to advertise, and then stopped, a victim of his own routine.

'Rachel, believe me, unopened bottles are a bad sign. Uncorked bottles mean people have been making a choice. They appreciate being able to do that. You only *think* all this stuff's going to get wasted, but none of it will. The wine will keep. They tell you it won't, but it will.'

'Rachel knows about wine,' the other woman said. 'It's her party, it's her wine.'

Rachel was sitting between them and her eyes were perfectly still.

'Have a bath in the fucking stuff if it bothers you that much. Listen to me – it's not worth worrying about.'

Rachel stood up and looked as though she barely had the energy to stand. I suggested coffee.

Rachel said, 'Good idea.' She began to prepare it, but I insisted.

'He *insists*, Rachel,' the woman said sarcastically.

The other helped me find the percolator and four cups. Rachel went through into the sitting-room.

'The idea originally was that we were a Gay Divorcee club. Rachel was in by default.' The woman washed and dried the cups. 'And now she's falling apart.' Remarks which are made with a supreme and unassailable confidence are said in a certain way: the tone of voice precludes all argument.

The woman lined the cups up on the table and turned their handles to face in the same direction.

In the sitting-room the curtains were drawn, but the windows open.

'Someone's smashed a bottle on the pavement and another on the path,' the woman at the window said. 'I told you it was a good party.' She held the curtains open an inch.

The painting above the fireplace had been turned to face the wall.

'And there's a burn in the arm of one of the chairs.'

And a small plant had been knocked over and someone had mounded the spilt soil in the hearth. Details. Amid which Rachel sat and wished herself elsewhere. Any life can be reduced to a handful of details, and these, now, were hers.

She took the coffee and said she would have been happy to have made it herself.

'He *insisted*, Rachel,' the woman at the window said.

I wanted to answer her, but didn't.

The woman who'd helped me told her to shut up.

I knew their names, but to me they were never more than the two women with Rachel.

We discussed cleaning up the house and found excuses to delay. Both women said they would be happy to stay and help, making it clear that it wasn't what they'd intended. The one at the window said she'd once calculated how many pieces of crockery she'd washed during her married life.

The other said there were agencies which sent people round to clear up on occasions such as this.

'The Morning-After Agency.'

'I didn't know. I – '

'I made it up. That's what they ought to be called. Perhaps it's what *we* should do.'

'Think of all the unwanted drink we'd collect.'

'A minute ago you said none of it went to waste.'

'Like the steaks. She let him take all the uneaten steaks away with him. Do you know how much that stuff costs?'

'No. Do you?'

'*Encore* hypothetical. Apart from which, that's not the point.'

Apart from which, there was a principle involved.

Rachel told them to stop arguing over *her* decisions. She said she intended cleaning the house herself and that she knew perfectly well that neither of them wanted to stay and help her. She sat with her half-filled cup on her knee and we all watched it, ready for it to fall. Another detail.

'Rachel, the longer we sit here doing nothing, the more chance there is of the ground cracking open and swallowing us up.'

Apart from which –

'It was a good party, Rachel. Everybody said so. Why should they lie?'

The women were beginning to leave.

Rachel asked if the plant which had been knocked from its pot had survived or died. Its stem had been broken and it would die. She asked if part of it could be repotted to grow again the following spring. She made no attempt to retrieve or even to examine the broken plant.

One of the women said it sounded wrong to talk of a plant as being 'broken'.

After half an hour of letting her know they were leaving, the two women finally went. One of them kicked the broken glass from the pavement to the gutter. There was little traffic and their voices carried back into the room.

During the remainder of the day Rachel worked hard at getting the house back into order. She poured the last of the wine away. I offered to help, but she said she wanted to do it alone. Listening to her work was like overhearing a private conversation.

She started in the rooms which had been least used at the top of the house and worked her way down. She went out to the path and then the gutter to sweep up the broken glass.

Gradually the house was cleaned and its debris collected in the kitchen. She filled sacks with empty bottles and paper plates. She found four shoes, a coat, two ties and a handbag and made a list of whom she thought they might belong to. She went through the rooms she'd cleaned and made another list of all the house's more recent imperfections, its spots of chipped paint and scratches. Finishing in the garden, she worked on the charcoal stains with a bucket of hot water and a scrubbing brush.

By six in the evening nothing of the party remained in the house.

By eight she'd been through it with a small brush and pots of paint and touched up all the chips and scratches. The house became as perfect for her as it had ever been. Nothing of the past, of what might lie beneath the surface, was allowed to show through.

When she'd finished she went into the sitting-room and turned the paintings back round. She said the man had started to remind her of her father, and having convinced herself of this, that the woman would soon come to resemble her mother. She asked me if I could think of anything in the house still to be done, something she'd overlooked.

Afterwards, she spoke of the party often, and the events of the short month which followed it were inevitably measured against the mastery and precision of its organisation.

She drank little for a week, and then resumed. The tablets which finally helped her sleep at three and four in the morning often kept her asleep until the late afternoon of the following day. People called to thank her, but whenever possible she avoided speaking to them, and accepted their own invitations without the slightest intention of going to see them.

She said finally that she was pleased the party had been a success. She'd been renowned in the past for holding good, successful parties.

In the past she'd been renowned for a great many things. Nothing had been beyond her. In the past she'd been another woman. People remembered her by the things for which she'd been renowned. She told them now what those things had been, and for most it was how they still preferred to know her.

2

There had been an accident in the street below, three cars bumper to bumper, all dented, one with its windscreen shattered. The front car would not start and the traffic coming from behind had edged forward to within inches of the rear car's raised boot; none of the drivers had wanted to lose the opportunity they believed those extra few inches might have given them. Six men and two women stood on the road and a small crowd had gathered on the pavement. Four of the men were in a group shouting and jabbing their fingers at each other.

'The end of the world is nigh,' Colin said, standing beside me, looking down.

Two policemen arrived and dispersed the crowd.

'A baton charge,' Colin said, pretending to hold a camera. 'Baton Charge through Lace Curtains – The End of the World.'

Only the flashing yellow light of the patrol car now suggested a sense of drama.

In the room behind us he'd set up a dozen of the seismographs, some as crude as the one he'd already shown me, some more recent and more technically complicated. The end result of them all – their mountainous outlines – was remarkably similar. Our every movement was recorded. We'd experimented seriously with them and then played with them. Our stamped feet and dropped books became the epicentres of upheaval. Much of what we were able to create was again distorted by the traffic outside and by our own unintentional tremors. Some of the instruments were too sensitive and their needles and markers swung wildly the whole time. Colin told me about each in detail, but without any of his former enthusiasm. We searched the rolls for the unexpected jump which might have been the accident.

'Rachel knows about this place,' he said.

How? I wondered if I was being accused.

'She never said. It made her revelation all that more impressive. Who knows? An innocent enquiry, an awkward silence, an excuse, a lie. It scarcely matters.'

He went round the room disconnecting some of the machines and tightening the clamps on others. Their needles stopped moving.

'She even said she was having second thoughts about coming to Africa with me. She won't, but I got the message. I won't bother with this place when I get back. Yesterday, because I had nothing better to do, I went with a local crew to watch the demolition of three cooling towers in the Midlands. A local mayor pressed the button on the first and then two schoolkids were brought on. They'd won a competition: "Why I Would Most Like to Destroy a Cooling Tower". Click, bang, puff of smoke, nothing.'

'And then I suppose you ran the film in reverse.'

'What else? Cooling towers and toppling chimney stacks – they only knock them down so we can show them rising back up from the rubble. I'm convinced some people have seen it often enough to believe it can be made to happen.' He became distracted by his inflatable cuff.

I asked him if Rachel had been to the flat.

He shook his head. 'When I said she "knew", I didn't actually mean she knew the number on the door; it might just as easily be a hotel room somewhere.'

Did she think he was seeing someone else?

'The thought had occurred to her. This' – he lifted his arm – 'told her otherwise. No, I don't think she believes that, either.'

Was she serious about Africa?

'She's too busy to leave everything behind for a fortnight.'

He went back to the window. The car at the front of the accident was being towed away. Two men in blue overalls performed the task as casually as though they were on an empty country lane. Three of the four men were still arguing; a policeman held the arm of one of them. On the pavement a new crowd had formed.

I asked him if he thought I'd told Rachel about the flat.

He said Yes and No, of course he had and of course he didn't believe it. 'The only reason we've lasted this long is because we've both known everything there was to know about each other, and because we each thought we had the advantage of knowing more than the other. Don't believe anyone who tells you it's impossible to know someone completely. You can know it by listening to them call you a liar; you can know it of some people by watching the way they pour you a drink or light your cigarette.' He went on absently with his examples, few of which pointed directly to Rachel.

'The last cooling tower had started twisting in on itself and then it stopped. The dust had cleared before it started up again and then subsided in a heap. For a minute the world stopped moving. It might be an added surprise, but it ruins the film running backwards, makes it somehow seem like more than the trick it is. There were four camera crews; it must have been a slack day everywhere else. The dog- and flower-show men were there for a little excitement.'

He slid a video cassette into the machine beneath the television and ran it forward, searching for the point at which whatever it was he wanted to show me began. When he stopped it to check, I heard the distinctive commentary and cheering of a boxing match.

'My latest acquisition, euphemistically entitled "The Noble Art": a collection of the final minutes of twenty or thirty knock-outs. You'd expect them to lose their appeal after five or six, but they never do. It's been put together by someone working for the BMA. At one side of the table there's a doctor saying the gloves are cushioned and that it's no more dangerous than crossing the road. What else? And at the other side there's another doctor reading out aloud a list of deaths and brain-damaged men. Four of the losers in the film died as a result of being knocked out, but I'm not entirely certain which they are. I suppose not knowing makes watching the ones who recovered, got up and walked away unharmed that bit more exciting.' There was still no excitement in his voice. He stopped the tape and stood back. 'I think this is one of the deaths.'

Two young black boxers punched each other in diagonal lines across the ring. Both had an eye swollen and cut, and sweat and water flew in a fine spray from their jarred heads. Their eyes rolled and looked like the eyes of frightened animals. A white referee in cream trousers and a white shirt walked around them and motioned with his arms. Even when they were apart the two boxers stared into each other's eyes. They paced in short nervous steps because it was impossible for them to stop moving. One, sensing an advantage, caught the other in the stomach and then the face in a repeated and quickening motion. A few seconds earlier he'd looked ready to fall himself. Now he was drawing his strength and energy out of the air and the rising crescendo of the crowd.

'Watch his knees,' Colin said.

The beaten boxer's legs suddenly folded and he fell into an exhausted praying position. His attacker continued knocking his head from side to side, unable to stop. The referee held an arm across his throat and still he continued. Only when the bell rang did he come to his senses and stop. Literally, come to his senses, and his thin weighted arms fell to his sides and he was unable to lift them again. He stood at the centre of the ring with his eyes closed as people climbed into it around him. The beaten boxer was still on his knees, and with his mouth open. His gumshield fell out, followed by a string of saliva. He shivered and tried to raise his head and open his eyes. Someone wrapped a towel around his neck, but the weight of it was too great for him and he fell forward with his arms outstretched and his face turned to the camera.

'He might even be dead now,' Colin said. 'Imagine that.'

Seeing him fall, the victor came back to life and began to jump up and down. The noise of the crowd grew even greater. Someone lifted the towel from the unconscious boxer and fanned his back with it. The ring was quickly filled and he was lost.

'What do you think?'

'Bullfighting.'

'The papers the following day said he was DOA. It wouldn't have done for the commentator to tell us that he was dead there and then.'

There were a dozen more fights; only the expressions on the beaten men's faces remained the same. Men went down who'd exhausted every muscle in their body; others won because they had one more ounce of strength than the loser, or because they found it and he didn't.

Colin stopped the film again and pointed to a background detail with a pencil. 'This is his mother and this is his wife. If he wins this fight he stands to pocket two million dollars; if he loses, half a million. He's from Puerto Rico. What they're watching is someone earn more in twenty minutes than the previous generations of their family have earned in two hundred years. Look at their faces.'

Both women were praying and cheering. Both were also crying, but whether in happiness or anxiety it was difficult to tell. In the breaks between rounds the young boxer sat in his corner and smiled and nodded to them as he was hurriedly serviced with towels and water ready to begin again. One of his seconds fed him his gumshield as though he were feeding sugar to a horse. At the sound of the bell for the new round, both his mother and wife lifted their hands to their mouths. The camera followed the boxer back into the corner of the ring.

'Does he win?'

'What do you think? Look at his eyes and then look at his opponent's. He's a man to whom half a million dollars represents the whole world. He's not stupid enough not to want the big purse, but at the same time he isn't clever enough not to be happy with the smaller amount. He said before the fight that it was going to be his last.'

188

The man was knocked down a minute later with blood between his eyes.

The referee stopped the fight and declared the other man the winner. The Puerto Rican boxer propped himself up on one knee and looked across the ring. He was lost in the crowd climbing in between the ropes to congratulate the winner.

In the last fight on the film the loser was slammed against a cushioned corner and then fell through the ropes to the ground. The camera moved back to look down at him. He pushed himself up and then collapsed. The referee counted him out. He covered his face with his clumsy hands and cried.

Colin ran the film backwards. The man flew gracelessly back through the ropes and up against the cushion; the look of surprise on his face was exactly the same in reverse. The film ended.

'Have you ever tried talking to someone in pain?' Colin said. 'Someone in agony, real agony, someone perhaps dying? They talk back. They always try to talk back to you. Have you ever noticed that? No, of course you haven't. The simple fact is they're too frightened about what's happening to them *not* to try and talk back. Talking to you, to anyone, is something they know about, something to cling to. They'll talk about anything, literally anything, simply to keep up the pretence. It's the hole in their chest they don't know about, the fact that they can't breathe; but talking they know. For them, to stop talking might be the last decision they ever make. I know. I've seen it. I've only recently started to understand it, but I've seen it.'

In two days he would be in Africa. This part of his life was already behind him.

'"Why I Want to Blow Up a Cooling Tower",' he said, putting another film into the recorder and then stepping back as the first of three flimsy structures turned from brick to cloth and collapsed.

3

Three days after the party, and for the first time since she'd originally shown me them, Rachel took out her collection of carved
whalebone and ivory. She dusted each piece and then arranged
them around the room, clearing spaces amid Colin's mementoes.
She said it had occurred to her that now was the time to make an
inventory of the pieces. She also spoke about researching something
of their history. A ledger had once existed in which her great-
grandfather had kept a precise account of the details of each piece:
prices paid, from whom acquired, where the whale or walrus had
been killed, by whom (if possible), and how long the work had
taken. There had also been a list of the wives, mothers and
sweethearts to whom some of the pieces had been dedicated. All
that remained now were their chiselled names, partially hidden in
some cases, and in others woven into the design.

'I've stopped feeling how I used to feel about them,' she told me.
She asked for my response to the way she'd spread the pieces
around, and it was clear from the way she spoke that she was still
uncertain of how she felt. She'd even retrieved the stuffed mongoose and snake and put them on the table by the window.

She told me she'd visited Colin's grave, and that she might make
the visits part of her new routine.

Then she asked me what I thought about the pair of carved
walrus tusks on the mantelpiece. Information relating to the other
pieces might have been lost, but she knew everything there was to
know about the tusks. They had become the new centrepiece of the
collection.

The grave looked as clean and tidy as the last time she'd seen
it. She said that putting flowers on it would have spoiled its
appearance.

She took out a sheet of paper and read me details of the tusks. She
told me the weight of the walrus from which they'd been sawn and
then tried to imagine how big it might have been by comparing it
with the furniture in the room. She wondered if the figure had been
an estimate, or if someone had actually weighed the carcass by

190

lifting it using a pulley. A similar pulley, perhaps, to the one which had been used to raise the dead polar bear above its frantic cub on the deck of the ship. A similar pulley to the one in front of which the crew had posed for their celebratory photograph.

She told me about a woman to whom she'd spoken in the cemetery. On her first visit after the funeral of her father, the woman had been unable to find his grave. An attendant had given her the letter of the row and the number of the grave along it, but she hadn't even been sure of the part of the cemetery in which the row began. Afterwards, she'd remembered it by using some of the more spectacular headstones on other graves as markers. 'Dove, cherub, cherub, scroll, bible, bible, dove.' Rachel had remembered the symmetry of the rhyme. The woman took flowers every week. She said she hadn't seen her father for eight years before he'd died and had hated him for a further ten beyond that. She knew what she was doing with her weekly visits, but couldn't explain to Rachel.

Rachel said she intended seeking professional advice on cataloguing her collection.

Earlier, one of the two women who'd stayed the night of the party had called and invited her out to dinner. Rachel told me the excuse she'd given her. She said she intended taking the mongoose and snake out of the window and destroying it.

Later, she said she'd been watching some of Colin's films and that she remembered quite clearly the occasions they'd been made. His belated gift to her on the first of her birthdays she'd spent with him had been a two-hour film of the day itself: Rachel waking, opening her presents in bed, eating a birthday breakfast; her lunch in a restaurant, rowing on a lake, sitting on a bench in new clothes and fondling a new necklace, pretending to read a new book, speaking to passers-by; having a party, dancing, drinking, kissing Colin. The last shot had been of a clock indicating midnight.

She'd destroyed the film the day she heard of Colin's death and became a widow. She had never been able to think of herself as a widow, simply as a woman whose husband had died. There was a big difference.

4

Three days later she set up a projector in her bedroom and played on to the wall the film of herself dancing and undressing. She watched it several times and then moved with the figure on the wall until finally her own flat nakedness was superimposed on the jeans and sweater she wore. Her four arms moved out of time with each other until she became more adept at synchronising them, making the effort seem more one of memory than intuition. She fastened her hair up in an approximation of the style it had been when the film was made and once again became a part of it.

When her old self was naked except for the boots and had moved to kneel over the bed, she too knelt over the bed. She watched herself distorted by the surfaces over which the film now ran, and when it ended she was left with two of her arms stretched over the crumpled sheets and two more fastened around her head.

She told me what she'd been doing. She wanted to screen every one of the films and separate those of Colin's projects from those of herself and them both together. She made up titles for the hours and days she had rediscovered.

She arranged the films in chronological order and thus destroyed an even stronger order. She timed them and made notes on the subject of each. The contents of Colin's study were slowly spread throughout the house.

'In this production I am the Queen of Sheba; in this, Cleopatra.' It was what she'd said to him as the films were being made. He'd told her that the whole point of making them was that she was Rachel.

She held the aluminium cases perfectly balanced, one in each hand. There were other assessments to be made.

Some of the film sequences of Rachel were interspersed with unused pieces Colin had collected in the course of his work. These she edited until they contained her alone, and in doing so she destroyed another order. That order no longer mattered to her; what mattered now was that a new one should be quickly established, and that it should conform strictly to her own design.

'Telling me I'm living in the past because of what I'm doing would be pointless,' she said. 'Telling me that would only indicate a complete lack of understanding.'

Telling her anything would have been unwelcome. She began to stay up during the night screening the films. When she'd seen them all she was disappointed. She said she thought there were more. She asked me how many I'd seen, and when I told her she said she'd become the equivalent of an open book.

'I was always photogenic. That's probably why he chose and married me. Artists and photographers always marry beautiful women, or leave ugly women for them. Only writers go out of their way not to. Writers pretend they're looking for brains in a woman, but what often happens is that they adopt a middle course and go for plainness in the hope of suggesting inner beauty. That's how you can spot the frauds. Look at most television writers: they have beautiful wives – or at least wives who become beautiful. Absolute fucking rubbish, all of it.'

She might have been right about Colin.

'Left profile or right profile? Right. Look at all the films: he knew. How can it be a perfect record? How can it be what he wanted?'

She didn't possess even a snapshot of herself since his death.

Her screening of the films became the most intensely private thing she'd ever done.

'You think I'm looking for something,' she said accusingly. 'I'll have to be the one to suggest it, but that's what you think.'

I thought she was looking for a way to dismiss everything the films contained.

'I might even have a fixed screen installed in one of the second-floor rooms.'

The past had finally caught up with and then run into the present in a series of sudden and painful shunts.

She made it clear when she wanted to be left alone. She behaved like a woman who'd spent a lifetime perfecting her gestures of dismissal.

I heard her voice in the few films to which there was sound.

'You think it's unhealthy,' she once said.

'I haven't said anything,' I said.

'I'm telling you what you *think*, not what you said.'

I told her to keep the films. I told her that I thought keeping the films was a good idea. That they were good films, worth keeping.

She spent an hour one afternoon clearing out the conservatory. She made a mound of all the magazines and articles she'd collected and burned them. The fire left another stain on the brickwork, and in trying to clean it she dug out more of the slender bricks and could not fit them back into the pattern.

She scribbled out names from her address book and diary and then tore pages from both. She burned these in a bin inside the conservatory.

'Nothing's changed,' she said. She meant herself and her former self, her arms and breasts and legs, her chin, neck and face. She performed part of the dance.

It was best for her to want to believe that nothing had changed when in fact nothing had remained the same.

She danced around me. I tried to remember if there had been a soundtrack to any of the films in which she'd laughed.

5

Colin was killed in a car accident in Lomé on Boxing Day.

I tried to remember the list of places he'd already visited during his previous trips to Africa. I didn't even know where Lomé was. Lomé was the capital city of Togo. The only other place mentioned in the pocket atlas I consulted was a town called Sokodé; in addition, there were the Togo mountains and the River Mono.

Squeezed in a strip fronted by the Bight of Benin, it became the most distant part of the world. It seemed then like one of those insignificant parts of the world where someone was most likely and least likely to die.

In the telex, the word 'auto' was used instead of 'car', making his death seem even more distant.

The details themselves became irrelevant and then misleading. They were the markers of an event; of a place and of a time; but not of his death.

'They're telling me he's been killed in a road accident,' Rachel said. 'Is that what they're telling me?' Her indignant disbelief would bring him back to life.

In a road accident, in a hired car, on a bad road, travelling to or from a political rally. These were the secondary details. Potholes in the road, no lighting, dust, overhanging trees, people in the car with him.

'Was he driving? Was it his fault? How? How did he die? You know how good a driver he is. It's not him, it's not Colin. He isn't the one who's been killed. They can't all have been killed. Does it say?'

To have tried to tell her anything would have been an unnecessary cruelty.

She'd worked during the afternoon of Christmas Day. She'd been out briefly to a nearby party on Christmas Night. She'd expected to hear from Colin on Boxing Day; he'd called on Christmas Eve. She'd expected there to be a time difference, but Lomé was only one degree east of London. He'd explained all this to her.

Their last conversation consisted of Colin trying to pinpoint for her exactly where he was. She wanted him to wait while she found a map, but that was impossible. He told her how difficult it had been for him to get through to her.

It had never mattered to her before to know precisely: America had been America; Europe, Europe.

These were the details: the details of not knowing, and of knowing precisely without having to be told.

She sat in the house on Boxing Day and watched a silent television. I contacted a few people who might need to know. She told me not to, saying that it was still Christmas.

She read the telex fifty times in the certain knowledge that it contained nothing she hadn't fully understood before she'd finished reading it for the first time.

She wanted to talk, but not about anything in particular. She said she felt dispossessed. She asked me if I could think of anything specific she needed to do. She asked me what people had said when I'd called to let them know.

Two other people had been injured in the accident.

It had taken place on an unmade road twelve miles north of Lomé.

Someone had a photograph of the car and the ditch into which it had fallen. I never saw the photograph. There were buildings of corrugated iron, wire-less telegraph poles, a compound which had been prepared for an electricity generating station (the machinery for which had never been installed), a crowd of children and women, people picking from the wreckage once the body had been removed.

I never saw the photograph.

The two injured men were taken the twelve miles south to a hospital in Lomé – perhaps the only hospital in Lomé.

Their stories of how the accident happened were contradictory. They avoided all mention of the fact that all or some of them might have been celebrating and were drunk. When they were asked, they denied it vigorously.

After an explosion, the first, most powerful shock wave moves quickly outwards through buildings which only register its effect and are then blown apart by it a second later. It is a full second in which everything might be realised, but in which nothing can be done.

The chief exports of Lomé would be fruit, perhaps minerals, perhaps sugar, newsworthy unrest, upheavals, war, military coups, perhaps labour to neighbouring countries.

Perhaps nothing. Perhaps only bad news.

196

In the small atlas there weren't even the red and blue lines of air travel and shipping lines.

The heart of darkness was not possessed by mining companies with mineral rights, but by people looking into the blank spaces of small, inadequate atlases.

On the night of Boxing Day she didn't sleep.

On the morning following she didn't speak, and in the afternoon she spoke without stopping, recreating in the only details she knew everything that had happened between them during the previous months. She made the months into years, and then the years into emptinesses around the smallest events.

She'd known about the flat in Shepherd's Bush for a month before she told Colin she knew.

She bought a more detailed map and we studied Togo together. The name was wrong: it belonged in the Pacific; it stopped being a place on a map, nowhere.

Details of the return of Colin's body.

A letter from the least badly injured of the two other men, both of whom were flown home three days later. There was nothing they could tell her that she wanted to hear.

She didn't sleep for four nights. She slept instead for short hours during the day.

Details of the preparation for the funeral, lost in the distance between involvement and participation.

Details of the week following the funeral. Details of being certain, and then of never having known.

I stayed in the house with her. People called, people phoned.

There was an inquiry, but its conclusions meant as much to her as the sympathy in which they were couched. Colin was being hidden from her. The wives of the two injured men might hate her because of how close their own husbands might have come to being killed.

The inhabitants of Togo were probably killed every day and their relatives probably never even knew.

Togo was eight degrees and thirty minutes north of the equator. She'd only crossed the equator once, on her way to Brazil.

We took down the Christmas decorations four days early.

The time of year during which everything had happened made it seem even more unreal to her.

Even then, before the events which led her to the clinic, she was beginning to create small parts of the routine by which she would afterwards be able to continue.

Much later, I tried to remember if I knew anything of the

occasion Colin was supposed to be covering in Togo. Presumably it had been of wider interest, because of the involvement of far greater powers. I remembered that the man who should have gone was in Australia for a month.

I knew also, the second I saw the message, that Colin had not *simply* died in a car crash –

– had not *simply* been the unfortunate victim of –

– had not *simply* died when the car in which he had been travelling had –

The details had always been confused with the variations.

Rachel knew it too.

'They're telling me he's been killed in a road accident. How could he have been driving the car with his injured wrist? They said he'd been driving. How could he have been driving? How could he have held the wheel and changed gear? (An automatic transmission? Still not –)

Supposing they collected every tiny piece of the shattered windscreen and pieced the jigsaw together to reveal the concentric circles of imaginary bullet holes.

Supposing they could see what he'd seen, what he might hypothetically have swerved to avoid. Supposing they could recreate what he'd been thinking.

Supposing they knew about the second of grace following the explosion.

A fortnight after the funeral a card arrived addressed to Colin from his doctor asking why he'd missed a routine hospital appointment. A later date was suggested. It made Rachel laugh. It was as ridiculous and as irrelevant as the size of Togo or the position of Lomé, or knowing that it was joined by an invisible line to somewhere east of London; or that its population was under three million and that they lived in an area of 21,000 square miles, fifty per cent of which was listed as 'Waste, City Areas, etc', or that the 'etc' would have included the road on which Colin had died, driving or being driven, accidentally or otherwise, in a hired car.

'The doctors can tell me they've found a cure,' she said.

Neither of us would have believed it.

She'd had a calendar on the kitchen wall which had contained the motto *'The End Of One Passing Moment Is The Beginning Of Another'*. It sounded glib and trite, and something not to have to think about. She'd read the mottoes out aloud on the first of each month. Above the one about the passing moments was a picture of a woman wearing a bikini, walking with a panther on a leash.

Even then there had been details.

6

Ten days after she'd taken out and arranged her collection of scrimshaw around the sitting-room, Rachel collected the pieces together and once again packed them away.

'I've started not to like it again,' she said. 'It's a bone yard.'

It was the first thing she'd said to me in almost three days.

While packing a comb she'd snapped off several of its fragile teeth, and then, in an uncontrollable frenzy, had broken beyond repair a dozen of the other more delicate pieces. After telling me, she showed me the chippings she'd collected in a bag. Instead of guilt or anger at herself, she adopted the aggrieved, almost reconciled tone of someone who had been burgled. She immediately put the rest of the collection out of reach and then considered without any real conviction the possibility of the broken pieces being repaired. She took the fragments out of the bag and held them in the bowl of her hands. When she'd finished making excuses she threw them into a corner of the room, where they hit the wall and scattered.

Afterwards, she said that her cataloguing of the collection had come to nothing. The museum curator she'd consulted several days previously had told her that her aims would be better served by allowing someone who knew about that kind of work to undertake it. She'd accused him of trying to get her to hand over the collection to him. She'd expected him to have lunch with her, but instead she'd been granted an interview of under half an hour in his office. The half-hour had been much interrupted and she'd been made to feel as though she were wasting his time.

She said the pieces of scattered bone reminded her of runes.

Even the films had started to depress her.

'I'm definitely selling the house. It feels like a positive thing to do,' she said. 'I've been in touch with the same agent. I'm calling him again tomorrow.'

Her eyes returned to the broken carvings.

'He'd expected me to have some of the pieces with me. He told me that people who didn't know about that kind of work were often likely to overestimate its real value. It was something he couldn't even guess at without seeing the pieces themselves. He said the insurer's valuations were often a mockery of the true worth of the pieces – of the individual pieces – which he himself, the almighty authority, would have to see.'

Hence her brief but uncontrollable destruction of the century funnelled towards her birth, the happier lives of people she had never known, but who she now felt certain had foreseen what was happening to her.

She insisted on finding a pattern in the pieces of scattered bone before gathering them back up.

'He told me that whales are the first creatures mentioned in the Bible. He actually knew – *knew* – about my great-grandfather's company. He knew more than I did. It was his job to know. Smug – '

The following day she avoided me. And the day after that. On the third morning she spoke to me and told me she'd had an almost identical dream for the past three nights. In it she'd left the house in darkness, walked barefoot through the garden to the conservatory and, using a sledgehammer, had destroyed it completely in less than a minute. She'd been amid the wreckage, swinging wildly, and at the same time standing back from it, applauding herself. As she remembered it, everything in the dream had taken place in complete silence: there had been no one to restrain her; no noise of smashed glass, the crumpled aluminium frame, the shattered pots; no lights at neighbouring windows, no knowing smiles of people proven right. The fact that she was barefoot also seemed to hold some significance for her.

'Do I even possess a sledgehammer?' she asked.

I said that I couldn't imagine Colin ever having needed one. There were tools in the basement, but not the tools of a man who took his capabilities as a handyman seriously.

She went on to describe the dream in greater detail. She said that when she'd stood back from the conservatory and watched it being destroyed, the pieces of shattered glass had risen into the air like small disembodied flames, had been extinguished in the darkness and then had fallen back around her like heavy drops of rain.

'You think I'm confusing it with the clinic,' she said.

I began to tell her that the rising pieces of glass might have reflected –

'And my feet are always wet when I get back into the house. There's a point when I'm walking down the garden when the whole thing looks like a block of ice and I can see myself in it. I can even see the hammer. How much do those things weigh? And each night is exactly the same, right down to the way I feel about it afterwards.'

Which was?

'Relieved. I don't even want to destroy the thing. Not even subconsciously. That's a joke, incidentally.'

I asked her if she thought there was any connection between

what had happened in the dream and her destruction of the scrimshaw, but instead of answering she changed the subject. There was a newspaper on the table between us and she turned it to face me. Its leading article dealt with the overthrow of a Caribbean dictator and his departure with his wife and a plane-load of crates packed with banknotes to an unknown destination. The first act of reprisal of the liberated population had been to kill the élite members of his personal bodyguard. This they did by surrounding them in mobs and stoning them to death. There had been film of the violence on the television news the previous evening. The body-guards held machine guns, but these they pointed in the air and tried to make not using them appear like a friendly act. Even when they were dead on the ground their arms and legs still twitched at the impact of each rock and brick that was thrown.

'Appropriate, don't you think?' Rachel said. 'A nice Biblical ending.'

I told her Colin would have been interested.

'Wouldn't he just. And the word is "excited". As in "Colin would have been excited." '

I turned the paper back to face her. My reaction made her laugh.

'It would have been a good year for Colin,' she said. 'This, the space shuttle, record year for air disasters, another Royal wedding, everything else, all things considered. What do you think?' She became unsure of herself again and looked away to avoid being answered. She studied the conservatory through the open door. 'I might even have a pond sunk and fill it with fat colourless fish, something to look at when there's nothing else to look at. I'd have them instead of a cat because they'd be lazier than a cat and then I wouldn't feel too bad about doing fuck all myself all day. What do you think? That's twice I've asked you what you think.'

Buy a sledgehammer.

'Let he who is without sin cast the first . . . Perhaps they honestly believed they were – without sin, I mean. Perhaps they'd made a faulty equation between what they'd suffered before and how they thought they were going to live from now on.' She read the article as though it contained the answer to her suggestion.

There were pictures of the prince and his fiancée kissing on the lawn of Buckingham Palace, surrounded by photographers. They'd been on the television, too, kissing a dozen times in the space of a minute for the benefit of the cameras.

'It's all been done before,' she said, and pushed the paper from the table to the floor. 'There must be a limit to fairytale fucking romances. What do you think? One a decade? More? Less?' She positioned her feet on the paper and pulled the top sheet in half.

8

The next day she went out and returned with her pockets full of cuttings from the hothouse in the park. She spread them across the table in display.

'I stole them,' she said proudly.

Most of the leaves and stems were already crushed and discoloured.

I told her she would probably have been given them if she'd asked.

'That wasn't the point of the exercise. Do you think I want them? One. I want one.' She selected a bunch of leaves, sniffed at it and discarded it, trying several others until she found the one she decided she wanted. 'There are more.' She tipped the contents of a carrier bag on to the table. 'I took a pair of scissors to save time. There was no one there. I could have taken ten times as many. I'd like, just for once, to grow something spectacular. Just once. So I can tell people when they ask.' She became distracted by the scatter of leaves and dying stems and then went on about where in the house the plant might grow best. She plucked the leaves from the stalk in her hand, dropped it and chose another. She brought in a plant pot filled with earth and pressed the inch of green into it. 'It'll die,' she said. 'I ought to root it in a rooting compound first. I'm too impatient to be a good gardener.'

There was a book on houseplants in the kitchen and she tried to identify what she'd stolen and potted and was convinced would die. She decided finally that her trophy was too exotic to be in the book. She tapped the pot to settle the soil and then pressed it flat with her thumb. She stood it on the window sill and lost interest in it.

'It's easier than it looks,' she said, referring to her theft. 'Or perhaps I *was* given them. Perhaps I walked in and charmed the gardener until he was begging me to take them. Wouldn't you rather be able to guess than to know for certain?' She took the pot from the window to the sink and swamped it with an inch of water. 'It's probably dead already,' she said. 'Why should it live? It's not going to get any warmer. Anyone with an ounce of sense would realise that the end of September was hardly the best time to get something to grow.'

She was wearing the same simple sleeveless dress she'd worn for the past week. She wore sandals inside and out, and left them wherever she kicked them off. She'd sorted through her wardrobes again and there were piles of clothes on the landing.

Later in the day she took the pot from the window sill outside and threw it against the wall. I heard her apologising to the plant for what she'd done to it.

She admitted afterwards that she'd been given the cuttings, but that the gardener in the hothouse had told her he doubted if they would survive without the artificially high temperatures. She asked me if I still believed that knowing was preferable to not knowing.

9

The day after was the nine-month anniversary of Colin's death. Rachel told me and then asked me not to say anything. She said that strictly speaking a 'nine-month anniversary' was a contradiction in terms. Anyway, the twenty-sixth of September; an almost apologetic shrug.

She went out and I watched the film of her and Colin having their picnic by the river. There was no sound, only the two of them running over the study wall, moving out of shot, and then Rachel alone, the camera moving with her to keep her the focus of attention.

Seeing her as she had once been, watching her run and wave and laugh, felt sacrilegious.

In the film she lay down with him and the camera was badly angled, allowing them to be seen only intermittently as they rose briefly above the long grass. When they stood up, Rachel smoothed down her dress and leaned into the blade of light which shone through the window behind me. Unseen, Colin returned to the camera, lifted it from its stand and moved towards her with it. She lowered herself back to the ground, shook out her hair and then retied it for her future audience. Then she knelt looking up at him, almost as though she were praying to him, as though at any second she might throw herself forward and grasp his legs, or take his feet from his shoes, kiss them and then wash them with a cloth dipped in the river. There was nothing she might not have done for him. She reached out and touched his shin, and the simplicity and strength and purity of her affection for him caused the camera to flinch and catch a square of unfocused horizon and sky before returning to her face and uncovered shoulders.

10

And the next day, two days after she'd come home with the cuttings, and the day after she'd danced four years ago through the grass along the wall and into a pattern of the present, Rachel went from the garden into the empty house, half filled a bath with warm water, sat in it fully clothed and appeared to try to kill herself. It was not a particularly serious attempt at suicide; nor was it even a serious or sincere cry for help – which was how people saw it, which was how people needed to see it in the absence of any other explanation.

The act itself was lost in the days which led up to it and in its aftermath of routine and speculation, acceptance and disbelief.

I believed her afterwards when she said that she neither knew nor cared what would happen: a suicide by someone testing the depth or the heat of the water, by someone for whom – perhaps for a minute, perhaps less – living and dying had appealed and repulsed in equal measure.

Half an hour beforehand she'd called three magazine editors to ask if they were interested in stories of first-hand experience of the after-life and of reincarnation. Even these were not the assurances of rescue they were afterwards thought to be, and only one of the women she'd called had made any connection and contacted the police; to the others she had already ceased to exist.

'Dispossessed', I heard her shouting, and felt another part of the past become a permanent feature of her future. She'd looked fifty years ahead and, for that minute at least, everything she'd seen had been unendurable.

A plainclothes policeman opened the door upon my return to the house, turning the handle as I reached for it, as though he'd seen me coming and had waited until the very last second for best effect.

No one had been able to contact me to let me know.

I'd spent six hours of a nine-hour day behind the wheel of a hired car, five of the six hours on motorways. Returning to the house and seeing the man, I felt as though I was arriving somewhere I'd never previously been.

She had been semi-conscious when found. She'd taken with her the small knife she'd used during the summer to skin and stone peaches. It was an old knife with a wooden handle, its short and slender blade worn even thinner by excessive sharpening. She'd made a single shallow stroke across one of her wrists after scoring superficial lines over the backs of both her forearms, drawing blood without any real loss. She'd also taken an overdose of her sleeping pills, and the empty bottles lay beside her at the bottom of the bath. I imagined her painless rehearsals on her forearms, watching the blood appear and waiting until it ran or smeared before dipping her arms into the water and waiting for it to begin again.

The detective held the knife and spoke about what had happened. I told him about the peaches and he made notes. He nodded as he wrote, as though the information helped him to understand more clearly the reason for what she'd done. He was already well advanced in the process of recreating her for the purposes of his own inquiry.

He told me about the phone calls. He wanted to tell me what he would rather be doing, where he would rather be. He wanted to tell me about something he might have planned with his wife and children, something urgent now that the autumn nights were drawing in and it was dark at eight.

He moved around the room, briefly inspecting its contents.

He told me where she'd been taken and how satisfactory her condition was.

I went upstairs. There were still damp shoe-prints on the landing and the bath was still half filled with scarcely tinted water. There were still flecks of blood on the tiles, against which someone had pencilled an arrow.

From the second-floor landing there trailed strips of unwound film, knotted to the banister and thrown over to hang. Their empty canisters lay like giant coins by the study door.

When I went back down, the detective asked me what else I knew, and this time he listened without taking notes. My only choice would have been to tell him everything or nothing. He told me how many times he'd been in the same situation before.

In Colin's study everything had been swept from the desk and shelves and lay in a heap on the floor. The pictures and certificates had been pulled from the walls and their frames had been smashed.

There were people outside in neighbouring gardens looking up at the house.

The detective told me how long ago the ambulance had left and guessed at when I'd be able to see her. He said something dismissive

208

about the spectators and I almost told him it was what she would have expected. He spoke of everything as being straightforward from then onwards; for the purpose of his report, straightforwardness had become the desired aim.

Downstairs, I offered him a drink. I almost asked him if he wanted to leave, to return to his waiting wife and children. He was impressed by Colin's record collection. He said the neighbours had given him all the details he needed. I asked him if there was anything I needed to do, things I shouldn't touch. He laughed and said that as far as the public was concerned, police work was littered with myth. I agreed with him: the comfort of involvement in someone else's routine.

When he'd gone I emptied the water from the bath and wiped the tiles clean.

In another of the first-floor rooms a conversation was taking place on the radio – like an obvious trick in a film – someone to overhear, a scream and a gunshot, a door thrown open and a radio play going on and on. Apart from those few low voices, the house was silent. Above me, the unwound film hanging from the balcony looked like the flimsy streamers thrown from the railings of an ocean-going liner as it slipped slowly from the land into the solitude and exile of the sea.

11

'You brought flowers,' she said.

I held them out; they were large daisies, yellow and white, children's ideas of flowers. They felt like the most useless thing I could have taken her. Or perhaps not; perhaps without them there would have been nothing to say, nowhere to begin.

'They don't think flowers are a particularly good idea,' she said. 'It doesn't make any difference, but it's what they think.' She indicated the flowers in vases and bowls beside the beds on either side of her.

Her headrest was tilted into a half-sitting, half-lying position, and the sheets were drawn in a sharp line across her chest, making her look smaller. Both her arms were bandaged from wrist to elbow. She saw my glance and raised them.

'Nothing to see,' she said.

There was nowhere beside her own bed to put the flowers and so I laid them in their paper cone on the floor.

Opposite me a screen had been drawn half the length of the bed; I could see the visitors sitting around the beds on that side, but not the patients they had come to see.

Rachel saw me looking. 'Causes for concern,' she said. 'They enjoy it.' She laid her arms along the fold of the sheets. 'They bandaged them from top to bottom to make the real damage less conspicuous, less obvious. They probably think I backed down at the last minute. It didn't even take a minute. Before you came, one of the nurses actually suggested to me that serious suicides open the vein lengthways along their inner arm. It makes sense. Apparently, the nick across the dotted line of the wrist is for television plays and magazine stories only. According to her, that is. There was no point in trying to explain it to her, but you at least can see my point. There would have been no other way – not for me personally. It might sound stupid, but I feel better now than I have done for weeks. I suppose you've been in the study.'

I told her I had.

'Is much of it beyond retrieval or repair?'

'Most of it looks salvageable.' I didn't tell her that I'd spent the previous evening rewinding many of the films she'd thrown from their cans.

'I got carried away. No I didn't. I knew exactly what I was doing, and now I want it all back, everything. Don't look for any sense in it.'

When I caught the eyes of the other visitors we smiled at each other. Several moved from bed to bed making conversation with new acquaintances.

I'd been told they would keep her in until only the following day.

'Look.' She turned down the sheets a few inches to reveal bruising on her ribs, and indicated a fainter discolouration on her throat. I could only guess at the necessary violence by which the marks had been caused.

The woman in the next bed began to complain loudly at the late arrival of her visitors. She shouted across the ward to ask a nurse if she'd seen them. She wore glasses with excessively thick lenses which gave her eyes the appearance of being two more open mouths.

The nurse approached us, took the flowers from the floor and left.

The woman in the next bed continued to ask her unanswered questions and made everyone around her feel uneasy, as though they were somehow a part of the conspiracy to keep her visitors from her.

'She has a dozen a day, and they only come because of the fuss she makes if they don't.'

The woman heard the remark and turned to face us. The nurse returned, set down the vase and told the woman not to be so impatient.

'I sometimes think,' Rachel went on, waiting until I wasn't looking at her, 'that from now on everything's going to be the same, that nothing's ever going to change.' The flowers in the vase were lopsided and she pointed this out. 'Imagine what would happen if we could all be the people we started out to be.'

The woman's visitors finally arrived and she demanded to know why they were so late. I asked Rachel if she knew what the woman was in for. Everyone in the ward knew; the room was filled with people knowing everything there was to know about everyone else; other people's illnesses and suffering were part of their own process of recovery.

'I'm a real tonic to them all,' she said. She lifted both her arms and let them fall. She smiled and held my hand. 'Don't ask,' she said.

One of the woman's visitors gave her a hand-mirror and she studied herself, straightening her hair and bed-jacket and complaining at her appearance.

211

'I found this,' Rachel said. She gave me an Instamatic photograph of Colin lying on the ground with a Dalmation standing over him, one of its paws on his chest, its tail made indistinct by movement.

'Bird? I'd always assumed he was a setter or retriever.'

'No. That was Bird.' She took back the photograph and looked at it closely, as though a doubt had been raised. 'He was with me when he was killed on the road. They hear you, dogs like that, but it counts for very little if they've already made up their minds to do something else. I couldn't even lift him. The man who hit him had to drive us home. He wanted to come in and explain to Colin, but I wouldn't let him. Bird. You probably confused him with being some kind of bird dog.'

'Probably.'

'They're too faithful for their own good.'

Probably.

The woman in the next bed complained of feeling sick and asked one of her visitors to call for a nurse. They looked at each other for a moment before one of them, a man, stood up. 'Shout,' the woman told him, but instead he walked quickly along the ward to the small office in which the nurses sat drinking their tea and looking out at us, acknowledging the smaller responsibilities of which they had been temporarily relieved.

Rachel watched him go. 'Everything.' she said, 'I want it all,' and, turning away from me, she slid her bandaged arms back beneath the sheets.